RACE
TO·THE
SUN

RACE
TO·THE
SUN

REBECCA ROANHORSE

RICK RIORDAN PRESENTS

DISNEP • HYPERION   LOS ANGELES   NEW YORK

First Edition, January 2020
3 5 7 9 10 8 6 4 2
FAC-020093-19338
Printed in the United States of America

This book is set in 12-point Dante MT Pro, and Aeris A Pro/Monotype
Designed by Mary Claire Cruz

Library of Congress Cataloging-in-Publication Data

Names: Roanhorse, Rebecca, author.
Title: Race to the sun / by Rebecca Roanhorse.
Description: First edition. • Los Angeles ; New York : Disney-Hyperion, 2019.
• "Rick Riordan Presents." • Summary: Guided by her Navajo ancestors, seventh-grader Nizhoni Begay discovers she is descended from a holy woman and destined to become a monsterslayer, starting with the evil businessman who kidnapped her father. Includes glossary of Navajo terms.
Identifiers: LCCN 2019000566 • ISBN 9781368024662
Subjects: • CYAC: Adventure and adventurers—Fiction. • Monsters—Fiction. • Navajo Indians—Fiction. • Indians of North America—New Mexico—Fiction. • Navajo mythology—Fiction. • Family life—New Mexico—Fiction. • Friendship—Fiction. • New Mexico—Fiction.
Classification: LCC PZ7.1.R57773 Rac 2019 • DDC [Fic]—dc23
LC record available at https://lccn.loc.gov/2019000566

Reinforced binding
Follow @ReadRiordan
Visit www.DisneyBooks.com

To my daughter, Maya,
and all the other Native kids who deserve to be heroes

CONTENTS

THE ORIGINAL AMERICAN GODS

Changing Woman. Rock Crystal Boy. The Glittering World. The Hero Twins.

If those names don't ring a bell, you've been missing out on some of the coolest mythology* anywhere. But don't worry. Thanks to Rebecca Roanhorse and *Race to the Sun*, you're about to plunge headfirst into the fabulous, scary, wonderful story world of the Diné, also called the Navajo. Even if you already know something about traditional Navajo tales, you're going to squee with delight, because you have *never* experienced them like this before.

Meet Nizhoni Begay. (Her first name is pronounced Nih-JHOH-NIH and means "beauty.") In many ways, she's a typical New Mexico seventh-grader. She just wants to be good at something, to get some respect at school. Unfortunately, nothing works. Her bid for internet fame is a fail. Her chance to become a sports superstar ends with a basketball in the face. She can barely manage to hang on to her one good friend, Davery, and prevent her artsy younger brother, Mac, from getting beat up by his nemesis, Adrien Cuttlebush.

And as if that weren't enough, Nizhoni has another small issue. Recently she's been seeing monsters. Nobody else seems

---

* Just to be clear, when I use the word *mythology*, it is in its first and most basic sense, meaning stories about gods and heroes, not in its later, more secondary application as something false or made-up.

to notice, but Nizhoni is pretty sure that even Mr. Charles, the rich guy who is offering Nizhoni's dad a new job in Oklahoma, is *not* human. Worse, it seems that Mr. Charles has sought out the Begay family because he considers Nizhoni some kind of threat. . . .

I *love* this story, and not just because it's a funny, brilliant page-turner with unforgettable characters and an ingenious quest. The point of Rick Riordan Presents is to publish and promote great voices from cultures that have been too often marginalized or erased by mainstream culture. *No one* has suffered from this more than Native and Indigenous peoples. As Rebecca says in her author's note, it's important for Native kids to be able to see themselves in fiction, but it's equally important for people from all backgrounds to read about Indigenous characters who aren't just a collection of stereotypes or long-dead figures from the past. Native cultures are alive and well and vibrant. Their stories can tell you about the *original* American gods and heroes, those who inhabited and embodied the land for thousands of years before the Europeans brought over their interloping Zeuses and Aphrodites and what-have-yous.

I'll tell you something I haven't shared before: Piper McLean, the half-Cherokee character in my Heroes of Olympus series, was inspired by conversations I had with Native kids during school visits, of which I did hundreds over the years. They asked me repeatedly whether I could add a Native hero to Percy Jackson's world. They wanted to see themselves reflected at Camp Half-Blood, because they simply never found themselves in popular kids' books. Piper was my way of saying, "Absolutely! I see you. I value you. You can be part of my world anytime!"

But my perspective is *not* a Native perspective. It was one thing to include Piper as part of the heroic ensemble, to share Percy Jackson's world with kids from all backgrounds and send a message that heroes can come from all sorts of places. It would be quite another thing to write entirely from a Native protagonist's point of view about the mythology of his or her own culture. That sort of story needed to come from a Native writer, and I yearned to find books like that and put them into the hands of young readers, Native and non-Native alike. There are so many wonderful Indigenous mythologies. They deserve to be read, shared, and spotlighted.

For Native kids, seeing themselves reflected in books is critical. Seeing themselves reflected in the very authors who create those books is exponentially more empowering. I am thrilled that Rebecca Roanhorse agreed to write *Race to the Sun* for Rick Riordan Presents. It is a much-needed addition to children's fiction, and I hope it's the first of many!

For all kids, reading about other cultures' mythologies is a way to expand their imagination and their empathy. There's an old Czech proverb: *Learn a new language, gain a new soul.* Mythology is similar. The traditional sacred stories of every culture can offer us a new window onto the world—a new way of seeing and understanding. As a bonus, when written by someone as talented as Rebecca Roanhorse, mythology is wildly entertaining!

But I've said enough. I'll let Nizhoni take it from here. Welcome to Dinétah. Keep your hands and feet inside the novel at all times, or some monster might bite them off. If you're really good, maybe the Begay family will take you to Pasta Palace afterward for some Spaghettini Macaravioli!

Rick Riordan

ONE

♦

I Can See Monsters

My name is Nizhoni Begay, and I can see monsters.

In fact, I'm looking at one right now.

The monster is a pale man with thin blond hair, slightly bulging eyes, and unusually red lips. He's tall and skinny, and he has on a black suit and tie. (Monsters wear human skin more often than fairy tales would lead you to think. Scales and horns and claws are strictly for beginners. Trust me, I'm an expert on these things.)

This monster is sitting in the second row of the packed bleachers of my seventh-grade coed basketball game, looking completely normal. Normal except for the fact that he's wearing a suit when everyone else is wearing a T-shirt that says GO, ISOTOPES! or GO, BEAVERS! depending on which team they're rooting for. Normal except there's a circle of empty space around him despite the gym being filled to capacity, like nobody wants to get close to him. Maybe they feel there's something creepy about him, too, but they aren't sure what it is.

I watch as a lady in a bright purple tracksuit moves in front of him, waving a red-and-black pom-pom dangerously near his face. Pretty sure if she keeps that up, she's a goner. Monsters don't take kindly to people invading their personal space.

Okay, I made that up. I don't actually know how monsters feel about personal space, or whether they eat ladies in purple tracksuits, and I'm not so much an expert as much as a reluctant amateur. I mean, I've only been able to sense monsters for a few months. It started as a strange feeling while watching a lady massaging the avocados at the farmers' market, and there was the definite bad vibe from the old dude with the scaly feet and Jesus sandals at the Taco Bell. And just like in those instances, every instinct I have is shouting at me that this guy in the bleachers is *not* normal.

The tiny hairs on the back of my neck rise. A chill—like the time my little brother, Mac, dumped a snowball down my shirt—shudders down my spine. Out of habit, I touch the turquoise pendant I have taped to my chest underneath my shirt. I'm not supposed to wear it during basketball games, but knowing it's there helps me feel brave.

"Nizhoni!"

The way this school year has been going, trying to be brave has become almost a full-time thing. When I left my big public school and transferred to ICCS (short for Intertribal Community Charter School and pronounced *icks*), I really thought things would change for me. And by *change*, I mean I'd have lots of friends and be popular. After all, every student at ICCS is Native American, just like me. But I've been at ICCS for two years now and nothing is different. I'm still not popular, and I'm definitely not cool. I'm just—

"Nizhoni Begay!"

Coach! I whip my head around, because of course I'm not listening (Hello! Monster!), and she is right there in my face. So close, in fact, that drops of spittle fly out of her mouth and hit my cheek every time she shouts my name. I surreptitiously wipe off the spit, trying not to look completely grossed out, even though it's pretty gross.

Coach is no monster, but she has issues with personal space, too—she's always in mine. She's also a little short for basketball—but no one would ever tell her that, because she makes up for being height-challenged by being really loud. Coach is Hopi, so it's not her fault she's so short. Besides, she's scary in other ways. I'm not worried she will eat my eyeballs for hors d'oeuvres or anything. (Eyeball hors d'oeuvres are very popular with monsters. I read that somewhere, FYI.)

Coach snaps her fingers inches from my nose. "Are you even listening?"

I nod. Total lie. Besides, it's time-out. Nobody listens during time-out.

"There's five seconds left in the game!" she yells. "Your focus should be on me"—she points at herself with two fingers—"and your teammates." She gestures at the group of seventh-grade boys and girls now huddling around me. "We need you to pay attention."

"Sure thing, Coach," I chirp obediently, but honestly, all I can think about now are eyeballs stacked like meatballs on a toothpick for easy snacking.

Coach is talking again. "Okay. Davery is going to pass the ball in. Who wants to take the last shot?"

"I'll do it!" I say, raising my hand.

3

The rest of my team groans in disbelief.

"Put your hand down, Nizhoni," Coach snaps. "You're standing right beside me."

"Oh, right." I lower it. "But I can take the last shot."

Coach looks at me. The whole team looks at me. I stand a little straighter to seem extra tall. I, in fact, am not height-challenged. I have a good inch and a half on Coach.

"I'll take the last shot," I repeat. Firmly.

"Are you sure, Nizhoni?" Davery whispers. He's my best friend—okay, my *only* friend—and always has my back, but right now he looks a little worried. His brown eyes are narrowed in concern behind his glasses and his lips press together thoughtfully. He runs a nervous hand over his short-cropped curly hair.

"Easy as pie," I insist. "You pass the ball to me. I'll be at the top of the key, and—*swish!*—Isotopes win!" I bust out my most confident smile.

Davery just crinkles his brow.

"Does anyone *else* want to take the last shot?" Coach asks, looking pointedly at the rest of the team. Everyone looks down or away or anywhere else but at Coach, because no one wants that kind of pressure. "Anyone?" she asks again, desperate.

I clear my throat loudly.

"Okay," Coach says, resigned. "Davery passes the ball to Nizhoni. Nizhoni, you take the shot. Be ready!"

Movement in the bleachers catches my eye. It's the monster.

I watch as he makes his way past the other spectators. He's pushy, knocking into people's knees without even saying

Excuse me. Rude! But then, monsters aren't known for their good manners. Some folks give him a dirty look as he shoves his way through, but most just move aside, rub their arms like they're cold, and mutter unhappily to the person next to them.

I lose sight of him as the crowd rises to their feet.

I twist my neck this way and that, straining to see where he disappeared to in the midst of screaming fans, but he's gone. Lost in a sea of black and red.

Coach claps just as the buzzer sounds, signaling the end of time-out.

Everyone on the team extends an arm into the middle of the circle, touches hands, and yells, "Isotopes!": a rallying cry for what must be the worst mascot in the history of mascots—expect maybe for this one team I heard of called the Fighting Pickles. But really, who even knows what an isotope is? Davery once tried to explain it to me—something to do with the history of nuclear technology and atomic bombs in New Mexico, blah, blah—but I fell asleep halfway through.

Coach is yelling. We hurry to take our spots. Davery is at midcourt with the ball in his hands. I run to the top of the key and get ready for the inbound pass.

I try to visualize the winning shot I'm about to make, like Coach tells us to. I can see it all—the crowd chanting my name, my teammates hoisting me on their shoulders and leading me around the gym in victory, just like a champion in a sports movie. Everyone will know me. I'll be a superstar! Fame! Glory!

I take another quick peek at the crowd, double-checking for the monster in the suit. Nothing, nothing . . . No, wait . . .

There he is! Bottom row, courtside, twenty feet away. His eyes are red and he's staring right at me!

Four things happen all at once.

1. I scream.

2. The ref blows the whistle.

3. Davery shouts my name.

4. And I turn toward him just in time for the basketball to hit me—*smack!*—right between the eyes.

◆

TWO

Blood Everywhere

I wake up flat on my back, blurry faces hovering over me.
My own face feels warm and sticky, and I reach for my nose.
My hand comes away coated in blood. I blink away tears as
I recognize Coach, Davery, and a few other teammates star-
ing down at me. A low murmur of disappointment in the air
tells me that the game is over. I hear the shuffle of thwarted
Isotopes fans leaving the gym.

And then I remember. I prop myself up on my elbows
and look around, but I don't see the monster in the black suit
anymore.

I sneak a glance at the scoreboard. The score was tied
before, but now the Isotopes are down by two, which
means . . . we lost.

I groan, more from embarrassment than pain.

"Take this," Coach says, shoving something cold and
lumpy in my hand. An ice pack.

"What happened?" I ask, pretty sure I already know but
hoping I'm wrong.

"You don't want to know the details," Davery warns me.

My nose hurts so badly it feels like it's going to fall off.
But I guess it's not, because Coach grunts and says, "Walk it

off, Begay. You're fine." Then Coach walks away herself. My teammates, who've been staring at me with various levels of horror, disgust, and disappointment, leave, too. I hear someone mutter, "What a loser."

"Thanks for caring," I mumble after their retreating backs.

"You okay?" Davery asks. He holds out his hand to pull me up.

"I'm fine," I say through a bloody nose, holding the ziplock bag full of ice to my face. Once I'm on my feet, I see that the gym has pretty much emptied out. Discarded popcorn bags and paper plates litter the bleachers.

"Coach tried to call your dad, but nobody answered," Davery informs me.

"She shouldn't have bothered," I mutter. "I'll just walk home."

Davery looks concerned, but I shrug it off. I know my friend feels bad for me, but I'm used to Dad not being able to make it to my basketball games, just like he wasn't able to attend my first-grade school play, when I had my first speaking role as a giant fungus in *The Very Hungry Caterpillar: An Interpretive Dance*. It's no surprise that he's too busy to pick up his injured and humiliated daughter who was clumsy enough to get hit in the face with a basketball and lose the game.

"How bad was it?" I ask Davery, bracing myself for the truth.

"Oh, your average humiliation," he says lightly. "Ball to the nose, blood everywhere. The Beavers get the rebound *off your face* and go down and score. The crowd goes wild." He cups his hands over his mouth and makes cheering noises. Then he drops his hands and adds, "Isotopes lose, in a dramatic upset. Nizhoni Begay is banned from ever setting foot in the ICCS gym again."

"Ugh."

"Yeah, 'ugh' is right. What happened? You were totally spacing out back there. I thought you were going to make the winning shot."

"I thought I was, too." At least, that was the plan. To be honest, I'm not very good at basketball, just like I'm not very good at most things. I even flubbed my one line in *The Very Hungry Caterpillar*. But an opportunity like that, to get all the glory, and have the fans scream your name? I had to try, right?

"I was really hoping to launch my bid for school fame," I confess as we start to walk toward the gym doors. "I've given up on being internet-famous, but school-famous still felt within the realm of possibility. A game-winning basket would have been a perfect start."

Davery snorts. "Well, that plan is a total loss. The only thing you launched was a thousand sad memes."

I chew my bottom lip, thinking. "Do you think this means all sports are out of reach now, or just basketball?"

"What did you have in mind?"

"I could try to join the lacrosse team."

"You don't know how to play lacrosse, either."

"A ball, a stick, how hard can it be?"

"Don't let the Haud Squad hear you say that."

The Haud Squad is the group of Haudenosaunee girls who rule the lacrosse team. Since their people invented the game, that makes sense.

"Okay, lacrosse is out. What about the swim team?" I barrel on. "Wait, do we even have a swim team?"

"Nizhoni . . ." Davery says, shaking his head.

"Cricket? Volleyball? Synchronized swimming?" I fling my free arm out in a ballet-like move. Davery ducks at the last minute to avoid getting hit in the head. Whoops! "Okay," I say, "maybe not synchronized swimming."

He sighs. "Why do you need to be famous, anyway?"

I stifle a groan. Davery wouldn't understand. His parents love him, dote on him, and turn up for everything he does. They were front and center for *The Very Hungry Caterpillar*. They even came to watch him present a book report once, which was, admittedly, a little awkward, since they were the only parents there and had to sit on those tiny chairs next to Laurie Wilder, who kept asking Davery if he was "really Indian." (Davery's mom is African American and his dad is Navajo, and small-minded people like Laurie can't fathom that folks can be part of two cultures—ignorance like that is another reason Davery and I both left our old public school and transferred to ICCS.) But at least Davery's parents cared enough to come. My dad didn't. And my mom . . . well, she's been gone since I was a toddler.

I clutch the turquoise pendant under my shirt. It's the only thing I have left of her besides the one picture of her, my dad, my little brother, and me that Dad keeps on the fireplace mantel. I still don't know why she abandoned us, and Dad won't talk about her, so I don't even get the benefit of his memories. Just this necklace. Sometimes it's enough, but more often it's not.

So I'm that kid. The one with no mom and a barely there dad, and some therapist would probably say I crave attention or approval or whatever, and that's why I try so hard to be popular. But it's not just that. It's something . . . deeper. Something more important. Yet every time I think I'm ready to try to explain the truth to Davery, I can't make the words come out. So instead I say, "Are you kidding me? Heroes get all the glory. Single-handedly winning the game at the last moment with a clutch shot? My eyes get teary just thinking about it. Besides, everyone knows you when you're the school hero. Maybe then people will learn how to pronounce my name."

We pause in front of the gym doors and Davery gives me a dubious look. "Like it's hard to say Nih-JHOH-NIH." He plants his hands on his hips. "I noticed how distracted you were in the game. What's really going on with you?"

For a second, I want to blurt it all out. But the words sit on my tongue, cold and uncomfortable, like the time I stuffed a whole bag of marbles in my mouth on a dare and they kept trying to escape from my cheeks. Almost died from that one. Didn't!

I want to tell Davery about the weird feeling I had about the man in the black suit, the surety that he wasn't human and the fact that, at least at that moment, his eyes were red. Explain that it isn't the first time I've sensed a monster. But I don't. The truth is, Davery is smart and funny and could have any friends he wanted. He hangs out with me because we've known each other since preschool—his dad and mine are old buddies from Fort Lewis College. It's probably just a matter of

11

time before he decides being with me is a liability he doesn't need. And then I'll be alone.

No, I can't tell him about the monsters and let him think I'm even weirder than he already knows I am. Besides, if I were him, I wouldn't believe me, because I can barely believe it myself.

"There's nothing going on with me, and I was distracted because I'm hungry. Feed me and I'll be fine."

"Hey," Davery says, "maybe we can go get froyo? Rainbow sprinkles to celebrate your humiliation?"

I laugh, accidently snorting dried blood up my bruised nose. "Ouch!!!" I know Davery's just trying to cheer me up by offering a delicious distraction, and I'm all for it. Rainbow sprinkles are my favorite.

"At least the bleeding's stopped," he says. "But your uniform is toast."

I glance down at my good old Isotopes jersey. The front of my shirt looks like a ketchup convention gone awry. Dad is not going to be happy. Although, on second thought: "It does look pretty heroic, right?"

"It looks like you lost a fight with an angry tomato."

Okay, so maybe not quite heroic.

"What gets bloodstains out?" I ask.

"Soda pop will get it out."

"Like from the vending machine?"

He nods. "It contains carbonic acid, which breaks down the proteins—"

"Okay, okay," I say, waving a hand. "Stop science-ing me. How do you know these things?"

"I like to read."

"I guess that's what happens when your dad's a librarian." The head librarian of the whole school district, in fact. Davery spends a lot of time in the main branch as a result.

"Even if he wasn't, I'd still like to read. I like knowing things." He frowns at the look on my face. "You should try it sometime, Z. That, and doing your homework. It's not so bad."

"Maybe, but doing homework is not how I'm going to find my true destiny." I push the exit door open and motion for him to go first, sighing over yet another missed opportunity to be a middle school superstar. Before I follow him out, I take one last look back at the nearly empty gym.

The custodian has already appeared to sweep up the mess, his broom moving steadily back and forth across the wood floor.

And there, at the top of the bleachers, is someone else. The man in the black suit.

Red eyes staring right at me.

THREE

◆

The Opposite of Rainbow Sprinkles

I have never been so happy to see my dad's white Honda Accord waiting in the pickup lane. He'd gotten the coach's message and come after all! I double-time it over and wrench open the car door, ready to slide into the passenger's side.

"Occupied," says a bored voice from that seat. Black hair hanging in his face, sneakers covered in doodles, llama-face T-shirt that says I JUST WANT TO FOCUS ON MY ART RIGHT NOW in a purple thought bubble. My little brother, Mac.

"Move it, Marcus," I say, using his full name for emphasis. "I'm oldest. I get the front seat."

Mac doesn't even look up from whatever art thing he's animating on his iPad. "You're only older by ten months, which means we're practically twins—"

"We are *not* twins."

"—which means I should get equal time in the front seat."

I huff, irritated, but decide it isn't worth fighting over.

"Hey, Mr. B," Davery says from behind me.

"Hey, Davery," Dad says, distracted. He's wearing a crisp blue dress shirt and has a fresh haircut, his black hair carefully combed back over his ears. He's texting on his phone, head down, and not paying attention to us. "How was the game?" Dad asks me, not even bothering to turn in my direction. "Your coach called and left a voice mail, but honestly, I can't understand a word that woman says. She was going on and on. . . ."

"Fine, Dad. I'm fine." *Just covered in blood, that's all.*

I open the back door, slide the flat pile of Dad's moving boxes up against the far side, and scoot in. I motion for Davery to get in the back seat, too, and he slides in next to me. It's a tight fit, but we manage. "Is it okay if Davery comes to froyo with us?"

"We're going for froyo?" Mac asks, looking up excitedly.

In the rearview mirror, I see Dad's face crinkle up like he's in pain. "I'd like to, Z, but my new boss is in town and he's coming over for dinner. I really need to get home and prepare—"

"He's not your new boss yet," I protest. Even worse than being humiliated and seeing monsters, we might have to move from Albuquerque to Tulsa for Dad's new job in a few months, when the school year is over.

"Nizhoni," Dad says, sounding exasperated, "we've had this conversation before. If you and your brother want me to be able to pay for things like fancy basketball sneakers and art classes"—he shoots a pointed look at Mac—"then I need a better-paying job. And that job is in—"

"Oklahoma," Mac and I finish for him, in unison.

He stares straight ahead for a minute, clearly not amused. "Landrush Oil and Gas is a major company. If they offer me the job, I'm taking it. End of story." He looks back down at his phone and starts texting again, and I know for sure I've blown my chance at rainbow sprinkles.

"Isn't Landrush that company people are protesting for putting in that pipeline?" Davery asks, low enough that Dad can't hear him.

I nod miserably. Another reason Dad should definitely not take this job. But when I tried to talk to him about companies like Landrush ruining the water and land, he told me folks have to eat, and unless the protesters were going to pay his rent, he wasn't interested. "He won't listen," I tell Davery. "And, sorry, but it looks like froyo's a no-go."

"It's okay, Nizhoni," Davery says, opening the door and sliding back out of the car. "My dad's still at the main library. I'll just head over there. Text me later?"

I slump in my seat and wave him good-bye.

Dad pulls out of the pickup lane to merge with traffic. Now he's talking with the phone up to his ear, which, last time I checked, is illegal to do while driving in the city of Albuquerque, New Mexico. But it also means he's not paying attention when I lean forward to talk to Mac.

"I saw something," I whisper to my brother, the only person who knows about my secret. "A you-know-what."

Mac's head snaps up, revealing a worried expression, which immediately transforms into a grin. "Whoa! What happened to your face?"

"What happened to *your* face?" I ask. Because Mac has a huge black eye, which, sadly, is not that unusual for him.

"What do you think?" Mac mutters, doing his signature hair flip that drops his bangs down over his eyes, hiding the evidence.

"Adrien Cuttlebush?" That's Mac's nemesis. He's a seventh-grader, like me, and Mac's only in sixth, but they know each other from summer camp, where Mac did something to Adrien that he won't fess up about. Ever since then, Adrien has had it out for him. Cuttlebush once flushed Mac's entire sketchpad—a new one he'd just gotten for his birthday—down the boys' bathroom toilet, one sheet at a time. *Rip. Flush. Rip. Flush.* Brutal. And another time, he tried to flush Mac *himself* down the toilet, but the assistant principal intervened before Adrien could get more than a sneakered foot in the bowl.

"I told you I'd help you fight him," I say. "No way are you gonna be able to take on him and his goon squad all by yourself."

"What are you going to do, Nizhoni?" he asks, sounding bitter. "Bleed on him?"

I wince. Low blow. I've been trying my best to keep Mac safe from his nemesis, but I'm not very good at that, either.

He grimaces, like he's sorry he snapped at me. "So did the monster—?" He points at my nose.

"Monster-size basketball!" I say quickly, cutting him off. Mac tends to talk before he thinks. I don't want Dad to know I see monsters. He has enough to worry about, what with the new job prospect and all. "Right to the face."

"So what did you see?" Mac whispers. We both look over to make sure Dad's not paying attention. Yup. Totally into his phone call about boring surveyor stuff—no way he's listening to us. Or looking—he still hasn't said anything about my bloody uniform, and I doubt he's even noticed Mac's puffy eye.

"Definite monster." I hand my brother the ice pack, because my nose feels better. "Wait . . ." I wipe blood off the pack with the only clean corner of my shirt. "Here."

He gives me a grateful smile and holds the bag to his bruised skin. "What did he look like?"

Mac keeps thinking the monsters are going to be covered in scales or grow tentacles or something, but most of the time, they appear normal.

They just don't *feel* normal.

"He looked human, but I could tell." And then I lean closer to whisper, "He was in the bleachers at the end of the game, and I swear he was watching me."

Even now I feel a trickle of fear.

"Did you do anything? Make eye contact?" Mac's face lights up. "Did he take a bite out of anyone?"

"We definitely made eye contact. His eyes were red."

"Wow! Like, glowing red? Or just, um, bloodshot like he didn't get enough sleep?"

"I don't remember. It happened pretty fast, and then I got injured." When I say it like that, it sounds pretty weak. But I know I'm not wrong. I just can't explain the way it feels.

"Was he staring at you before you got face-bombed?"

I shiver as a million tiny ice-footed ants march down my spine. "Do you think he knows I can . . . ?" It never occurred to me that the monsters might be able to single me out the same way I can identify them, and now I'm extra freaked.

We turn onto our street and our house comes into view. I blow out a breath, relieved to be safe.

We only live a five-minute drive from school. Most of the time I just walk home, since Dad's too busy to come get me. But I guess that call from Coach did work. And he even picked up Mac from art class. Probably because he needed to make sure we were home for this dinner.

"Your monster spotting seems to be happening more and more lately. Maybe we should tell someone," Mac says quietly.

"What am I going to say? There was a guy who looked like a pretty normal guy but was really a monster? And get this, he was *staring* at me? You think anyone will believe me? Or care?"

"Too bad there's not a real-life Ghostbusters hotline, but for monsters! With the cool hearse and the plasma boxes and . . . Hey, who's that?"

We pull into the driveway in front of our pretty basic and totally average-looking modest adobe house. But the car parked out front—a big black Cadillac Escalade—is not basic or modest at all. Tinted windows, oversize rims . . . it looks like something out of the movies. The kind of car the government sends to pick you up, and then you're never seen or heard from ever again.

It gives me the creeps.

"Did the neighbors get a new car or something?" Mac asks.

No way that's our neighbor's car. Ms. Abeyta drives a lime-green Prius with a bumper sticker that says YOU CAN'T FART WITHOUT MAKING A LITTLE ART. I don't really see her upgrading to a Caddy.

"Let's go back, Dad," I say, suddenly sure we don't want

to be here. I can't say why, but I know that car means nothing good. "I—I forgot my homework in my locker. Gotta go back!"

"What?" Dad asks as he swipes to end his call. "Don't be silly. That's my new boss, Mr. Charles. I was texting with him before. He arrived early, and he's going to take us out to dinner. So I don't have to cook! Isn't that great?"

I can't see anything through the SUV's dark windows, but I can feel an evil presence nearby, just like at the game. The hairs on my neck rise. The chill puts goose bumps on my arms. I squeeze Mac's shoulder.

"Ow!" he whines.

I point with my chin to the car, making *Something is not right* eyes. Unfortunately, Mac thinks I'm making *I need to go pee* eyes, so he says, "Just hold it, Nizhoni. We're almost inside."

I try again, but now he's looking at the SUV.

Someone gets out: a Black man with a shaved head and deep brown skin like Davery's. He's wearing a white suit, and a holster is showing under the jacket. "Is that a gun?" I squeak.

"Bodyguard," Dad says, laughing a little nervously. "Mr. Charles is very high up in the oil and gas industry, which makes him a target for protesters. In fact, it's kind of strange that he would come all this way just to interview me, but he said he was in town and he really cares about all his employees, even the lowliest surveyors." Dad's forehead wrinkles up, like he's just now realizing how unusual this is. "I, uh, guess they do things differently in Oklahoma," he says with another little laugh.

A second person gets out of the car. This one's a Native American woman, but not Navajo like us. Maybe from a Plains tribe. She's just as tall and muscled as the first bodyguard, with the same white suit and the same gun.

"Two bodyguards," Mac says incredulously. "Who *is* this mysterious Mr. Charles?"

I make a little hiccup sound when I see there's one more person getting out of the car. Tall. Blond. Unusually red lips. Black suit. Mirrored sunglasses.

"That's him," Dad says as he unbuckles his seat belt. He exhales, like he's preparing himself for battle. He puts on a bright fake smile and opens the door. "Come shake hands, kids."

"Mac!" I whisper, squeezing his shoulder harder. "Stop him!"

"Stop who? Dad?"

I nod, frantically. Dad's halfway across the yard, hand outstretched. Seconds from contact.

"That's him!" I whisper.

"Who's 'him'?"

"The one I saw at the gym. The guy who was watching me."

"But . . ." Mac frowns, confused. Then he goes all bug-eyed as he finally understands.

"Dad! Noooooo!" we both scream, banging on the window glass. But it's too late.

He reaches out, and we watch as our dad shakes hands with a monster.

◆

FOUR

Remain Calm

"What do we do?" Mac squeaks.

I'm not sure, but I do know one thing. "We remain calm. We have the upper hand right now."

"How do you figure?"

"He won't want to blow his cover in front of Dad, right? So as long as we play it cool . . ." I glance over at Mac. His expression reminds me of that time we went to the amusement park and he insisted on riding the Cyclone right after he'd eaten three chili dogs. Part super-excited, part terrified, and part ready to barf. "I said play it cool, Mac. *C-O-O-L*. Right now you look decidedly uncool."

"I'm trying," he says. He takes a few deep breaths, nervously shuffling the ice pack between his hands.

Dad is eagerly waving us over.

"We better go," I say. "Dad's waiting."

"He's going to want us to shake hands," Mac reminds me.

Dad always wants us to shake hands with everyone. Once, we went to this honoring ceremony for Native American veterans. There were at least thirty of them there from all different tribal nations, and Mac and I had to walk the entire line and shake every single hand. I was really annoyed at first, because I was hungry and everyone knows that elders get to eat first, so it was going to take forever. But then it turned out to be kind of cool to meet all those people and see their medals up close. One grandpa had even been a Navajo Code Talker in World War II. I think he must have heard my stomach growling, because he slipped me a chocolate chip cookie on the sly. I was so grateful, and ever since then, I haven't minded shaking hands so much.

However, this time I mind a lot.

"No way I'm touching a monster," I protest.

"What else can we do? Run for it?"

"Yeah, that'd be real cool." I sigh. "Come on. I've got an idea. Just follow my lead, okay? And whatever you do, don't touch him." I don't know much about monsters, but it seems like common sense. Who knows what could happen? They could slime on you, suck out your soul, eat your eyeballs. The terrible possibilities are endless.

We get out of the car together and walk slowly over to Dad, Mr. Charles, and the two bodyguards in white. I see Dad focus on us and his eyebrows shoot up. Looks like he's finally noticed my bloody shirt and Mac's black eye. But he doesn't have time to say anything before Mr. Charles speaks.

"So this must be Nizhoni and Marcus," Mr. Charles says enthusiastically, giving us an oversize grin. "But holy heck, what happened to y'all? You both look like you've been wrestling longhorns!" Despite his fancy suit, he's got a twangy accent that shouts *Aw shucks* and *Gee whiz* like a fake cowboy in an old movie. I don't trust it.

"Sports injury." I narrow my eyes at Mr. Charles and

wait to see if he says anything. After all, he was there. But he doesn't let on that he knows, and it's hard to figure out what he's thinking behind those sunglasses. His face is just politely curious, and maybe a little grossed out. What kind of monster gets faint at the sight of blood?

"Well, shoot. Sorry about that, but it looks like you survived," says Mr. Charles. "Nice to meet you both!" He thrusts his right hand in front of me. It looks perfectly normal, but I remind myself that it's not, that this a disguise. Underneath that perfectly normal-looking skin is something truly awful—something scaly or tentacle-y or . . . or . . .

"Better not," I say, trying to sound regretful. I hold up my hand and wiggle my fingers. Thankfully, there's still some blood underneath my nails and dried bits flaking off my palm, so I have the ideal excuse.

"Go get cleaned up, Nizhoni," Dad says, gesturing to the front door. He nudges Mac to shake hands.

"My hands are full," Mac says. He clutches his iPad closer to his chest, eyes wide. "Sorry."

"Don't be ridiculous," Dad says, and takes his iPad away. And just like that, Mac runs out of excuses.

I gulp, worried . . . and watch as Mac reluctantly reaches out and shakes Mr. Charles's hand.

I squeeze my eyes shut, shoulders tense, and wait for Mac to scream in pain. Or freeze and fall over. Or for his eyes to flash green and for him to start talking in a robot voice, hypnotized by Mr. Charles's touch.

But when I open my eyes . . .

Nothing happens.

Charles lets go, and then Mac moves over and shakes hands with the two bodyguards—first the man, who introduces himself as Mr. Rock, and then the woman, who says her name is Ms. Bird. And nothing weird or scary happens. Nothing at all.

Well, besides Mac looking back at me over his shoulder and giving me a huge thumbs-up.

"What happened to playing it cool?" I mutter under my breath.

"Hurry up and get ready, Nizhoni," Dad says. "And put on something nice. Mr. Charles is taking us to the Pasta Palace for dinner."

Did I hear that right? The monster is taking us to my favorite restaurant for dinner? Is that even allowed?

Behind me I hear Mac ask the woman bodyguard, "Is that a real gun? Can I see it?"

And now I am thoroughly confused. I still have that feeling that makes the hairs on the back of my neck stand up, but Mr. Charles hasn't done anything that would make me think he was evil. Was I wrong about him being a monster? Was I wrong about Dad and Mac being in danger? Was I wrong about everything?

◆

FIVE

A Very Interesting Family

I wash up quickly, getting rid of both the lingering blood and the gym-socks smell from basketball, and like Dad said, I pick out something nice to wear. Not too nice, in case the monster calling himself Mr. Charles attacks us or something and I have to make a run for it. But clean jeans, my favorite Frank Waln shirt, and a pair of Nike N7 sneakers. I'm leaving my bedroom, pulling the door closed, when I notice something odd.

Mr. Charles is standing in our living room by himself—no Dad or Mac, and no bodyguards. He's in front of the mantel, where we keep some family photos. He picks up the largest, peering at it closely before setting the frame down and examining the next. I know which picture it is from here—it's the one of my whole family, including my mom. Mr. Charles flips the frame over and turns the clasp that holds the photo inside. He starts to slide out the paper. Wait . . . he's stealing it?! He shouldn't even be touching it! It's special, and he needs to keep his monster paws off.

"What are you doing?" I snap.

He looks up, sunglasses still on, and calmly slides the photo back into the frame and sets it down. "Hello, Nizhoni."

26

His blond hair looks almost silver in the late-afternoon light coming in from the windows, and he smiles self-assuredly, showing a mouth full of perfect white teeth. He pulls something from his pocket and palms it so I can't tell what it is.

"Did you know that your name means 'beauty' in Navajo?" he continues. "Well, of course you did." He chuckles. "It's your name."

"Where's my dad?"

"You have a very interesting family," he says, gesturing back to the photos and ignoring my questions. "Is that your mother?"

I glare at him. No way I'm telling him anything.

"I never met her, of course, but she is known to my . . ." He pauses, as if searching for a word. ". . . associates."

"Monsters?" I blurt out.

His face freezes for a moment, but then he grins. "I see you and I don't have to play games. That's good. I like that we can be honest with each other." All traces of his hokey cowboy accent are gone.

I knew it! All my feelings were right! Mr. Charles *is* a monster. But on the heels of my triumph comes dread. Why is a monster interested in my family, and how would he and his so-called associates know about my mom?

"As long as we're being honest," Mr. Charles says, "let me tell you why I'm here. To explain that, I'll have to start with your mother. Did you know her side of the family goes way back in Navajo history? All the way back to the goddess Changing Woman? She's—"

"I know about Changing Woman. But we call her a Holy

Person, not a goddess," I say, lifting my chin and trying to sound brave. "I mean, as long as we're being honest."

My shimásání—that's what I call my grandmother on my mother's side—taught me that Changing Woman created the clan system of the Navajo people. The system tells us who we're related to, and it's one of the first things Mac and I had to learn. Since I carry three of the original clans in my lineage, being descended from Changing Woman isn't as strange as it might sound.

Mr. Charles's greasy grin gets bigger, if that's even possible. His bright teeth look sharp behind his lips. "Such a smart girl," he says, in a creepy fake-compliment voice. "Then I assume you also know that your mother's ancestry can be traced directly to one of Changing Woman's sons."

I don't remember my shimásání ever saying anything about Changing Woman's *son*. And how does this white dude from some oil and gas company know anything about Navajo stories, anyway? A chill crawls down my spine.

"Perhaps I don't have to explain why I'm here," Mr. Charles goes on. "Perhaps you already know." He raises an expectant eyebrow.

"To take us to the Pasta Palace?" I blurt out, fear making me say something ridiculous. Real smooth, Nizhoni.

He laughs. Twirls whatever it is he has in his hands. It's a long black object that glints in the afternoon light, but I still can't get a good look at it. "You can probably guess that I'm a very powerful man. I run a corporation worth billions of dollars. On my private estate, I have dozens of people at my beck and call. I'm not used to being thwarted. And yet, it was recently brought to my attention that there is a girl, the daughter of our former enemy, who could impede my plans for the future." He steps closer.

My back is up against my bedroom door. I'm not trying to be brave anymore. In fact, I'm considering screaming. Through the living room window I can see my dad outside, chatting with those bodyguards. Isn't he wondering why I haven't come out yet? What his boss is doing? Unless Mr. Charles used some power to make Dad forget all about me . . . not that he needs much help in that department.

"Well, imagine how upset this news made me," he says. "I've worked so hard for all that I have." He puts his sunglasses on top of his head, and I see that his eyes are bloodred. He stares at me and my whole body freezes up. His gaze is powerful, dangerous. I felt it before, at my basketball game, and I feel it again now. "With the hope that I could prove my associates wrong, I had to come see for myself. It was easy enough to set up a meeting with your father. And when you recognized my true identity at the basketball game . . ."

I shake my head and start to say something, but he cuts me off.

"Oh, don't bother denying it. We're being honest here, remember? I found that it was true. You are your mother's daughter. And I'm sorry, Nizhoni, but I can't afford to have one girl, one tiny speck of a girl, ruin everything."

"But I can't ruin anything!" I protest. My heart is beating a mile a minute, and I just want out of here. "I see stuff sometimes, I admit it, but that's all."

"*Stuff?*" He chuckles, waving my words away. "It's okay,

Nizhoni. You can say it. You can detect monsters. But interestingly enough, your brother cannot. In fact, I thought he might take after your father instead of your mother and be perfectly mundane. But then Marcus shook my hand, and I felt his unrealized potential. He's special, too."

I knew it was a bad idea to shake his hand! A burst of anger overrides my fear, and I shout, "You better not touch my brother!"

"So fierce. What a good sister you are! But don't worry about Marcus. I want him alive. His power is different from yours, and once it manifests, he will come in quite handy for my business needs. You, however . . ." He shakes his head sadly. "It does pain me to hurt youngsters, it really does. But best to do it now, before you grow up and truly become a problem. I am so very sorry, Nizhoni, but I'm afraid . . ." He stops twirling the object in his hand and points it at me. It's long and flat and made of black stone, and it looks sharp at one end.

My heart thuds hard in my chest when I realize he's holding an obsidian knife.

". . . I need you dead."

SIX

◆

No Spaghettini Macaravioli for You!

I don't even think before I run full tilt at Mr. Charles. His startled eyes are the last thing I see before I kick that knife right out of his hand. It goes skittering across the tile floor.

Whoa! Where did that move come from?

But I'm not done. I head-butt Mr. Charles in the stomach. He goes *Whooof* and stumbles back. And for good measure, I execute a perfect elbow strike to the cheek, just like I learned in the self-defense class Coach taught in PE last year. I've never been able to do it before, but this time it's a direct hit. And it's fast! I'm fast! Mr. Charles definitely makes an *Uggghhh* sound.

"Nizhoni!" my dad yells from the open front door, horrified.

I pause in my vicious monster-fighting onslaught to look over. It's not just Dad, but also Mac and the two body-guards pushing through the entryway. They're all staring at me, mouths open, eyes big as frybreads. Well, I can't see the bodyguards' eyes behind their reflective sunglasses, but something tells me they're huge.

"What on earth . . . ?" My dad rushes forward to help Mr. Charles. The man is bent over, one hand holding his stomach and the other rubbing his cheek. "I am so sorry," Dad murmurs as he helps Mr. Charles stand up straight. "I have no idea what is wrong with her."

Wrong with *me*? "He had a knife!" I exclaim. "I was protecting myself!"

Dad looks around. "I see no knife."

"I kicked it away," I say. "It's on the floor over there." I gesture vaguely in its direction.

Mr. Rock bends over and picks something up. "This?" he asks, holding up a sharp, deadly . . . mechanical pencil.

"It was a knife!" I insist.

Mr. Rock presses the fraction of lead sticking out of the top of the pencil, and it breaks off with an audible *snap*, showing how thin and fragile it is. Mac makes a low whistle and mouths, *Way to play it cool, Z.*

"But—but . . ." I take a step toward Mr. Rock, ready to search his pockets. *Of course* he switched out the knife for the pencil, *of course* he's hiding it. He works for Mr. Charles, doesn't he?

"Not so fast," Dad says, holding out an arm to stop me in my tracks. He grabs my wrist like a vise, and the low rumble in his voice tells me I'm in big trouble. The only thing worse than the rumble is when he calls me by my full name.

"Don't you think you've caused enough trouble, Nizhoni Marie Begay?"

Welp!

Mac mouths, *You are so grounded.*

I narrow my eyes. Oh, no. I'm not getting blamed for this

one. "Dad, he had a knife, honest! He was threatening to kill me! Why else was he in our house—?"

"I came in to use the little boys' room," Mr. Charles says with an embarrassed *Aw shucks* chuckle.

Oh, please. Surely Dad's not falling for that. I mean, do monsters even pee?

"Then why were you studying our family photos?" I ask with a growl.

"I was admiring them," he says. "You have such a lovely family."

Aha! More lies! Everyone knows Mac is funny-looking.

I ask, "Then why did you need a pencil?"

He crinkles his brow, puzzled. "You asked me for an autograph. Don't you remember?" He holds up a small flip-top notepad. Mr. Rock pumps the eraser to load fresh lead and hands the pencil to Mr. Charles, who signs a piece of paper with a flourish. He tears it out and holds it out to me.

"Thanks," I mutter, taking the paper automatically. I look down at it and see that he has very nice handwriting. That seems odd for a monster. . . . Wait, monsters give autographs? Double wait, I never asked for his autograph. He's totally lying!

Dad simmers.

Mac mouths, *Loser.*

"Dad!" I start to protest, but he's not listening.

"To your room!" he says, quietly but firmly pushing me down the hall.

"I swear he had a knife!" One last protest.

We're at my bedroom door, and he marches me across the

33

threshold, plants me by the bed, and turns to me. I've never seen him so mad. His face is bright red, his eyes are wet like he's about to cry, and the veins in his neck are pulsing with parental rage.

"I have never been so embarrassed in my entire life!" he hisses through gritted teeth. "How could you attack my potential new boss, who I'm trying to impress? And then make up some wild story about a knife?!"

"But—"

"No!" He holds up a hand. "You're done talking, Nizhoni. In fact, you're done, period. You are staying here while the rest of us go to Pasta Palace and have a nice violence-free dinner. You are not to leave this room, and I'm taking your phone, too, so you can spend time thinking about what you've done. Do you hear me?" He raises a shaky hand to his face and pushes his short hair back. "And I am going to apologize profusely and try to save my job. I know you don't want us to move away, but you've gone too far. Much, much too far! I hate to say it, but I am ashamed of you."

And just like that, all the fight goes out of me. I feel like a worm. Worse—the end of a worm. Worm butt, that's me. I feel my stomach sink, and tears rush to my eyes.

My father gives me one last look, a look of pure shame, before he closes my bedroom door right in my face. I stand there for a minute, staring at the back of the door. I can hear Dad making more apologies to Mr. Charles and that slimeball laughing it off and asking if I cause trouble in school. Unfortunately, I also hear Mac helpfully volunteering that I once had to attend a Saturday anger management class at my old school for punching Elora Huffstratter in the nose. But Mac neglects to mention that Elora Huffstratter, a white girl, said my mom left us because I was a dirty Indian. Then she made war-whooping noises like something out of a bad Western. So, as far as I'm concerned, Elora totally had it coming. I would do it again in a heartbeat, even if it meant another Saturday anger management class.

Mac has totally bought into Mr. Charles's act. My little brother has no idea that we're both in danger, and I can't warn him without my phone.

More voices and footsteps, and they're all leaving. I hear the *click* of the front door as it closes. I rush to my window to watch everyone pile into the big black Escalade and drive away. Everyone except Ms. Bird, who turns and heads back to the house. I open my door a crack to see her plop down on the living room couch and pick a magazine off the coffee table. Looks like she's getting left behind to make sure I don't escape.

And just like that, my day of average humiliation becomes a day of spectacular humiliation.

No family, no phone, and everyone believes a monster's word over mine.

I flop on my bed and maybe, just a little, because nobody's here to see it, I cry.

SEVEN

◆

Mr. Yazzie

No matter what I do, sleep won't come. I toss and turn and flip and flop, utterly miserable. I try to get more comfortable, fluffing my pillows and smoothing my blankets until they're all lined up with the sheets the way I like them, but nothing works. Still wide-awake. Because, honestly, how could I sleep after what Mr. Charles said to me?

I replay the conversation in my head, trying to make sense of it. According to him, my dad is totally normal but my mom is *a former enemy*, because she's directly related to Changing Woman's son, whoever that was. And that makes me a threat. But how can I be a threat? I did land a pretty spectacular head butt to his stomach, but he wanted to kill me even before that.

Maybe I should run away. But I can't leave Mac behind. Charles wants him for something. What did he mean by *He will come in quite handy . . .*? My empty stomach flops at the thought of Mac being brainwashed—or worse—by a monster at this very moment.

But if Dad doesn't believe me, what am I supposed I do? His boss can lie all he wants, but when I told the truth, I got punished.

"I do not deserve this," I say aloud.

"There are very few things we do deserve," says a voice from the top of my bookshelf. It sounds croaky, a bit like that of an old man who's smoked too many cigars.

I sit straight up, blinking furiously.

"Haven't you ever heard that saying," the voice continues, 'Life is a box of chocolates?' Oh dear, no, that's not it. 'Life is a bed of roses?' No, no . . . What is the blasted saying? I know: 'Life's not fair'!"

Am I hallucinating? Did the basketball to the face knock something loose?

"Did . . . did someone speak?" I ask hesitantly.

"Why, of course someone is speaking. *Me!*"

I slide off the bed and make my way warily toward the source of the voice. It's coming from the top shelf of my bookcase, where I keep my favorite stuffed animals. I know I'm a little old for them, but some have been my friends for so long, I just couldn't bear to give them away when Dad came around with the donation box right before Christmas.

"Who's there?" I scan the shelf for a hidden speaker. Maybe Mr. Charles bugged my room. But the voice sounds nothing like his, and I don't see anything suspicious. . . . "Hello?" I ask cautiously.

"Yá'át'ééh!" someone responds in Navajo.

I reach up and quickly part the animals, pushing aside a purple bear and a pink narwhal named Cupcake, to find the owner of the voice.

In the middle of the shelf sits my stuffed horned toad,

Mr. Yazzie. But Mr. Yazzie is no longer a toy. He's a very real, very alive lizard—spiky head, beady black eyes, and all. And I'm pretty sure he's smiling at me.

"Are you—" I whisper in awe.

"A na'asho'ii dich'izhii?"

"Uh . . . I was going to ask if you were a talking horned toad."

The little guy frowns. "Na'asho'ii dich'izhii means horned toad, and I am most certainly talking, so I believe the answer to your question is yes."

"Is this for real? I mean, how did you get here? Where did you come from?"

"Why, from *you*, Nizhoni. You picked me out at the Museum of Indian Arts and Culture gift shop. Have you forgotten?" He looks crestfallen.

"Not at all!" I rush to reassure him. "I just remember you being a bit different."

"Oh, yes. You mean"—he pokes his side with a little claw—"not alive."

I nod. While others might scream or faint when a formerly stuffed horned toad speaks to them, I've been raised to take seemingly supernatural things in stride. Up to now, talking animals hadn't been a part of my everyday life, but my shimásání told me that there's more to the world than we humans can see, and it's best to keep an open mind. So that's what I'm doing—keeping an open mind. A slightly freaked-out open mind.

"Well, quite right," Mr. Yazzie says. "Of course. Thank

you, by the way, for choosing me. It gets a bit boring, living in a museum. I mean, it's not that I don't enjoy a seeing a new exhibit every once in a while, but honestly, even lizards like a bit of adventure. And let's face it—living things don't belong in a museum."

A couple of years ago, Dad dragged Mac and me to the Museum of Indian Arts and Culture in Santa Fe for a lecture on contemporary Navajo jewelry. The lecture was pretty good, but Mac wouldn't stop fidgeting, so Dad had sent us out to browse in the gift shop. He even gave us some spending money. Mac went straight for the art books, of course, and I loved looking at all the bright scarves and silver jewelry, but what really caught my attention was the shelf of stuffed toys based on animals native to the Southwest. There had been a lot of great choices, but the palm-size horned toad was my favorite. He had a sand-colored hide and a wide, flat body, with a mane of small horns that flared around his face like a fierce cross between a lion and a dragon. The tag attached to his short tail said that horned toads were considered a blessing and symbol of protection by traditional Navajos. If you caught one, the little grandfather (as we sometimes call horned toads) might help you in the future. Best of all, he was soft and fluffy but tough and prickly at the same time, kind of how I saw myself. We were kindred spirits.

But that was before he started talking to me.

"I don't mean to be rude," I say, "but how long have you been . . . alive?"

"Oh dear, where are my manners? Allow me to introduce

myself. I am Theodous Alvin Yazzie." He holds out a little claw to me.

"Yes, I know." I gently pinch his claw between my thumb and finger and shake. "I gave you that name."

"You did?" he murmurs. "Indeed, indeed. How could I forget? That's what sitting on a shelf will do to the old brain. Don't suppose you have any coffee?"

Of course my previously stuffed horned toad wants coffee. Totally normal.

"I'm not allowed to drink coffee. Dad says it will stunt my growth. But if you really want some, maybe later I could warm up some instant. . . ." If I ever get out of my room, that is.

He makes a disgusted face. "Instant? Bah."

I've never understood the appeal of a drink that smells like gym socks and dirt, but adults—and talking horned toads, apparently—take it quite seriously. Wait, why am I thinking about coffee? Focus, Nizhoni! Recently animated stuffed animal here! "So why are you talking to me?"

He smiles. Or at least I think he does when the sides of his wide mouth curl up like that. He could just have gas for all I know. "Because you need me. To help you fight the monster."

"You mean Mr. Charles?"

"Most assuredly."

"I seem to be the only one who can tell. My dad thinks I'm making it up."

"Because he's not familiar with the old stories," Mr. Yazzie says with a melancholy sigh. "Or he has forgotten them in his grief over losing your mother."

I wonder how the lizard knows so much about my

dad . . . and my mom. Everyone seems to know more about her than I do. It's getting frustrating.

"The elders don't pass things down the way they used to," continues Mr. Yazzie, "and the young people don't care to learn. Back when I was just a small toad, we were taught all the old stories—the Four Worlds that came before this one, First Man and First Woman . . . My personal favorites are the Hero Twins," he says. "No one tells any of these stories very much anymore, so people have forgotten how to live in the world." He sighs again.

"I'm sorry," I say, seeing his spiky mane droop sadly. "I mean, I'm sorry no one's learning the stories. My shimásání taught me some when I had my kinaalda." Then something occurs to me. "In fact, now that I think about it, I saw my first monster soon after that."

"Your coming-of-age ceremony surely awakened your powers," Yazzie says matter-of-factly. "So shall we go slay the monster, then? But I'm getting ahead of myself, aren't I? Never lock a gift horse in the house. . . . No, you can lead a horse to fodder. . . . No, no. . . . Oh, yes. We must not put the cart before the horse!"

He looks so happy, recovered from his moment of melancholy, that I hate to bust his bubble. But bust I must. "I'm all for fighting Mr. Charles, but I'm stuck in my room, if you hadn't noticed. Besides, what can one girl and a once-stuffed horned toad do against a monster with a knife? No offense about the stuffed part."

Mr. Yazzie huffs a bit, as if he was indeed offended by the stuffed part, but he says, "He had a knife, did he? Of course he did, being a monster and all. Don't expect him to fight fair. We'll just have to procure you some weapons of your own, won't we?"

"Weapons?" That sounds promising.

"Yes! But we'll have to go get them." He looks at me. "Do you have the map?"

"What map?" I ask. "I don't have any map." Maybe the weapons are buried somewhere, like a treasure chest. "Maybe we can Google Map it?" I ask hopefully. Well, once I get out of my room and have my phone back.

"My dear," he says, puffing out his collar a bit, "we are looking for the Glittering World, which, I can assure you, is not on any Google Map. Umm . . . what exactly *is* a Google Map? Never mind. The map must have been lost. We'll need a new one."

"How do we get a new one?"

"Na'ashjéii Asdzáá can help us."

"Who?"

"Her map," Mr. Yazzie continues, ignoring my question, "will show us the path to the House of the Sun. Once you get there, you will ask him politely for the right weapons."

"I am trying to keep an open mind," I say carefully, "but you say 'him' like the sun's a person, and last time I checked, the sun was a huge star millions of miles away in outer space." Or at least I *think* that's what the sun is. Where's Davery with his science facts when I need him?

"The Sun is much more than a star in the Glittering World. There, the Sun has a fine house at the end of the Rainbow Road. Lovely, really. I've been there often. Well, a few times, anyway. But, a warning, he can be rude. His nickname *is* the Merciless One."

"Umm . . . maybe we should skip his place, then?"

"No. If you want your weapons, that's where we must go."

"Can we do all this before my dad gets home? Because if he finds out I went on some crazy quest to a glittering rainbow place for monster-killing weapons when I wasn't even supposed to leave my room, I'll be grounded until high school." It's supposed to be a joke—my way of dealing with all the scary things Mr. Yazzie's telling me—but the horned toad doesn't laugh.

"If you don't succeed, Nizhoni," Mr. Yazzie says, his tone serious, "you won't have to worry about high school."

I swallow the lump in my throat.

Mr. Yazzie peers at me with one big eye. "This is important, Nizhoni. I want you to understand that the dangers we will face are very real. You must be prepared. Throughout history, other people have tried to fight monsters and failed."

"What happened to them?"

"They disappeared and were never heard from again. I can only assume they perished."

"'Perished,' as in 'd-died'?"

"Well, yes. What do you think happens to monsterslayers who fail to slay monsters? They're called monsters for a reason, and it's not because they're warm and fuzzy." For a long moment, Mr. Yazzie looks at me without saying anything. Little beads of sweat trickle down the sides of my face.

"Death is always a possibility," he says finally, "but this is your destiny. You must put a stop to this enemy, and not only for your own sake, but also for your people. If you are brave enough, and determined enough, I will do what I can to help. Are you willing to try?"

My destiny. I'd thought my destiny was to be a sports hero or an internet sensation. But instead, I'm supposed to be a fighter. For my family.

What did he call me? A monsterslayer? That sounds kind of cool. It's not what I'd expected, but I'm okay with that. I mean, I'm not okay with dying, but this is a chance to do something real, something important. It's what I've been waiting for all this time.

I nod, crossing my fingers that I'll be up to the task. "Okay. I'll do it."

"Very good. Then wake up!" And with that, Mr. Yazzie gathers his powerful legs beneath his reptile body and leaps from the shelf.

Straight at my face.

◆

EIGHT

It Helps to Be a Sensitive Artist

I wake to a quiet knock on the door. I open my eyes, feeling like I'm pulling myself out of a vat of thick honey. And then it all comes back to me in a flash. I remember Mr. Yazzie and the horrible way he launched himself at me, and I bolt straight out of bed. I look around wildly, hands clutching at my cheeks, feeling for damage. I'm not sure what damage a pet horned toad could do, but wild ones are quite fierce, so I imagine it could be bad. But no, my face is fine. Well, except my nose is still sore from basketball. I breathe a sigh of relief.

Another knock, this time louder.

"Who's there?" I ask warily, half expecting to hear a strange little croaking reply.

"Nizhoni? Can I come in?"

Just Dad. Not a talking lizard. Relief . . . Or maybe not. Because if it isn't Mr. Yazzie at my door, then I must have been asleep and dreamed the whole thing and there's no one to help me fight Mr. Charles.

"Nizhoni?" Dad asks again. "Please let me in."

I make a quick pass by the bookshelf to see if a certain stuffed animal is where he should be (he is—looking completely not alive) and go over to unlock the door before flopping back down on the mattress. I try to fake being calm, though my heart is beating out of my chest. Mr. Yazzie seemed so real. . . .

But I don't have time to contemplate it further, because Dad pushes the door open, and a most wonderful smell enters the room along with him. The aroma is emanating from a round foil take-out container with a white cardboard top that reads PASTA PALACE.

"I brought you dinner," Dad says, holding the food out to me.

"Thank you!" I lock the weird dream away for now and concentrate on licking off the drool already gathering in the corners of my mouth. "I take back half the mean things I was thinking about you."

He shakes the container slightly and laughs. "Only half?"

"Is that Spaghettini Macaravioli?" I ask, pushing myself up to a sitting position and fluffing the pillows at my back.

"I believe so." He smiles, handing me the foil pan and a plastic fork. I peel off the top, and the most beautiful pile of spaghetti, macaroni, and ravioli covered in red sauce appears before me. Italian heaven! I dig in as he takes a seat next to me on the bed.

He watches me for a while, then gets a funny expression. I pause, my mouth full of melty cheese and three kinds of pasta. "Do I have it all over my face? Is that why you're staring?" I wipe my mouth with my sleeve.

Dad laughs. "No, no. You're fine. I just . . ." He sighs. "What were you thinking, Nizhoni? With Mr. Charles."

I groan. I should have known that dinner would come with strings attached.

"I need to understand why you attacked him," he says. "I know you've had some problems with kids at school in the past, but this just doesn't seem like you."

"He had a knife," I explain calmly. I'd practiced using a reasonable voice before I fell asleep and dreamed of Mr. Yazzie. It comes out very convincingly, if I do say so myself. Although, with food in my mouth, it sounds more like *He hab a wife*, which, admittedly, would not merit a self-defense maneuver. But Dad seems to get the idea.

Yet I can see from his expression that he still doesn't believe me.

"You think I'm lying," I say, feeling distinctly worm-buttish again.

He folds his hands in his lap and looks down.

I consider telling Dad all the things Mr. Charles said about mom's family, but every time I bring her up, Dad gets super sad. Like sitting-around-staring-at-bad-TV-and-forgetting-to-make-dinner level of sad. Until I know more about what Mr. Charles was saying, I don't want to mention my mom. So I limit my explanation. "He said I could ruin his plans and that he had to kill me."

Dad's frown lines deepen to valleys on his forehead. "Why would a wealthy oil executive like Mr. Charles feel threatened by a twelve-year-old girl?"

"I don't know, but—"

"And *kill you*? With all of us standing right outside?"

47

"I know, but maybe the knife was magic. . . ." That idea just occurred to me, and it's not a bad one. The knife did not look like a normal one.

"Nizhoni," Dad says in his no-nonsense voice. "Stop it. Your story doesn't even make sense."

I take another bite, but I don't feel much like eating anymore. My shoulders slump, and I poke listlessly at a ravioli. A single tear treks down my cheek and lands in a mound of cheese.

"There's nothing wrong with having a big imagination," Dad says. "Your mom sure did. Always seeing monsters lurking everywhere."

I jerk my head up so fast I almost drop the Spaghettini Macaravioli to the floor. Dad is talking about Mom! "What?! You never told me that."

"She was an artist, and artists need big imaginations. That's probably where you get it from."

"Dad," I say, setting my food aside, "this is serious. I need to know everything about Mom seeing monsters. Because I—"

"I always knew Mac had a big imagination," he goes on, "but I think you do, too. Both my kids are artists at heart."

"Dad, you're not listening!" I say, irritated. "About Mom and the monsters—"

"But no matter what, Nizhoni," he says, his tone sharpening, "you can't go around attacking people. Fortunately, I was able to smooth things over at dinner. . . ."

I moan in frustration, but it doesn't register with him. It's like he can't even see or hear me. Did Mr. Charles do something to him, or is he just my normally self-absorbed dad who never listens when I talk about my problems?

"I think I'm done," I say, thrusting the Pasta Palace container back at him.

He takes it and carefully puts the lid back on. "I'll save this for tomorrow's lunch." He stands up. "Oh, and here's your phone." He pulls it out of his pocket and puts it on my nightstand. "But I don't want you to use it tonight. Get some sleep, and we can talk more later."

But we never do talk, because by tomorrow, it's too late.

◆

NINE

Aliens and Bigfoot and Monsters, Oh My!

Dad's already gone to his job at the state surveyor's office by the time Mac and I walk to school in the morning. Mac's going on and on about how great Pasta Palace was and how I missed out on the best night ever, and it takes all my patience not to roll my eyes.

"I can't believe you sat across the table from a monster and you don't even care."

"I care," Mac says, defensively. "I just don't think he's a monster."

I stop in my tracks. "What? Now you don't believe me, either?"

"Mr. Charles was a pretty nice guy. He asked me tons of questions, and he even wanted to see my drawings."

I throw up my hands and start walking again. "Because he was trying to figure out if you have a special power!"

Mac perks up. "Cool! Hey, if I do have a special power, I wonder if I could use it on Adrien Cuttlebush."

"What special power?"

"I don't know. You're the one who just said I had it."

"Mr. Charles said . . . Oh, never mind." It isn't worth telling him more if he isn't going to believe me.

"You don't have to worry about him, anyway. He and Mr. Rock and Ms. Bird are going back to Oklahoma today."

"They are?" That's unexpected. Why would they give up so easily?

No, I don't believe it. They're up to something.

"You worry too much, Z," Mac says. "Always seeing things that nobody else does. I think it makes you a little . . ." He widens his eyes and twirls a finger next to his temple.

I was about to describe my dream about Mr. Yazzie, but now I don't want to. If Mac already thinks I'm nuts, what would he say about a stuffed horned toad that came to life?

School comes into view and Mac speeds up. "I want to make it to class before Cuttlebush gets here," he explains as he fast-walks to the front doors. "Catch you later. And don't worry about being cray-cray. All the best people are!"

"Thanks," I mutter as I watch him go off to wherever sixth-graders go. Part of me is shocked that Mac doesn't believe me anymore, but the other part suspects it has something to do with his being around Mr. Charles last night. The monster must have some powers of his own.

I head straight for the school library. Davery is already there, setting up a display on the big table in the middle of the room. He's putting out little cardboard cutouts of a hogan and a Popsicle-stick corral full of cotton-ball sheep. In front of his display is a sign that says: TRADITIONAL DINÉ (AKA NAVAJO) HOUSE. He steps back, admiring his crafty work.

"We need to talk," I say, grabbing his bicep.

"Whoa!" he protests. "I'm working here." He shakes me

51

off and does an arm flourish like a talk show host. "Ta-da! What do you think?"

"It's important."

"No, no." He flourishes again. "*This* is important." He holds a hand to his chin and squints. "Do you think I got the sheep right? Are they too fluffy?"

"There's no such thing as too fluffy."

"Nizhoni . . ."

"Fine." My eyes want to glaze over, but Davery is my best friend, so I take a moment to look more closely at his display. "It's actually pretty cool," I admit. "It kinda looks like my shimásání's place on the rez. The sheep camp, anyway."

He beams.

"Okay, now can we focus on my problem?"

"Fine, fine." He reaches over one last time to adjust the sheep wool. "No such thing as too fluffy . . ." he mutters.

"I have something important to tell you," I say. "But it's a secret, and you can't tell anyone else. Do you promise?"

I've been thinking about this all night and all morning, and I decided that spilling the whole truth to him is my only option. I could really use some backup. I need someone who can strategize with me, and clearly I can't count on Mac anymore.

Davery turns his full attention to me. He truly is the best. If anyone will believe me, it'll be him.

I squeeze my eyes shut, take a deep breath, and say, "I see monsters."

Silence.

I wait for Davery to say something. When he doesn't, I pry one eye open and take a peek.

He's got his thoughtful face on. Lips pursed, eyes narrowed, head tilted slightly to the right like he isn't sure if I just spoke English or another language.

"Like, right now?" he asks in a worried whisper.

"No, silly," I say. "In general. They're disguised as real people. It's the reason I messed up in the basketball game yesterday," I rush on. "Well, not the whole reason, because honestly, I'm sort of a lousy shot. Anyway, the point is, I was totally distracted by this monster in the stands. And then, even worse, he showed up at my house last night, and guess what? He's my dad's new boss! He pulled a knife on me, so I used the elbow bash Coach taught us in self-defense class last year—the one I could never do— but this time I was like something out of *Street Fighter*! But nobody cared, and everyone thought I had lost my mind, andIdidn'tgetogotoPastaPalace!!!" I take another breath. "It was awful."

His thoughtful face has changed to his slightly disturbed face, which is essentially the same thing but with way bigger eyes.

"You don't believe me," I say, deflated. I knew it. I should never have said anything. Better to keep my imagination to myself.

"On the contrary," Davery says. "I *do* believe you. I know how much you love that restaurant."

"You really believe me?!" I shout.

"*Shh!*" We both turn. The librarian is staring at us, finger to her lips.

"Sorry," I whisper.

"My apologies," Davery adds. "No matter the emergency, there's no excuse to disturb the sanctity of the library."

The librarian beams.

"Suck-up," I mutter, only loud enough for his ears.

He looks slightly offended, because the truth hurts.

"Come with me," Davery says, marching to the reference section.

This part of my middle school library is nothing to write home about. Two long shelves of outdated encyclopedias, a few dusty donated tomes, and three aging desktop computers. Budget crisis or something, and ICCS is a charter school, so we don't always get the greatest supplies. Davery sits down at one of the computers and starts typing in a password.

"This is the password for adults," he explains in a whisper. "It'll let us access more sites."

"Won't you get in trouble?" I ask.

Davery doesn't even look up. "My dad gave it to me. He's proud that I like to research stuff outside of homework. It's like I'm doing an extra-credit assignment."

"Good point. So what are you going to look up?" I ask.

"Stories about people who have seen monsters."

"You're gonna find a lot of wild stuff, I bet. How will you tell the truth from the fake news?"

"Leave it to me," he says, as he *tap-tap-tap*s on the old keyboard.

"Can't your dad convince the school to invest in some iPads or laptops for the library?" I observe. "This is sad."

"I'm trying to concentrate," he says. "Here we go!" And he pulls up the front page to the *National Inquisitor*. The headlines scream out at me:

Woman Abducted by Cat-Headed Alien; Says His Name Was Marty

"Fake news," I murmur. Davery keeps scrolling.

Man Spots Bigfoot at the Laundromat

"Wait!" I say. I lean over Davery's shoulder, reading. He leans in, too.

The man claimed that Mr. Sasquatch, as he insisted on calling him, was washing some Spider-Man pajamas as well as a very nice pair of satin boxers.

"Well, that one's definitely true," I observe.

"Yeah," Davery agrees. "Everyone knows Bigfoot is real."

"But Mr. Charles is not a Sasquatch, so keep looking."

Davery scrolls some more, but none of the stories are help-ing. "Maybe we should try something else."

"Try googling his name: Mr. Charles. And the name of his company: Landrush Oil and Gas."

Davery types the information in and hits Enter. The screen fills with all kinds of articles and photos. Stories about Mr. Charles meeting the president of the United States, with shots of them shaking hands. Several pieces about Mr. Charles and Landrush Oil and Gas being sued by tribal governments to stop them from using their land for fracking. And more pictures of protesters outside the Landrush headquarters with banners and signs that say things like NO PIPELINES ON SACRED LANDS and HONOR THE TREATY RIGHTS.

"He seems like a really bad dude," Davery observes.

"There's one other thing I want you to look up. Na'ashjéii Asdzáá."

"Can you spell that?"

I do my best to spell out the name Mr. Yazzie told me in the dream. I must do a good job, because Davery hits Enter, and over six hundred entries come up.

"Spider Woman?" Davery asks.

"One of the Navajo Holy People," I say, reading over his shoulder. "Oh, great. How am I supposed to find *her*?"

Davery starts to say something but is cut off by the first-period bell. Students begin to stream into the library. He hits the red X in the corner to close the browser before anyone can see what we were researching. A boy in a blue hoodie asks if we're done with the computer, so Davery slides out of his seat and we head for the door.

"So," Davery says nonchalantly, "if you're googling Spider Woman, does that mean you're coming back during lunch period for Ancestor Club?" He excitedly points to his display, and now I notice his Navajo sheep camp sits next to three others made by different kids: a Pueblo plaza scene, a Lakota tipi, and a Haudenosaunee longhouse.

"I forgot about Ancestor Club," I admit, feeling slightly ashamed. "But in my defense, I've been focused on the monster."

Davery crosses his arms, unconvinced. "You know this is

important to me," he says. "I've been trying to get the club together for ages. It's only our second meeting and you're trying to bail?"

"No offense, Davery, but it's not normal for seventh-graders to be so obsessed with their ancestors." I think fleetingly of what Mr. Yazzie said about young people no longer learning the stories, and I wince at my words.

"I am not obsessed. I started a club. It's no big deal. Are you going to come or not?" He might have been saying it was no big deal, but I can tell by the tone of his voice that it's a Really Big Deal.

"Of course I'm coming," I say in my most chipper voice. "Wouldn't miss it!"

He grins, looking relieved. "It'll be great. Maya's bringing in a corn kernel necklace her Pueblo grandmother taught her how to make." His brow crinkles. "You should start thinking about what you're going to contribute. You can't just keep coming and eating the free cookies, even if you are the best friend of the club president."

Ugh. Being Davery's best friend and the promise of free cookies were the only reasons I went to the first meeting of the Ancestor Club. This Apache kid named Darcy brought these chocolate chip triple-chunk lumps that her mother made, and they were to die for. It was a very convincing argument to learn more about my culture.

Come to think of it, maybe it could be helpful. "Mr. Charles also said some strange things about my mom," I tell Davery. "I think maybe she could see monsters, too."

"That sounds like another good reason to come to Ancestor Club, Z. We could try to find out more about your family."

Second bell rings and I let out a groan. I am so late for homeroom. "Gotta go, but I'll be back," I promise. "Any chance Darcy's bringing more chocolate chip pieces of heaven?"

"Actually," Davery says, "I brought the cookies today. They're vegan. And organic. And sugar-free."

"That's not a cookie, that's a pile of sawdust!" I mime choking and falling over until Davery rolls his eyes.

"See you at noon, Z."

I stop pretending to gag and wave Davery good-bye. As if the monster wasn't enough, now Davery is trying to kill me with his cookies, too.

TEN

◆

Operation Break Some Rules

I somehow make it through the morning's classes, although all I can think about is Mr. Charles, my mom, and my weird Mr. Yazzie dream. Well, that should be all I can think about, but the truth is, by 10:30 a.m., my mind is focused only on food. Because in my hurry to get out the door, not only did I skip breakfast, but I forgot to grab my lunch of leftovers from the kitchen counter. By the time the bell rings at 11:45 a.m., my stomach is making rude noises and visions of ravioli are dancing in my head.

With no bag lunch and no money for school lunch, I'll be stuck eating Davery's super-healthy sawdust special, and that is just not going to work for me. Whatever the opposite of mouthwatering is, that's what my mouth starts doing whenever I think of his cookies.

We are strictly prohibited from leaving school during the day except in the case of emergency. And even then, you have to be signed out by a parent. But I can't think of a bigger emergency than getting a decent lunch, and there's no way I'm calling my dad to have him come and sign me out. He's probably out in the field doing a survey anyway, and cell service can get spotty in the wilds of New Mexico. Even if I could get through to his phone, he'd be too far away to come back to school and he'd be mad at me for forgetting my lunch to begin with. No, if I want to eat, I'm going to have to break a few rules.

I decide to sneak off campus. My house isn't that far. It's a fifteen-minute walk, which would be a five-minute run, and I can be back for Ancestor Club before Davery even notices I'm late. Well, not too late, anyway.

Easy peasy, lemon squeezy. I decide the best escape route is out the side exit and across the baseball field. It's not a fool-proof way. Sometimes a few kids hang out there—the ones who like to ditch classes—but they usually stay behind the bleachers. If so, they'll be easy to avoid.

No such luck today. Near the backstop behind home plate, I think I spy Adrien Cuttlebush, the bully who gave Mac a black eye. He's there with his friends, laughing about something. I skirt the field, hoping he's too busy showing off to notice me. If it were any other time, I'd stop and give him a piece of my mind.

Once I'm free of school grounds, I break into a jog. I don't mind running. I may not be as good at team sports as I want to be, but I'm a pretty good long-distance runner. I don't get tired easily, and it feels good once my blood starts moving and I shake off that initial sluggishness. I check my watch: 11:52 a.m. My house comes into view in eight minutes flat.

I'm so busy thinking about my impressive running time that I almost don't register the big black SUV parked in front of my house. As soon as I notice it, I pull up short and look around for cover. The only hiding place is my neighbor's overgrown chamisa bush. I duck down behind it. But then I remember I'm mildly allergic to chamisa.

Great.

I can feel a sneeze coming on, but I pinch my nose to hold it back.

My dad's car is in the driveway. Why is he home in the middle of the day?

I hear a door slam. My front door? I peek around the bush and my stomach drops. There's Mr. Charles, on his smartphone, striding away from my house. So much for him going back to Oklahoma. Close behind, Mr. Rock is rolling a trunk on a dolly. Ms. Bird clicks the key fob and the SUV's back pops open. Mr. Rock heaves up the trunk and pushes it into the car.

Where's my dad? I wonder.

"Careful," Mr. Charles says absently as Mr. Bird opens the back seat door for him. "We don't want to damage the merchandise."

Merchandise? What kind of merchandise does an oil executive need?

Then I get a sick feeling in the pit of my stomach. Maybe they're robbing us!

Mr. Charles turns back to his phone conversation. "The boy won't be a problem. He fell right into my hands last night. We should be able to secure him easily enough. . . ."

Secure him?

"The girl, however . . ."

He means *me*!

". . . she recognized me from the beginning. Takes after her mother—a real fighter. But if her father asks her to come along peacefully, she'll comply." He climbs into the car and Ms. Bird slams the door closed.

Little puffs of yellow chamisa pollen drift down into my face.

I grab for my nose a second too late.

Achoo!

I freeze, wincing. Ms. Bird could have heard—she's still outside the car. I wait for a second. Then I peek around the corner, and sure enough, Ms. Bird is staring right at my shrub.

Don't notice me, don't notice me.

Mr. Charles rolls down his window and leans out. "Is there a problem?" he demands impatiently.

"I thought I heard . . ." She cocks her head to the side, listening.

"You 'thought'?" Mr. Charles snaps. "Well, that's your first problem. I don't pay you to think. I pay you to *know*. So do you *think* you heard something, or do you *know*?"

Ms. Bird's eyes narrow. I hold my breath. And my nose.

"Well?" he demands again, irritated. "I don't have all day."

"It was nothing, sir," she says, turning abruptly. She climbs back into the driver's seat.

I breathe a sigh of relief. That was close.

I hear the engine start up, and then, with screeching tires, the SUV pulls away from the curb. Once it turns the corner, I sprint to my house.

I open the screen door to find that the front door is unlocked. I push it in as gently as I can, but the hinges still make a squeak that seems loud in the hushed afternoon. "Dad?" I call.

Nobody answers. I hope they didn't knock him out or tie him up or something.

I run through the house, looking for Dad and checking to see what's missing.

But everything is in its rightful place . . . except for my father.

The realization hits me like a punch to my gut. *Dad was in that trunk. Did they kill him?*

No, no. Charles said they were going to use Dad to make me comply.

But was he drugged? Hurt? Where were they going with him? I wish I had taken down the SUV's license plate number. . . .

I feel panicky, and my hand shakes uncontrollably as I pick up the landline. I'm just about to punch in 911, when I imagine the conversation:

Emergency services. Name and address, please. Nijoanie? How do you spell that? Your father's been kidnapped by his boss, you say? A monster? Well, we all have problems at work, honey, but . . .

Who are the police going to believe? Some random brown kid, or a famous executive with his blond hair and a fancy suit that reeks of money?

No adult is going to buy this story. I've got to take down Mr. Charles on my own.

There is someone who might help—the only one who seemed to know anything about fighting monsters. I rush to my room, head straight for my bookcase, and feel around the top shelf until my hand closes around a plush horned toad. I pull him out.

"Mr. Yazzie?" I say, my voice shaking. "If you're real and not just a dream, please wake up. I'm in trouble. The monster I was telling you about? He took my dad and said he's going to kidnap me and my little brother, too. Or maybe just . . . *kill* me!"

I shake Mr. Yazzie gently, but nothing happens. My breath is coming hot and fast and I want to cry, but I won't. This is a time to be strong.

I'm still wearing my backpack, and I place Mr. Yazzie in the big outside pocket. Might as well bring him along for luck.

My stomach grumbles, reminding me why I came home. I'll need my strength if I'm going to have to deal with monsters. My lunch bag is still on the counter, right where I left it. It's lying on its side like someone knocked it over.

I pick up the bag and an apple rolls out. A Red Delicious. Dad loves them, but he knows I can't stand them. Why would he pack one in my lunch? I pick up the offending fruit, and I'm about to set it back on the counter when I see it: Carved into the apple, the yellow flesh showing through the red skin, is one word.

RUN!

My feet feel unsteady and my head gets a floaty feeling. I blink several times, take a deep breath, and look again, sure I imagined it. But the word is still there.

R-U-N. RUN!

My dad left me a secret message.

Through the still-open front door, I hear the rumble of a car engine outside.

I look out the screen door to see that the black SUV has returned, and Mr. Charles is getting out of the back seat!

"I forgot the photo. I'll just be a minute," he says to Ms. Bird, and he jogs toward the house.

The photo! The one he was so interested in yesterday, of Mac and me with my mom and dad. I don't get why it's so important to Mr. Charles. He probably wants to use it to track us or something. All I know is that there's no way I'm letting him get his dirty hands on it.

I run to the mantel and grab the picture frame.

I hear the screen door opening.

I race for the back door, dropping the apple as I go. I fly out into the yard just as the screen door closes. I vault the rear fence and race down the alley to school, my breath loud in my ears and my monster senses tingling. I don't stop, and I don't look back.

ELEVEN

◆

The Ancestor Club Meeting Is Indefinitely Postponed Due to Reasons

"Mr. Charles kidnapped my dad!" I shout as I skid through the library's double doors.

Six pairs of eyes turn to stare at me.

Maya drops her corn necklace. A single kernel goes clacking across the floor, the only sound in the entire room. Well, besides me.

I'm panting and sweaty, I'm screaming about somebody kidnapping my dad, and I'm clutching a macaroni noodle picture frame in one hand. I can see how this might make me look weird.

"I mean . . . uh . . ." I clear my throat. "Davery, can I speak to you for a minute? Alone?"

He pushes back his chair and gets to his feet. I rush over, grab him by the arm, and pull him away from the other Ancestor Club kids.

Their eyes all watch me, astonished. "Just kidding about the kidnapping thing. Keep going with your presentations." I flash them a winning smile.

"What's happening?" Davery hisses once we're out of earshot. "And why are you tardy?"

"Oh my God with the tardiness. That is not important."

"Punctuality is always important."

I groan. "Focus! I saw Mr. Charles again. He was at my house."

"When? Wait, you left school grounds? That is strictly prohibited."

"Never mind that. Listen to this!" I tell him what I saw, what I heard. Everything, including the message carved into the apple.

Little lines form on his forehead. "That *is* pretty disturbing."

"Duh."

"Do you have the apple?"

"No. I dropped it. But I have the picture."

Davery frowns. "Well, now he knows you were there."

"It's better than letting the photo fall into his hands, right?"

"Probably," he agrees. "But now that he knows you saw him at your house, he may not wait until after school to get you. He may come here."

As if on cue, the overhead speaker crackles to life. We pause, listening as our principal, Mrs. Peterson, comes on. "Would Nizhoni and Marcus Begay please report to the office?" she asks in her feathery voice. "Nizhoni and Marcus Begay. It's a . . . family emergency."

"Oh no," I whisper. "Mr. Charles."

Davery blinks. "What are you going to do?"

"My dad said to run. So I'm going to get Mac and run."

"I don't know, Nizhoni. Maybe you should go to the police. Or tell Principal Peterson."

67

"You know the police won't take my side. Not in this town. And Principal Peterson's already compromised. Nobody's going to believe me when someone like Mr. Charles tells them I'm lying."

Davery doesn't argue. He knows I'm right.

"I better go," I say. "I've got to stop Mac from going to the office."

"Do you have a plan? I mean, what are you going to do after that?"

"Do you remember how I had you google 'Na'ashjéii Asdzáá'?" I ask, an idea forming in my mind. "Well, it's sort of a long story, but I need to find her. I had this dream. . . . Someone told me she could help me get weapons to fight monsters. Now that Mr. Charles has my dad, I think that's what I have to do."

Davery doesn't even look at me funny. He just marches us back to the computer, types in his secret password, and searches for "Na'ashjéii Asdzáá" again. "It says here that not only did she bring weaving to the Navajo people, but she is a helper and protector, too." He scrolls some more. "Her traditional home is at the Spider Rock in Canyon de Chelly."

"Oh." I blush. "I honestly thought it would be harder to find her."

"Apparently not. She is near Chinle, Arizona, on the Navajo Nation." He quickly pulls up a map. "It looks like you can take the train as far as Gallup, New Mexico. From Gallup, it's another ninety-one miles to Chinle."

"Ninety-one miles?" That's too far to walk. "We'll just

have to take the train now and figure it out once we get there. Maybe they have Uber. . . ."

Davery pulls up the Amtrak schedule. "Okay, there's a train leaving in an hour. Can you get to the station downtown?"

"I'll have to find Mac first, but we'll make it."

I watch as he fills out passenger information forms for Mac and me. When he gets to the payment screen, he doesn't even pause, just types in the numbers.

"When did you get a credit card?" I ask, surprised.

For the first time, Davery looks guilty.

"Davery Dallas Descheny! You better explain."

"It's my big brother's," he says sheepishly. "I use it for buying games online, and I pay him back with my allowance. But this is an emergency, right? The principal said so."

I lean over and hug him, squeezing until he coughs. "You're the best."

"Yeah, I know. So"—he hits Print—"three tickets to Gallup."

"Three?" I ask, confused.

"One for you, one for Mac, and one for me."

"You're coming?"

He nods. "I can't have my best friend running off to fight monsters by herself." Smiling, he adds, "Besides, you might need a credit card again."

I grin, ready to burst with happiness and relief. He hands me two of the printed tickets.

The loudspeaker crackles on, and Mrs. Peterson comes

on again, repeating her request for Mac and me to come to the office.

Davery's got his thinking face on. "I'll stay behind, try to hold them off for a while."

"How are you going to do that?"

"I'll think of something. You get Mac and head for the station. I'll meet you there. You've got your phone?" Davery asks.

"Yes." I pat my pocket.

"Text me if there's a problem. I'll get there as soon as I can."

I give Davery one last shoulder squeeze before I fast-walk past the Ancestor Club kids, who stare openmouthed at me again, and rush into the hallway to look for my brother.

TWELVE

◆

Like that Time at the Water Park
but Way Better

I can't find Mac anywhere.

My heart's beating so fast it's hard to think past the panicked thumping in my chest. What if he's already in the principal's office? Would she hand him over to Mr. Charles without a note from my dad? Maybe the monster forced Dad to write one. . . . What if I'm all alone now?

But then the loudspeaker comes on again and Mrs. Peterson, sounding increasingly annoyed, orders Mac and me to come to the office. This time she adds, "Now!"

I exhale, relieved. My brother's still free.

But if that's the case, where is he?

Not in the school, or he would have gone to the office.

Which could only mean . . .

Adrien Cuttlebush.

I take my family picture out of the frame and tuck it in my back pocket along with our train tickets. I wish I could keep the frame, which I made for my dad years ago, but it's too bulky, so I regretfully drop it into the nearest garbage can and head over to the baseball field.

Sure enough, Adrien's still there, along with his three friends. And in the middle of their circle stands one terrified-looking Mac. His backpack is lying by his feet with the tip of his iPad sticking out, and his new box of fancy colored pencils has spilled on the ground.

Rage rises in me, turning my vision red. I clench my fists. Nobody messes with my little brother on my watch! But just as quickly as the rage came on, doubts begin to swirl in my mind. What if I mess this up the way I messed up the basketball game? And confronting Mr. Charles. And everything else I do.

I shake it off. Doubts or no doubts, I have to help Mac.

Besides, I have monster-fighting skills now. This will work! Right?

"Hey!" I shout, stalking forward. "Leave him alone!"

Adrien and his buddies turn to look at me.

"Well, if it isn't Nizhonee Baloney," Adrien drawls in that irritating voice he has, deliberately mispronouncing my name. "Heard about your epic fail at the basketball game."

"My nose, my nose!" one of the other boys squeaks in a voice that sounds absolutely nothing like me. Okay, he sounds exactly like me.

I can feel my face heating up in embarrassment.

"Hey, Marcus," Adrien sneers, "too bad you have to have your sister come and protect you. Especially when everyone knows she's a loser, too."

They burst into belly-clutching laughter, as if Mac and I are the most hilarious kids they know.

I remember what Dad said about not attacking people, no matter what, but I can't help it. I just want Adrien to shut his stupid face. So, like I did last night with Mr. Charles, I lash out. My fist flies before I can even think to stop myself. But Adrien's way more agile than Mr. Charles was, and he dances out of range. My glorious punch passes in front of his nose, missing by inches. Momentum makes me stumble forward. My foot gets caught on Mac's backpack strap, and I trip. And *smash!* I fall face-first into the dirt with an *Umphhhh!*

Adrien and his friends laugh even harder. A little blood trickles out of my nose. Visions of yesterday's humiliation flash before my eyes.

"Quit it!" Mac shouts. "Leave us alone!"

"Or what, Marcus? You gonna draw mean pictures of me?"

"Marcus Be-gay!" Adrien shouts. "Oh, please be gay!"

"Gay! Gay! Gay!" they chant, like the brainless homophobes they are.

Mac growls. Like, literally growls. I've never seen him this angry before. His hair is hanging down over his eyes, but I can tell he's been crying, and he wipes his runny nose violently on the sleeve of his jacket. His whole body is shaking.

"You're a joke," Adrien says. "You and your loser sister." He reaches down and scoops up Mac's colored pencils, the special ones like our mom used to use. Mac saved up for them all last year. They are his favorite things in the world, even more precious than his iPad, and when I hear Adrien snap one between his fingers, it feels like something just snapped inside me, too.

Mac screams, an animal-like, bloodcurdling cry of rage. He slams his hand onto the ground, palm flat. And it might be my imagination, but I swear the ground shakes under my feet.

A low rumble rolls across the baseball field, like an army of badgers tunneling through the earth, and then, suddenly, all the sprinklers turn on. There have to be a dozen of them, and they burst into life, shooting water in thin razorlike streams right at Adrien and his friends.

"Ow!" one of the boys says as the malevolent sprinkler rips across his chest with a pointy blast. "That hurts!"

"What the heck?" Adrien says as water beans him right in the eye.

"Are the sprinklers . . . attacking us?" the other boy says incredulously.

And I realize that's exactly what they're doing. The jets are all pointed at them, zipping back and forth in sharp slashing cuts, or pulsing bursts aimed at their eyes. Adrien stares, jaw gaping, and one sprinkler shoots a stream right into his mouth. He sputters and spits, stumbling backward. Another sprinkler pops out of the ground just as his heel hits the edge, and Adrien Cuttlebush goes sprawling on his back into the fresh mud around home base.

He scrambles to his feet, trying to fight off the water assault. His friends attempt to help him stand, but they are all slipping and sliding now, the ground soaked through. The four of them go down in a big *splat*. Adrien has to crawl to the dugout fence before he can pull himself up.

Once he's on his feet, he looks back at us with terrified eyes. I shrug. It wasn't me.

Mac still has his palm on the ground and a determined look on his face, confirming that it was him. Adrien must realize it, too, because he and his friends start running across the field, back toward school, clearly shaken. The only problem is, there are sprinklers all over the field, so every few feet, they get creamed by another burst of water, and then another, until they practically fall over the outfield fence trying to escape.

I want to laugh, but Mac's eyes are glazed over like he doesn't even know I'm here.

"Mac," I say, shaking my brother's shoulder gently. "They're gone. You can stop now. Mac? Mac!"

He blinks like he's coming out of a trance, then looks up at me. His face is wet with tears and he's got a serious snot bubble, but I don't say anything mean, because, duuuude! What just happened?

"You just made the sprinklers attack them, right?" I ask, my voice hesitant. I mean, if I hadn't seen it with my own eyes, I wouldn't have believed it.

He swallows hard and then nods.

"Have you ever done anything like that before?"

He shakes his head.

And I realize that whatever Mac did to control the sprinklers must be related to the powers Mr. Charles was talking about last night.

"I—I've made water move before," Mac confesses. "Like in the bathtub. B-but I thought maybe I was just imagining it."

"You *weren't* imagining it," I whisper, a smile breaking over my face. "You have a special ability. Just like I do."

He sniffs up the snot bubble (thank God!) and brushes his hair from his face. "The monsters . . . So you really can see them?"

"And fight them." Although, admittedly, my trying to hit Adrien didn't work. But maybe it was because, as much of a jerk as he is, he's just human, and not an actual monster.

"Cool," says Mac.

"Not necessarily," I say. "Mr. Charles knows about our powers. They have something to do with Mom's side of the family. And I'm pretty sure he wants to kidnap you."

"*Me?*" he squeaks. "What did *I* do?"

"It must have to do with all this." I gesture to the sprinklers that are now gently watering the outfield like they weren't tiny mutant water warriors five minutes ago. "Part of his company's business is fracking. You need a lot of water for that. I think that's why he wants you."

"But he didn't say anything at dinner last night. If he knew, then why . . . ?" His voice drifts off until his eyes bulge. "He *did* ask me if I liked to swim. Do you think maybe he was fishing for an answer?" He giggles. "Fishing. Get it? Fishing?"

Sometimes Mac is such a dork. But I've never been happier to hear his bad jokes.

"And what about you?" he asks. "Does he want to kidnap you, too?"

I chew my lip, not sure how much to tell Mac about what I overheard. But I decide he should know the truth, since we're both going to be on the lam.

"I don't think he wants to kidnap me. I'm in his way. I think he just wants me dead."

"*Dead?!*" Mac yelps.

"Yes." Which reminds me why I'm out here to begin with. We have to go. The principal and Mr. Charles are going to find us any minute now. I start gathering up the pencils and other stuff that spilled from his backpack. Among the piles of junk I find a semi-clean tissue and hand it to him so he can wipe his nose, but I leave a glob of something that looks suspiciously like a ball of chewed bubble gum in the grass where it fell.

"Dead, like *dead* dead?"

"Yes," I say, stuffing more pencils into his backpack, "and that's why we need to run."

"We don't need to run," Mac says. "We need to tell Dad."

And here it is. "We can't."

"Why not? Come on, Nizhoni, you can't keep this from him. Dad will believe you now, for sure."

"Because Dad already knows," I say. "He's the one who told us to run." It's not exactly a lie, but it's not the whole truth, either.

"Really?" Mac looks dubious and I don't blame him. But if I tell Mac what I saw, he'll worry too much, and I need him not to freak.

I dig our train tickets out of my back pocket. "How else would I have gotten these?"

"What are those?"

"Train tickets to Gallup."

"Gallup? Why—?"

"There's a lady near there who can help us. Promise." I don't tell him her name is Spider Woman, because I know that will send him down a whole other tangent, and we only have so much time.

Mac takes a moment to process it all. I hold my breath, waiting to see if he's going to believe me. Finally, he says, "If Dad said so . . ."

I smile, relieved. I stand up, holding out a hand to pull him to his feet. Then, before he can ask any more questions, I say, "I'm sorry I didn't help you beat Adrien Cuttlebush. All I did was make it worse."

He slides his backpack over his shoulders. "You did great. Plus, I didn't need you to save me," he says, standing up straight. "I took care of Cuttlebush on my own."

I grin, happy for my little brother. "You sure did. But how did you end up out here with them, anyway?"

He groans. "It's a long story, and you wouldn't believe me if I told you."

It must be embarrassing. I don't know how Mac gets himself into these situations, but I know not to push too hard. It's bad enough that he has to deal with bullies. I don't need to pile on him, too.

My phone buzzes. It's a text message from Davery.

Davery

Are you at the train station yet?

Nizhoni

No, but I found Mac.

Davery

Well, you better hurry. Everyone's looking for you. They even have school security out now.

Nizhoni

Whoa! The ICCS cops?!

Davery

Mrs. Peterson just walked into the library. She's talking to Maya now. GTG. I'll join you as soon as I can.

I swipe my phone off and drop it back in my pocket.
"What is it?" Mac asks.
"Time to go."

THIRTEEN

◆

Hot Cheeto Kryptonite

We make it across the field and off the school grounds surprisingly easily. I'm starting to think school security is really lacking. I'll have to give Mrs. Peterson some helpful pointers on improving it, assuming we survive. At the very least, I'll have Davery write her a strongly worded letter.

Mac and I pool the change in the bottom of our backpacks. Between the two of us, there is just enough for bus fare downtown. The ride is quick, and we make it to the Albuquerque train station twenty minutes before our train is scheduled to leave. I've only been to the station once, to pick up my cousin coming in from Flagstaff, and the big adobe building and the rumbling trains are both exciting and intimidating. The air is bright and hot and a little humid, like a rain shower came through recently. Sure enough, little puddles of water have gathered in the corners of the courtyard, the dark rocks around the tracks glisten like shiny black and gray diamonds, and everything smells like wet concrete. Plenty of people mill about, some in business clothes and some in tourist T-shirts, all crisscrossing the terra-cotta tile floor. We get a few curious looks, but most folks don't even notice two kids on their own waiting for a train.

Mac's stomach growls. I'm starving, too. I'd totally kill for one of Davery's dusty cookies right now.

Kill. I swallow around a hard lump that suddenly rises in my throat. I can't believe someone wants to kill me. Not a someone—a monster. But I'm not helpless, I remind myself. I have a power all my own that will let me know when he's near. And I can figure out the fighting thing. I won't let him get close enough to snatch me or Mac.

"I'm so hungry," Mac whines. "Can we get something to eat?"

I look around. There's a bright neon sign to our right that says TACO TOWN, and at the thought, my mouth waters. But there's one big problem. "We don't have enough money," I admit. "We spent the last of our change on the bus."

"Not even enough for a bag of Hot Cheetos?" he moans.

Flamin' Hot Cheetos are Mac's favorite. I once saw him eat a family-size bag all by himself. Dad said if he did that again, he would ruin the plumbing in our house, but Mac vowed that nothing would stop him, even busted toilets. Mac may have some kind of power over water, but Hot Cheetos are definitely his weakness.

"I hate this," Mac mumbles.

"I didn't plan this, you know," I say, feeling like he's being unfair. Here I am risking my life to save him from monsters, and all he can think about is lunch.

"Maybe you should have planned it better if you were going to drag me along." Mac sniffs. "I think I want to go home."

"We can't!" I say, outraged that he already wants to give up. I clutch my turquoise necklace, the one my mom gave me, and take a deep breath. "Look, Mac. You've got to stay strong. Think about Dad. He needs us. He needs you."

"I still don't get why he wants us to run." He scuffs his shoe on the ground. "I mean, maybe you're wrong, Z. Mr. Charles was nice to me last night."

"Because he wants to steal you and your powers."

He shrugs. "If he had some food, I might just go with him. I can't think past my stomach."

Mac's right. It's hard to concentrate when you're hungry. "Okay. Wait here. I'm going to try and find us something to eat. Maybe someone will give me their leftovers."

Mac flops onto a bright blue bench and hugs his backpack to his chest. "I'm probably going to die of starvation before the monsters can even find us," he mutters. "Here lies Mac Begay. RIP."

Confident that Mac will not, in fact, die of starvation, and even more sure that he'll wait for me on the bench— out of exhaustion brought on by too much drama more than anything else—I head into the main area of the train station. People rush back and forth, shoes clicking on the tile floors. Someone bumps me from behind, making me stumble. I look to see who it was, but they're gone, without even an *Excuse me.* More passengers are coming in through the doors, from a train disembarking on the platform outside. I squeeze into a corner to get out of the way, and I feel trapped. I stare up at the beamed ceilings overhead, trying to stop an onset of dizziness. The train station is huge and overwhelming, and I feel so, so small. Mr. Charles could be in this crowd right now and I might not know until it was too late. What good is monster sense when the enemy is already staring at you from only ten feet away? And, suddenly, I hate this, too.

"This was a bad idea," I say aloud to myself. "Mac's right."

A squeaky sound, like a mouse on an exercise wheel, catches my attention. I look through the crowd and see a lady pushing a cart, the kind they roll down the aisle on an airplane. On the side someone has written in a loopy cursive:

Station Snacks!

The lady parks the cart right in front of me. I watch as she scratches her butt, looks around, sniffs loudly, and then walks away.

Leaving the cart completely unguarded.

All by itself. Loaded with snacks. And not just any snacks. Bags of Hot Cheetos hang from plastic clips on the side. Cans of soda pop are stacked on the lower shelves. A veritable rolling feast of junk food is sitting inches from my face. The other passengers pay it no mind, walking around it as if it were just a big rock in their way.

Now, it's one thing to break a school rule, but it's a whole other thing to steal. I have never stolen anything in my life. I once thought about shoplifting a Milky Way from a Bashas' grocery store and was so overcome with guilt at the thought that I cried for an hour. My dad thought I was sick and took me to the Indian Health hospital, where I confessed my thought crime to a baffled doctor. He sent me home with a lollipop and a shake of his head.

I glance through the crowd at my miserable little brother,

who is still slumped on the bench where I left him, allegedly dying of starvation. *I'm not stealing it for me*, I tell myself. *It's for him.* And that's the truth, but my insides still churn with guilt, and I hate myself a little for what I am about to do.

I try to act innocent as I move toward the rolling fount of temptation. I keep my eyes peeled for the cart lady. But she has disappeared, nowhere to be seen. I spot the bathroom and realize she must have gone in there.

I do a first pass, walking close to the cart, whistling nonchalantly. I reach out a hand and let my fingers brush the orange-and-red bag of fiery goodness, but I don't take it. When I pull my hand back to my pocket, I'm shaking. I may throw up, I feel so bad, but Mac's so hungry, and so am I, and I don't know what else to do.

I reach the far wall and then turn, casual-like, and make my way back to the cart. I pull my hand from my pocket and let it swing. Closer to the cart, and closer.

I reach out for the bag, eyes halfway closed in fear (or shame!). I'm ready to grab it and go, when the worst thing that could possibly happen happens.

I'm busted!

My wrist is caught in a viselike clamp, someone squeezing the bones so hard I cry out. I want to wail and puke at the same time.

"Can I help you?" says an older woman's voice.

I open my eyes to see who's holding me down. It's the cart lady. She's wearing an Amtrak uniform. Her face is brown like mine, and her dark hair is pulled back in a tsiiyééł, a traditional

Navajo bun. Silver-and-turquoise bracelets shine on her wrists. Where did she come from, and how did I miss her?

"I was going to pay!" I shout, hoping for mercy.

"Well, then," the cart lady says, smiling at me, "there won't be a problem."

"My brother's really hungry," I blurt. My stomach gurgles loudly.

Her eyes narrow in concern. "Sounds like *you're* hungry, too."

Smooth move, stomach. I nod, embarrassed.

She plucks three shrink-wrapped bologna sandwiches, three bags of Flamin' Hot Cheetos, two chocolate milks, and one grape soda from her cart and drops them in a paper bag decorated with an arching rainbow. She hands the bag to me. "For you, your brother, and your friend."

"My friend?"

"The one who's coming to meet you. The smart one."

She must mean Davery, but how would she know about him? Maybe I'm so hungry that I'm hallucinating. All I know is that my mouth is watering and I'm pretty sure I could make a solid attempt at eating all three sandwiches on my own.

But then I remember that I lied to her.

"Thank you, but I can't pay for this," I confess, feeling more miserable than I even knew was possible. "I don't really have any money."

She nods, like she already knew I was making up the paying-for-stuff thing. "Of course you can't, but where I'm from, we never turn away hungry people." Her voice is as sweet and warm as honey on bread fresh from the pan. "We always share what we have, even if we don't have much. And we don't make people pay."

"Ever?" I ask, surprised.

"Well, sometimes," she admits, "but not every time." She winks at me.

Now I really do weep a little, not because I'm scared or feeling guilty, but because my heart feels like it's going to burst. I wipe away a tear, hoping the cart lady doesn't notice I'm crying over white bread sandwiches and bags of cheese puffs.

"But if I give this to you, you must remember that whenever you have food and someone else does not, you must feed them first. Or else you'll bring hunger down on others. Do you understand?"

"Yes," I say, not quite sure about the *bring hunger down on others* thing, but I know she's basically telling me not to be greedy and to share. Two things I can definitely do. As soon as I get some food in my stomach and I can think straight again.

She nods sharply, satisfied, and gives me a little push in the back. "Okay, then. Now go on, Nizhoni. Tell Mac not to eat too many Cheetos or he'll make himself sick, like last time. But hurry. The train is leaving soon. And make sure you read the note I put in your bag."

"Thank y— What?" I'm so shocked I almost drop our sandwiches. "How do you know our names? And—"

But the cart lady has already turned away and is quickly rolling her cart through the busy station.

"How do you know us?" I shout.

She's gone now, lost in the crowd of passengers.

A man in an Amtrak uniform hurries past and I reach out to get his attention. "Excuse me, sir," I say, "but do you know where the cart lady went?"

He frowns down at me, annoyed at being waylaid. "Cart lady?" he grumbles, reaching into his pocket for his phone. "There's no cart lady around here, kid."

"But there was," I insist. "An older Navajo woman, her hair in a bun. She gave me these?" I hold up our food.

He looks away from his phone to inspect my lunch. Then he sneers. "Bologna sandwiches? Okay, now I know you're lying. There's definitely no one giving away *that* kind of food around here. You must be seeing things."

I look down at the bag, which has a rainbow symbol on the side. It's proof that I didn't imagine her.

The man makes an irritated noise, like maybe I'm a kid trying to pull a prank or something. "Look, I've got to go. And if you're here to catch the train, you'd better get a move on and stop worrying about some lady who doesn't exist." He hurries away without a second look.

I guess not all the Amtrak employees know each other. I still wish I'd had a chance to ask the woman how she knew my name.

A train horn sounds, and the people around me stream to the nearest platform. I look up at the big arrivals-and-departures sign above me that shows all the destinations. Our train goes to Gallup, and it leaves in five minutes.

I check my phone to see if Davery has texted and maybe I missed it, but there's no message. He said he would get here as soon as he could, but he also said the principal was talking to

Maya. Maybe Mrs. Peterson was interrogating everyone in the Ancestor Club about where I had gone. I chew on my bottom lip, worried. But chewing on my lip reminds me how hungry I am, and I'm still clutching the rainbow bag, so I go back to where I left Mac on the turquoise-colored bench.

Only, Mac's gone! I panic, fearing Mr. Charles got him while I wasn't paying attention. Now what will I do?

"Mac?!" I shout, looking left and right, hysteria rising from my gut.

"I'm here," he says from behind me.

I spin around, half-relieved and half-furious. "Where did you go?"

"Calm down. I had to pee."

"Don't tell me to calm down when people are after us! " I thrust his share of the food at him. "I got us lunch. And next time I tell you to stay put, you need to stay put!"

"Don't be ridiculous," he says, ripping the chip bag open. "When nature calls, I'm going to answer." He points at me with a Cheeto. "You need to take a chill pill."

"I don't even know what that means!"

"It's a pill to make you chill. Seriously? You're in seventh grade and you don't know that?" He munches on a Cheeto, unconcerned. And he didn't even say thank you for the food.

At this rate, Mac's going to make me want to strangle him before the monsters even get their chance.

◆

FOURTEEN

All Aboard

The whistle blows and the conductor leans out, calling, "All aboard!"

Mac and I gather up our food and push it all back in the bag. We run to the train and climb the steps into the car. I've never been on a train before, besides the one at the Albuquerque zoo, but considering that one just goes around the exhibits and back, I don't think it counts. This one is the real deal, with two rows of wide seats, and carpeted aisles, and big windows. I check our tickets again and find our seats—two facing each other in a group of four. Mac and I will both get a window.

"Aren't you kids a little young to be riding the train by yourselves?" asks a voice behind us.

I turn to find the conductor standing there. He's a dark-skinned man with a broad stomach. It's difficult to read his eyes beneath his Amtrak cap and bushy eyebrows. But he isn't smiling.

"Uhhh . . ." I mutter uselessly. This is it. If he kicks us off the train, I don't know how we'll get to Spider Rock. Which means no Spider Woman, no map, no weapons, and no saving Dad.

"Our father told us to take the train," Mac offers matter-of-factly. "He's the one who bought us the tickets."

"Is that so?" asks the conductor. "Well, we do get unaccompanied minors on occasion, especially going back to Gallup. But—"

"You can call him if you want," Mac says. "Nizhoni has a phone."

The conductor scratches his cheek, thinking. I give him my winningest smile. Like the one that convinced Coach to let me take the final shot. *Please, please, please let this work.*

Just then someone in the seat in front of ours calls, "Conductor, could you help me read this train schedule, please?" I turn to see a middle-aged Navajo woman turning the folded paper in her hands like she can't tell which way is up. "I don't know why these have to be so confusing. . . ."

"Give me a minute, ma'am." He reaches for our tickets.

"But I don't know if I'm on the right train or not," the woman whines. "I really need your help *now*."

The conductor wrinkles his nose and, after a moment's hesitation, scans our tickets. "Tell you what," he says to us, marking our seats with paper stubs. "I'll keep an eye on you both. If you need anything, let me know." He flashes us a big grin.

"Sure thing," Mac says, throwing the conductor a thumbs-up.

Phew, that was close. I watch, relieved, as the conductor moves on to the woman, and we take our seats.

"What's wrong?" Mac asks. "You look a little freaked out."

"Nothing," I say. "Nothing at all."

"Hey, didn't you say Davery was coming? We're leaving any second. He better hurry."

"He'll make it," I insist, but I'm worried, too.

Davery's still not here when the train rumbles to life. I check my phone again, but there's no text. My stomach does a flip-flop. I thought I could do this on my own, but I'm scared.

Mac pulls out his iPad and opens his animation app. I look out the window one last time, just as the train lurches forward, and to my utter astonishment, there he is. Davery is running full speed across the concrete platform, headed for the closing train door.

And Adrien Cuttlebush is right behind him.

"Look!" I yell, pointing out the window. Mac whips his head up, and we watch Davery leap for the door. He makes it through just in time, one hand grasping the support pole and the other gripping his backpack strap. The door slides shut in Adrien's face, and I can almost hear his yell of frustration as he pounds a fist against its window.

Adrien's head swivels toward me, his eyes meeting mine, and that horrible sensation—my monster detection—springs to life. The hair on the back of my neck rises, and a chill like the trail of an ice cube scuttles down my spine. The train inches forward, and as we pass, Adrien opens his mouth and shows me a mouthful of sharp, pointed teeth.

He may not have been a monster before, but he definitely is one now.

But before I can process how Mac's bully became a carnivorous red-eyed creature, Davery bursts into the train car. I stand up and wave, and he comes bustling over, murmuring,

"Excuse me," to the other passengers as his swinging back-pack whacks them on the shoulders.

He slides into the seat next to me, huffing.

"What happened?!" I whisper-shout, trying to keep my voice down so the other passengers don't get too curious.

Davery holds up a finger.

I sigh impatiently.

His glasses are fogged up, and he takes a moment to pull a kerchief from his pocket. He rubs the cloth back and forth over the lenses, making sure to get every corner.

"Are you serious?" I say, exasperated.

He doesn't say anything, just rolls his eyes up to give me the *Patience, Nizhoni* look. I swear he practices that one in the mirror.

I cross my arms and flop back in my seat. I check the window again to make sure Adrien is gone, and I'm rewarded with a view of the quickly disappearing city of Albuquerque. From here until we hit Gallup, in about three and a half hours, it should be just wide-open vistas of juniper, red rocks, and windy mesas. No monsters. (At least I hope not.) I'm still not sure how we're going to get from the Gallup station to Spider Rock, but I'll find a way. My dad is depending on it.

Finally, Davery slides his glasses back on and gathers himself.

"I think you're correct about the monsters," he says matter-of-factly. "And I believe the particular monster that's chasing you, the one you were calling Mr. Charles, may in fact be a shape-shifter."

Of course! That explains Adrien Cuttlebush. If people

really smacked their foreheads in eureka moments, I'd be smacking mine.

"I saw him," I say. "More like I saw his teeth, to be exact."

"Did Mr. Charles have any compatriots? Helpers?"

"He had two bodyguards."

Davery nods. "I think he *and* his bodyguards are shape-shifters of some kind. That means we'll have to be vigilant. No one can be trusted. They could be a monster in disguise."

I shudder. "Are you okay?"

"I'm fine," Davery says, although his voice seems a bit shaky. "But it was close. He waylaid me at the bus stop by the school, tried to get me to tell him where you went. He had some fantastical story about Mac controlling the sprinkler system like a character from the X-Men."

"Who, me?" Mac says around a mouthful of bologna. I mean, Mac's water powers are cool and all, but when he's eating with his mouth open and has Flamin' Hot Cheeto crumbs flecking his lips, he's about as far from an X-Man as possible.

"We can tell Davery the truth," I say to my brother. "He knows about my monster-sensing abilities."

"You're saying Mac really *did* shoot water at Adrien and his friends by using his mind?!" Davery's eyes are wide with surprise.

Mac straightens in his seat, looking proud. "Well, when you put it that way, I do sound pretty awesome." And then he ruins it by burping loudly before taking another bite of his sandwich.

I take a deep breath. "There's more," I tell Davery.

"More?" he asks incredulously. "More than monsters and superpowers?"

I hand Davery his sandwich and Cheetos. He gives me a baggie of his vegan cookies in exchange and I put them in my backpack "for later." Like that will ever happen.

"Something else happened," I say. "Back at the train station." I tell them about the cart lady who knew our names and gave us the free food. "This was in the bag, too."

I pull out the rolled-up paper. It's a flyer for the upcoming Navajo Nation Fair in Window Rock, Arizona.

"An ad?" Davery asks.

"There's writing on the back," Mac says, taking another bite of his sandwich.

I turn it over, and sure enough, he's right.

"What does it say?" Mac asks.

"It looks like a poem or song lyrics of some kind," I say.

"Read it," Davery prompts me.

I start to read it to myself.

"Aloud, so we can hear it."

"Better yet, if it's a song, you should sing it!" Mac says.

"I don't know the tune, you dork." I start reading, just loud enough for Mac and Davery to hear me.

"Ancient powers lurk in your bones.
Four mountains bind you to your home.
Four days to find you are not alone.

"White shell, blue turquoise, abalone, and jet,

Two to remember, one to forget.
The last, take from the progenitor's debt.

"The spider reveals the rainbow road.
Two will pay what one once owed.
Beware, beware the friendly toad.

"A talking stone, a field of knives, a prom of thorns, a
    seethe of sand.
Thoughts take form, form becomes true.
To defeat the trials, you must know you.

"Who will pay the lost ones' price?
Blood and flesh will not suffice.
A dream must be the sacrifice.

"The Merciless One keeps vigil true.
Heir of lightning, overdue.
What once was old is now brand-new.
Only then will you be you."

When I'm done, we sit in silence until Mac says, "Sounds like a heavy metal song to me. All that blood and sacrifice stuff? 'The Merciless One'? Definitely metal."

"Nah," Davery says. "If it *is* a song, I think it's meant to help us."

"Help us rock out?" Mac raises both hands, making the horns sign, and bobs his head, swinging his hair around.

"Better than that," Davery says excitedly, ignoring my

doofus brother. "It's a puzzle. We know the powers that 'lurk in your bones' now, right? Those are your ancestral powers, the ones that come from Changing Woman's son."

"Okay," I say. "What about 'Four mountains bind you to your home'? There aren't four mountains near our house, and how could they keep us home, anyway?"

"They didn't," says Mac, more serious now. "We ran away from our home." He looks out the window wistfully and mutters, "I hope we can go back soon."

"It must mean some different kind of home," Davery says gently.

"And what about four days to find we aren't alone?" I ask.

"Well, we have each other . . ." Davery offers.

I look over the paper again. "Some of this stuff sounds creepy. Blood, sacrifice." I shiver a little. "We could really use some help right now. I wish that cart lady had told us more." I realize now that the woman was more than she seemed, but I'm not quite ready to share my thoughts about her with Davery and Mac yet.

"We'll figure it out," Davery says encouragingly. "The cart lady wouldn't have given it to you unless she thought you could. Let's focus on getting to Spider Rock first."

"Yeah, you're right," I say, yawning. But I'm not as confident as Davery. Plus, it's not his dad who got kidnapped, and I can't even talk about it, because I don't want to freak out Mac.

"Tired?" he asks.

"I didn't sleep well last night. And a lot has happened today. Plus, too many carbs for lunch."

"Does that mean you're not going to finish your Cheetos?" Mac asks, raising his eyebrows hopefully.

I hand him the half-full bag, and he pumps his fist in triumph. His moment of homesickness seems to have passed, which is a good thing, and now he's babbling to Davery about how XXtra Flamin' Hot Cheetos aren't actually as hot as plain old Flamin' Hot Cheetos, but lime Cheetos are hotter than both kinds, and how maybe his ancestral power, besides controlling water sprinklers, is eating really, really hot cheese snacks.

I listen for a while, but I've heard Mac's Cheeto flavor comparisons before. So has Davery, as a matter of fact, but he's too polite to point that out. The rocking motion of the train and the droning of Mac's soliloquy are making me drowsy. I lean my head against the window and close my eyes. *Just for a minute*, I tell myself. Things are too dangerous for me to be napping. But the lulling movement of the train proves too much, and before I know it, I'm drifting into a dream.

◆

FIFTEEN

Too Many Coats

"Nizhoni," a voice calls from inside the house. "Come inside! Time to wash up for dinner."

I sit up in my train seat, only I'm not in my train seat anymore. I'm in a sun-warmed pile of leaves, crisp and gilded in the yellow hues of fall. I'm surrounded by a pack of adorable black and brown puppies. I know this place. I'm at my shimásání's house.

Grandma's dog, Ladygirl, had a litter, and her three fluffy babies are running around and crawling over my lap as I sit under a golden-leafed oak tree in the early afternoon light. I laugh as the one I named Bandit sticks a wet nose in my palm, and I scratch behind her floppy ear like she wants me to. The other two puppies bark and wrestle and crunch leaves under their oversize paws, all under Ladygirl's watchful eye.

Grandma says rez dogs are special. She doesn't "own" them the way people in the city keep their pets. She and Ladygirl and the rest of the pack have a mutually beneficial agreement—Grandma feeds them, and they guard her house and the surrounding land. As long as both parties keep up their end of the bargain, the dogs will stick around, but Grandma told me they're free to leave if they find a better deal. I've seen her sneak gravy and meat scraps into their bowls, and there's fresh bedding in their doghouse under the back porch, so my guess is they're not leaving anytime soon.

"Nizhoni!" Grandma says again. "I need you inside. Now."

"I guess I can never escape chores," I tell Bandit, who has now decided to chew on my fingers. I extricate my hand from the puppy's mouth and head inside. Mac, my dad, and my grandpa are in the living room watching football. As I pass them, Mac lets out a dramatic groan. Looks like Colorado State is beating his New Mexico Lobos. Again.

Grandma's sitting at the big table that takes up most of the kitchen, a pile of potatoes and a bowl in front of her. She's got her favorite apron on, the one that says KISS THE COOK, which she picked up at the Gallup flea market because she thought it was funny. She looks up, her eyes narrowing in suspicion.

"What is it?" I ask.

"You were outside without a coat?"

"It's not that cold," I say defensively.

"You're going to catch cold if you don't wear a coat."

"I'll wear it next time."

She shakes her head. "Your mother was the same way. Never listening to me."

"I'm not like her," I say sharply. "I'll wear one next time."

Grandma picks up on my attitude. "You think you're so different, but you're not."

"I would never leave my family," I protest. I automatically reach for the turquoise pendant around my neck, but I can't touch it, because now I'm wearing a puffy orange jacket, zipped all the way to my chin. When did I put that on?

Another shout from the living room, this one in triumph. The Lobos must have scored.

I fan my face, feeling hot, because now I've got another coat on top of the orange jacket. This one is black-and-red plaid. Two coats, and I can barely move my arms. Plus, I'm starting to sweat.

"Uh, Grandma . . . I'm having some trouble here."

"Of course you are. Because you're just like her. Your mother was so headstrong. Never listened. I told her not to get married so young and have babies."

Whoa, Grandma's never said that before, and for a minute, I'm distracted from my coat dilemma. "Really?"

"But she loved your dad. Loved you and little Mac, too, so she had to go." Grandma drops a freshly peeled potato in the bowl. "Life has a way of messing up all your plans," she tells me. "Your mom had plans, too, and see how that worked out. It'll be the same for you. So you better wear a coat."

"I think I have enough!" Because now I'm wearing three coats, the last a thick tan canvas Carhartt like my dad wears to chop wood. Sweat is dripping into my eyes, and I'm trying to unbutton or unzip all my coats to get to my pendant, but I have mittens on, too, and I can't get a grip on anything. "Help!" I gasp.

My grandma just keeps peeling her potatoes, looking serene. "Listen to me, Nizhoni," she says. "You can never have too many coats."

SIXTEEN

◆

The Sleeper Won't Awaken

"Nizhoni," Mac says, punching me in the shoulder, "wake up! I think there's something wrong with the train."

I slowly come to, yawning and stretching and shivering from the cold. I rub my eyes and try to shake the fuzzy feeling from my head. That's right—we're on a train, running from a monster. I can't believe I even fell asleep at all.

Then again, I've always been pretty good at sleeping through big events. Once I missed a tornado warning when we were visiting some relatives in Texas, and I've never quite made it to the ball drop on that *New Year's Rockin' Eve* special. Maybe my ancestral power isn't monster sensing at all, but snoozing. Which would be just perfect. Mac gets water magic and spicy-food eating, and I get the power to nap during a crisis.

"Nizhoni!" Mac repeated. "Did you hear me?"

"Stop yelling. What is it?"

"Something's wrong with the train. It's taking us up the side of a mountain!"

And I'm awake! I push myself up and look out the window. The otherwise-normal Amtrak train is running steadily forward on the track, but in a totally not normal direction:

vertical. And it's not just any mountain—it's huge, with a snow-capped peak. In fact, it's starting to snow outside our window, delicate white flakes falling softly around us to blanket the desert floor. No wonder I dreamed about coats. The rest of the dream I'm not so sure about, but it makes me miss my grandma and her dogs.

"We must have gotten on the wrong train," I say. "We'll have to find the conductor and ask to switch at the next station."

"Uh, that might prove difficult," Davery says. He's sitting up, yawning and stretching, as if he, too, took a nap. And I notice Mac has sleep boogers in the corners of his eyes. We all must have fallen asleep. "There's no one on this train but us."

"What?!" I twist around. Where's the confused middle-aged woman? And I distinctly remember Davery thumping someone in the head with his backpack as he pushed his way down the crowded aisle. But now all the seats are vacant.

I turn to look the other way, toward the front of the train. Completely empty, too.

We're all alone.

"Do you think Mr. Charles and his monster crew did this?" Mac whispers fearfully.

"I should think not!" comes a grumbly and muffled voice. "*I* did it. But no need to worry. We are headed in the right direction."

I recognize it. "Mr. Yazzie?" Relief bubbles up in my belly as the horned toad from my dream crawls out of my backpack and settles on the seat next to me. "You have no idea how happy I am to see you!"

"Yes, dear child. I am pleased to see you again, too."

"Again?" Mac says, mouth dropped open like a sea bass. "Since when do you know a talking lizard, Nizhoni?"

"Amazing," murmurs Davery.

"So you both can see him?" I ask.

"And hear him," Davery says, nodding.

If Mac and Davery can see Mr. Yazzie, then he couldn't have only existed in my dream, if it was a dream at all.

"Mac, can you pinch me?"

He leans over the seat and punches my arm.

"Ow! I said 'pinch,' not 'punch'!" But at least I'm sure that I'm not dreaming. "I know this is going to sound weird, but Mr. Yazzie used to be a stuffed animal, my stuffed animal, but he came alive because horned toads are natural helpers and he knew I needed help."

"At your service," he croaks.

"Amazing," Davery says again.

"As for the talking," Mr. Yazzie continues, "all animals can talk. It's just that they speak a language most humans don't bother to learn."

"But we didn't learn it, either . . ." I say.

"Ah, but your ancestral powers have awakened. This gives you the ability to know all kinds of things that were perhaps once forgotten, including the language of animals. Now allow me to introduce myself," he says, turning to Mac. "My name is Theodous Alvin Yazzie."

"Nice to meet you," Mac says, extending his pinkie politely. Mr. Yazzie rests a claw briefly against his fingernail in a human-to-horned-toad handshake.

Davery also holds his pinkie out for a shake. "Ancestral powers, you say? I don't know about that in my case, but this isn't much stranger than anything else that's happened today."

"Now that introductions are out of the way, we must get down to business."

"What business is that?" Mac asks.

Sometimes my brother has the attention span of a gnat. "Monster fighting!"

"Congratulations, Nizhoni and Marcus. You are the descendants of Changing Woman and have been gifted the powers of her sons, the Hero Twins!" Mr. Yazzie lifts a small claw and throws a handful of what looks like gold confetti into the air. I watch the teeny bits of colored paper rain down on our train seats. Mr. Yazzie pulls a tiny party horn from somewhere and blows it. It makes an unhappy sound.

"It's the best I could do on short notice," he explains. "Whenever a new monsterslayer and born for water are awakened, I usually try to splurge on a banner, streamers, a few party hats."

"Whoa, back up. A monster what? And a born for who?" Mac asks, flabbergasted.

"Ah, I get it," Davery says. "Monsterslayer"—he points at me—"and Born for Water"—he points at Mac. "You're not quite twins, but you're pretty close."

"Ten months!" Mac pronounces triumphantly.

"Maybe you should start from the beginning, Mr. Yazzie," I say.

The lizard clears his throat. "It is said that, long ago, Changing Woman created the first four Diné clans from her own skin."

"The Diné. That's us," Davery whispers to me.

"I know that!" I snap.

"But she looked around and saw that there were many monsters who threatened her people. So Changing Woman gave birth to twin boys, Monsterslayer and Born for Water, to protect the Diné."

"The Diné. That's us," I whisper to Mac.

He rolls his eyes.

"Enduring many trials and hardships, the Hero Twins did just that," Mr. Yazzie continued. "And ever since, whenever the world has been threatened by monsters, new heroes have arisen. Descendants who have inherited the twins' special powers as well as the responsibility to fight evil."

"And this time it's us?" Mac asks excitedly.

Mr. Yazzie nods.

Mac lets out a whoop. "We're going to be superheroes!"

So it's true. Mac and I are related to the legendary Hero Twins.

I give Mr. Yazzie a smile, despite the fact that my insides are curling in worry. I've been waiting my whole life to be chosen for something, to stand out as someone special. But now that we're in this for real, with my father's life at stake and my little brother facing physical danger, it isn't what I was expecting. Like the time Dad promised he would get mint chocolate chip ice cream on his way home from work, but the store was out of that flavor, so he came home with vanilla and some off-brand chocolate syrup instead. Still good, but not exactly great.

"Didn't you tell me before that the heroes who fight monsters"—I shoot a look at Mac and choose my words carefully—"er . . . sometimes fail?" I ask Mr. Yazzie.

"It is true that this is a very dangerous mission you two have been given, and there are no guarantees of success. But you must fight regardless. There is no other way."

"I'm still willing to fight," I assure Mr. Yazzie, "but I want Mac to know what he's getting into." I turn to him. "This isn't a video game we're talking about, bro."

The light of excitement in Mac's eyes has been replaced with a steeliness that surprises me. "I know it's dangerous, Z," he says, "but when I used the water against Adrien and those other guys, it felt . . ."

"Right?" I prompt.

"Natural?" offers Davery.

"It felt *awesome!*" Mac finishes. "I want to do more of that. I'm in! Hero Twins power!" he shouts, throwing his hands up.

I grin, feeling better. Like the cart lady's song said, I am not alone.

"I'm in, too," says Davery.

"No, Davery," I say. "You don't have to be involved in this. You've already done—"

He holds up a palm to stop me. "Hey, I'm half-Diné, aren't I? I care about our people's future. And if I remember correctly, that cart lady gave you three lunches, not just two. So clearly I'm supposed to be involved."

As usual, my best friend makes a good argument, leaving me speechless. I give him a big smile of gratitude.

Then I look to the horned toad, who is nodding in approval. "Mr. Yazzie, I remembered what you told me about asking Na'ashjéii Asdzáá for a map to the House of the Sun. Davery and I looked her up on the internet and found out she lives at Spider Rock in Canyon de Chelly. So we bought train tickets to the closest town, Gallup. And I swear we got on the right train, but now . . ." I gesture around helplessly.

"Very good initiative, Nizhoni!" Mr. Yazzie says. "You're a natural at this, I see."

"Oh." That cheers me up even more, and Davery gives me an encouraging smile. I might be hero material yet!

Mr. Yazzie continues, "I took the liberty of informing the Diyin Dine'é of our destination, and they redirected the train. No need to be alarmed."

"You can talk to the Holy People?" Davery asks.

"Of course. So can you."

All three of us stare at him, mouths open.

Mr. Yazzie smiles. "Who do you think you were talking to at the train station?"

"You mean the cart lady, right?" I thought so. "That's how she knew our names."

"And how much I like Cheetos," Mac adds.

"And that I'm lactose intolerant," Davery remarks, holding up his grape soda pop can.

"The tricky part is that the Holy People don't always answer, or at least not in ways that you might recognize," says Mr. Yazzie. "But they are always there."

Always there . . . just like the monsters. "Can you tell us more about Mr. Charles?" I ask. "What kind of creature he is, and how we can defeat him?" *And what he might do to my dad,* I think. But Mac still doesn't know the whole truth, so I keep that part to myself.

"I believe Mr. Charles is related to a nasty kind of monster called a bináá' yee agháni. These are vicious bird creatures that the original Monsterslayer imprisoned at Tsé Bit'a'í, the volcanic pillar now called Shiprock. Mr. Charles is a shape-shifter, so he can take on the form of these birds, or he can look human, as you have already seen."

"Does he have scales underneath his skin?" Mac asks eagerly. "Tentacles?"

"All of those and more, should he wish it," Mr. Yazzie says somberly. "He is very powerful and quite evil. He and his kind will not be happy until they have destroyed the land. He must be stopped."

And I'm the one who must stop him, I think with a slightly terrified gulp. I'm up for the challenge, and glad to have Mac and Davery and Mr. Yazzie to help me, but I'm still scared.

As if sensing my worry, Davery pats me encouragingly on the shoulder.

"There's only three of them," says Mac. "We can take 'em, easy."

"It's only Charles and his two henchmen for now," Mr. Yazzie says. "But if he isn't stopped, he will free his kin, and they will try to break out the other monsters that are imprisoned beneath the earth. Once they are released, I'm afraid it will be too late."

"Too late?" I ask. "Too late for what?"

"To save the planet. They are devourers, you see. They will not stop until they have consumed every patch of ground and every drop of water, and pulled the guts of Mother Earth from the inside for their own uses."

Mac gnaws on the side of his thumb and says, "That's bad."

Understatement of the year.

"Plus, they eat people," Mr. Yazzie adds.

Davery coughs. "Did you say 'eat people'?"

"Yes, *eat*." He works his jaw like he's chewing something. "You aren't familiar with the word?"

"I know the word," Davery says. "It just seems a bit . . . excessive."

"Sounds right to me," I say, visions of eyeball hors d'oeuvres rolling around in my mind.

A loud horn blows as the train crests the mountain. We've been climbing the whole time Mr. Yazzie has been talking, and now we're moving through puffy white clouds.

The train slows to a gentle roll, and finally it stops, coming to rest in the middle of a meadow between several snowy mountain peaks. The ground is covered in a layer of fresh powder. Mist lingers, making everything look soft and inviting.

"It's beautiful here," I say.

"Don't be fooled," Mr. Yazzie warns us. "Beautiful things can kill you just as quickly as ugly ones. You must be careful. And trust no one!"

◆

SEVENTEEN

The White Mountain

We gather our backpacks and stumble out of the train into the snowy landscape. Our breath puffs in the air, and I zip up my hoodie, already missing the warmth of the Albuquerque spring. Out here it seems to be sunrise, but that doesn't make sense. We didn't spend the night on the train. . . .

Mr. Yazzie hops up on a nearby boulder and clears his throat.

"Welcome to Sisnaajiní!" he proclaims, flinging out his tiny arms. "The Mountain of the Dawn, the easternmost sacred mountain, and the home of the Rock Crystal Guardians and the Gray Dove Heralds." His voice rings through the snowy valley, and the last word of each sentence comes back to us in reverberating echoes. "Also," he adds, "the guardians had some very delicious corn cakes last time I visited. Really the best." *Best . . . best . . . best . . .*

"So there's more than one sacred mountain?" I ask.

"Yes," Mr. Yazzie explains. "There are four—one for each of the cardinal directions: east, south, west, and north. They were set in place by the Diyin Dine'é and equipped with a guardian and a herald to care for the land. They surround the ancestral home of the Diné people, and each represents a powerful part of Navajo history and culture."

"*Four mountains bind you to your home.* That's the second line in the song," Davery says, looking at the cart lady's note, which I'd let him keep to puzzle over. He scratches his ear thoughtfully. "It's starting to make sense."

"But why are we even here?" Mac asks. "I thought we were going to Spider Rock to see some lady?"

"I arranged for a little detour," says Mr. Yazzie. "So we can find gifts for Na'ashjéii Asdzáá."

"Who is that, anyway?" Mac asks.

"Her name means Spider Woman." He starts to say something, but I cut him off. "And no, she isn't related to Peter Parker."

He looks a little disappointed.

"She has a map we need, but we can't just show up empty-handed and start asking her for stuff," Davery says. "That would be rude."

"Indeed," Mr. Yazzie agrees. "So we will visit the Four Sacred Mountains and gather an item from each place. A perfect white shell from Sisnaajiní, a piece of turquoise from Tsoodził, an abalone shell from Dook'o'ooslíid, and a nugget of black jet from Dibé Nitsaa."

"All those are mentioned in the song!" Davery says excitedly, pointing at the sheet. "White shell, blue turquoise, abalone, and jet."

I look over his shoulder. Right under the part about the four kinds of stones, it says, *Two to remember, one to forget. The last, take from the progenitor's debt.*

"But what about the next part, about remembering and forgetting?" I ask. "And what the heck is a progenitor, and how

111

are we going to take from his debt? I thought debt was, like, something you owed people."

"I can't tell you," Mr. Yazzie says. "The song was meant for you to understand, not me."

"A progenitor is like your ancestor," Davery says. "But I haven't figured out the rest yet."

My breath is puffing in tiny frosty clouds in front of my face as I look around at the white mountain peaks that surround us. There are so many things to keep up with and so much to learn. Spiders and rainbows. Talking stones, fields of knives, and of course, the phrase that is bothering me the most: *Beware, beware the friendly toad.* I hate to think poorly of Mr. Yazzie, but I can't ignore the words of the song. I vow to trust him for now, but to stay alert.

"I'm really cold," Mac says, his teeth chattering as he tucks his hands into his long sleeves. "Is anyone else freezing out here?"

"F-f-for n-n-now, let's f-f-focus on the mountains and getting the f-f-four gifts we need," Mr. Yazzie says.

"Are you all right, Mr. Yazzie?" Davery asks. "I remember from biology class that horned toads don't do well in the cold."

"N-n-now that you m-m-mention it," he says, "I d-d-do seem to be rather ch-chilly. . . ."

I scoop up our tiny guide and tuck him into the neck of my hoodie, between my warm shirt and the fleece. I make sure he's cozy but leave enough room around him so he can still see out.

"Is he okay?" Mac asks.

"Horned toads freeze in cold weather," Davery says. "It's a hibernation response. He'll be fine in a few minutes, once Nizhoni warms him up."

"Maybe we should look around and try to find somewhere inside," I suggest.

"Do you really think that's a good idea?" Mac asks, peering around nervously. "We don't want to wander off the edge of a cliff or something."

"We'll be fine," I say, starting off toward the closest white peak on the edge of the meadow. "He said there's a guardian on this mountain, right? We'll just look for them while we wait for Mr. Yazzie to warm up."

"I don't know, Z," Davery says, looking uneasy. "The guardian may not be friendly. He or she could be the one Mr. Yazzie warned us not to trust. I mean, 'guardian' does imply there's something worth guarding. And this guardian person might not take too kindly to us stomping all over their mountain looking for . . . What exactly are we looking for?"

"A white shell," I say, remembering what Mr. Yazzie said.

"Uh, this doesn't look like the ideal place to find a white shell," Mac says.

"I hate to agree," Davery says, "but I agree."

I stop in my tracks, resting my hands on my hips, and look at my companions. "Maybe you two have forgotten, but we are on a quest here, not a ski vacation. And frankly, neither of you sounds particularly questish. In fact, you sound like you're already giving up."

Davery frowns. "I don't think 'questish' is a real word."

"It doesn't matter if it's a real word!" I say, feeling exasperated. "What matters is that we find that shell. Now!" I motion toward the mountain peak.

"Fine," Davery says, "but I have a feeling we're going to regret this."

"Stop worrying so much," I say. "We'll be fine."

And that's when the arrow comes flying through the air to *thunk* into the ground inches from my toes.

◆

EIGHTEEN

A Cold Welcome

We all stop in our tracks.

"I surrender!" Mac yells, throwing his backpack down in the snow and raising his hands.

Davery and I do the same.

"Who's there?" comes a boy's voice. Or at least I think it's a boy. It sounds like winter wind blowing through pine trees—a soft sound that carries a lot of potential. I shiver when it touches my ears.

"Say your names!" the voice demands.

I look around, but I can't see who's talking. "Hello?"

"We come in peace," Davery says calmly.

"Don't kill us!" wails Mac.

I swear, I cannot take my brother anywhere.

A figure materializes, slowly separating itself from the white fields of snow. At first I think it's a statue that I somehow didn't see before—a statue of a boy, maybe fifteen or sixteen, carved from a diamond. His skin, his clothes—everything is made of white crystal rock. He's wearing long pants, a loose shirt, a shell necklace and matching earrings, and he has a bandanna tied around his head and knotted to the side. The morning sun illuminates the angles of his face, the crook of his elbow, the bend of his knees, so that he sparkles like the prism Dad hung in the window to catch the light. But he can talk and move—and he's holding a bow and arrow in his hands, nocked and aimed directly at me!

"Davery!" I yelp, my hands squeezing his arm.

"I see him," he says.

"What do we do?"

He steps forward, his hands still raised, and says again, sounding more official than before, "We come in peace!"

The crystal boy narrows his eyes, and his hands grasp the bow a little tighter.

"I don't think that's working," I whisper through teeth clenched in a smile.

"Do you have a better idea?"

As a matter of fact, I do. "Mr. Yazzie," I say to my shoulder, "I know you're frozen and all, but it would be really good if you woke up about now."

"Who are you talking to?" the boy asks suspiciously.

"How can you talk if you're a statue?" Mac asks.

"I am *not* a statue," the crystal boy says, sounding like a slightly irritated wind blowing around the inside of a glass bowl. "I am the guardian of this mountain. I belong here. And you do not. More importantly, *I'm* asking the questions." He turns clear eyes toward me. "And I believe I asked who you were talking to."

"Oh, well, see," I say, trying to sound reasonable and not terrified, "it's my friend. He's a horned toad, but he's very wise, and he brought us here, but then it was so cold that he kind of froze, but I'm sure he'll wake up—"

The crystal boy gives me a look and I stop.

"You're talking to a frozen lizard?" he says ominously. "And you think *I'm* weird because I'm made of crystals. Who's the real weirdo here?"

"Well, when you put it that way . . ." I squeak.

For a minute, it looks like he's going to shoot us with the arrow on principle. Then his face breaks into a grin, and he lowers the bow.

"Why didn't you say so?" He returns the arrow to his quiver and drapes the bow over one shoulder. He takes a step toward us, and we all take a step back.

He laughs. "I won't hurt you. For now." He leans over to peer at the neck of my hoodie. "Yá'át'ééh, shicheii," he says. "Welcome back to Sisnaajiní!"

The crystal boy holds out a hand. I understand what he wants, and I lift Mr. Yazzie gently from his impromptu bed and place him in the boy's outstretched palm. The crystal boy blows across the toad's frozen body.

"Won't that make him colder?" Mac asks.

"No," says the crystal boy. "Watch!"

And sure enough, Mr. Yazzie stirs back to life, stretching and yawning like he's just awakened from a nice nap. He opens his eyes and looks up sleepily at the guardian of the mountain.

"Well, yá'át'ééh, my old friend," he says. "Don't suppose you have a place where we could warm up? Seems these old bones can't take the chill the way they used to."

"Of course, Grandpa," the crystal boy says. "And then I'd like you to introduce your friends."

The crystal boy, who tells us his name is Rock Crystal Boy but we can call him RC, leads us across the snowy field to a small house in the distance. The structure is eight-sided and sort of low and wide. I recognize it as a hogan, a traditional Navajo dwelling. It looks surprisingly snug and cozy, and a stream of blue smoke wafts merrily from the pipe protruding from the center of the domed roof. RC leads us inside, hanging his bow and arrow by the door. We all hurry in, grateful for the fire that's burning in the wood stove in the middle of the large, open room. There's a big couch, and a table and chairs, and RC tells us to take a seat. Minutes later, he brings each of us a mug of tea. He pours Mr. Yazzie's onto a plate for easy drinking.

"Now, if you could introduce yourselves," RC says.

"I'm Nizhoni," I say, waving.

Mr. Yazzie makes a strangled noise. "Not that way, child. The proper way. Give him your name and clans."

"You could have told me that. . . ." For once, I'm glad Grandma made us learn our clans and the Navajo way to greet people.

"Yá'át'ééh," I say, using my formal voice. "My name is Nizhoni Begay. My mother's clan is Towering House. My father's clan is Bitter Water. My maternal grandfather's clan is the Mud People clan, and my paternal grandfather's clan is the Crystal Rock people."

RC shakes my outstretched hand. "Crystal Rock clan, did you say?"

I nod.

"Then we're related! You are certainly my granddaughter!"

"But you're not much older than me," I say in as polite a tone as possible.

RC laughs. "Thank you for the compliment. I do adhere to a rigorous skin care regime. But I assure you, I am much older than I look. I've been the guardian of this mountain since the beginning of this world. What matters, though, is that we're related."

"Why does that matter?" Mac asks.

"And who are you?" RC asks.

"I'm her brother."

"Introduce yourself the right way," I say, elbowing him.

Mac holds out his hand to RC, stating his name and clans, the same as mine. RC smiles and shakes his hand, and then Davery follows suit. His clans are totally different than ours, and his mom's side isn't even Navajo. But as Grandma once explained to me, Navajo people like to know who you are, whether you're Navajo or not, so Davery saying his maternal clan is African American is just fine.

"You wanted to know why it matters that we're related?" RC asks Mac once the introductions are done. "Because that means we share k'é."

"And what is that?" Mac asks.

"Well, it's very complicated, but I think it is enough for you to know that it means I take care of you, and you take care of me, because we are extended family."

"I like that," Mac says.

I don't say it, but I like it, too.

"So perhaps now you can tell me why you've come to my mountain and what I can do to help you."

"Thanks! I mean, ahéhee'," I add quickly, remembering the Navajo word. It seemed like the right thing to say, since we're talking to a Navajo elder, and it must be, because Mr. Yazzie smiles at me encouragingly. I vow to practice speaking my language more often in the future.

"We are looking for a white shell to take to Spider Woman as a gift," I say. "Can you help us?"

"Not just any white shell," Mr. Yazzie adds hastily. "It must be perfectly formed. No chips, breaks, or scratches."

"There are many shells here," RC says, tapping his chin in thought. "I am very busy and cannot help you look, but I can show you where a perfect shell might be found."

Hmm. He doesn't look that busy, but maybe there are secret guardian duties I don't know about. RC stands up from his seat and walks to the small window facing east.

"See the white peak in the distance?" he says, pointing toward the snowcap with a push of his lips. "Walk that way, until you reach the base of the mountain, and you will come upon the white shells you seek."

"I still don't understand how there are shells on a snow-covered mountain," Mac says. "Don't people usually find shells at a beach?"

"It is said that, when the Holy People made this mountain to mark the easternmost edge of Dinétah," RC explains, "they adorned it with white shells to make it shine in the sunlight and mark its beauty."

"It *is* very beautiful," I say.

"We learned in school that this land was once underwater and all kinds of sea creatures lived here," Davery adds.

"So it is said," RC agrees. "The world may change around us, but if we look closer, we can always see its bones."

"Bones?" Mac yelps. "No one said anything about bones."

"And since it is such a beautiful morning," RC says, ignoring him, "I will walk with you a ways. Once you finish your tea, of course. And let me find Mr. Yazzie a sweater."

We all empty our mugs, and RC digs around in a box full of what looks like scarves, mittens, hats, and other cold-weather gear until he produces a tiny sweater the perfect size for a horned toad. It's snowy white, just like the mountains around us, and it looks thick and warm.

"This should do the trick, little cheii," RC says as he slips the sweater over the lizard's bony spine. The turtleneck catches on Mr. Yazzie's left horn, but after a sharp tug, it's on nice and snug.

"Why did RC call Mr. Yazzie 'little grandpa'?" Mac asks me.

"It's respectful," I explain. "He is our elder, after all."

"Are we ready?" the guardian of Sisnaajiní asks. We all say yes and he opens the door to lead us back out into the rosy dawn light and pink-tinged snow.

"If you don't mind," Mr. Yazzie says to me from the table. He gestures toward the little nook on my shoulder where I had tucked him earlier. "It was quite nice being up so high."

"Of course," I say. I reach out an arm and let him climb to his new favorite spot.

He snuggles in and says, "Onward!" and I follow everyone else outside.

The snow is deep around the hogan, and we have to slog our way through. It comes up past my ankles, making my sneakered feet cold. But the farther we get from RC's home, the thinner the snow gets until it's only a sprinkle of frost underneath our feet. We walk for a while, the white peak getting closer and closer, but the sun doesn't rise any higher in the sky. After what seems like hours, RC stops.

"That is what you seek," he says, pointing to something in the distance.

Now I can see that what had looked like a snowcapped mountain is actually a massive mound of white shells. Hundreds, maybe thousands. Okay, definitely thousands. Piled higher than my house. A three-story pile of shells.

And somehow I have to find the most perfect one in the bunch.

NINETEEN

◆

An Impossibility!

"That's a lot of clams!" Mac exclaims.

"Good luck!" RC pats Mac on the back. "I'll just wait here for you to finish. I'd help, but as I said, I'm very busy."

"He doesn't look busy," Mac mutters as we watch RC head back to his nice warm house.

"We're supposed to go through all these?" I say, dismayed. "There's no way."

"It does look daunting," Mr. Yazzie admits, "but it can be done. The mountain seems huge, but I know we will find the perfect shell. With a little patience," he says, hopping off my shoulder to land on the white mound, "and positive thinking."

"I appreciate what you're saying, Mr. Yazzie. I really do. But I just don't think positive thinking is going to be enough."

"Well, that's negative thinking right there!" Mac says, eyebrow raised in my direction.

"Nonsense, Nizhoni," says the horned toad, climbing higher on the mountain. A trail of white shells trickles down behind him. "It is a challenge worthy of a hero, which you are!"

"I thought being a hero meant I was going to fight monsters."

"One step at a time, young slayer," he says, already halfway up. "One step at a time."

"Come on," Davery says. He tightens the straps on his backpack and looks at the foreboding pile. "We better get started." He follows Mr. Yazzie up the hill.

"I still say it's impossible," I mutter, "but I guess we're doing this." I adjust my own backpack and take a deep breath. I step onto the shell mountain. The sharp edges of broken shells poke at the canvas of my sneakers. Ouch! I try to ignore the pain and take another step. I immediately start to slide downward. I flail my arms for balance, letting out a not-so-heroic yelp, before I lean forward and dig in. Every move I make cracks shells underneath my feet. I can feel a wail building up inside me. How am I supposed to find a perfect shell when each step breaks some? It seems impossible. Even more impossible than fighting monsters. At least that's exciting. This is just hard.

I look up and see that Mac, Davery, and Mr. Yazzie are already halfway up. "Wait for me!" I shout, scrambling forward, my feet slipping. I lean over and use my hands, and immediately the shells cut into my palms. I've barely begun and I already feel like quitting. But I remember what Mr. Yazzie said. *You wanted to be a hero,* I tell myself. *This is part of it.* So I start searching. But all the shells look the same. Nothing is standing out.

The sun rises hot behind me. It feels like there's a heavy weight slung over my shoulders, and that weight is making me tired and hungry. *Give up,* it whispers. *Why try so hard? No one will notice if you quit. No one really cares. You're only a kid, after all. You can't really fight monsters.*

For a moment, I want to do what the voice says, but I don't. My dad needs me. And I definitely don't want the world to be overrun with monsters. So instead of giving up, I close my eyes, take a deep breath, and imagine the shell I want. Unblemished white and shiny, the ridges aligned perfectly. It's so clear in my mind that I can almost reach out and touch it. I lean down, stretch forward, and let my hand graze a shell. And I know it's the one.

I open my eyes and look. A perfect, smooth white shell rests in my palm.

Yessssss!!! Victory!

"I found it!" I shout. Mr. Yazzie, Davery, and Mac look down at me from higher up on the mountain. I wave the shell over my head. "I found a perfect one!" They all hurry over, sliding down the mountain and sending shells scattering as they come.

Mr. Yazzie is beaming with pride. "I knew you could do it! One gift down, three more to go. And it only took half the day."

"Half the day?" I look up at the sky. I thought it was eternally dawn on this mountain! But sure enough, the sun is hanging high overhead, telling me it's noon. "I guess I lost track. . . ." My heart sinks. That's a half day more my father has been in captivity, and I still have no idea where he is. To keep myself from crying, I concentrate on wrapping the shell in a semi-clean tissue from my pocket and tuck it in my backpack.

"That wasn't so bad. Where to next?" Mac asks as we make our way down the shell mountain. This is like a game to him. I'm glad he doesn't have to worry about Dad.

Before Mr. Yazzie can answer, a dark shadow crosses between us and the sun. We all look up as something the size of a car swoops over our heads. Something with huge wings, a feathered tail, and a sharp black beak.

The giant bird circles and then lands fifteen feet in front of us. Its feathers are a glossy midnight black, and it fixes us with an unblinking eye as it opens its mouth ominously.

"Birds eat horned toads," Davery murmurs.

"Do you think he's here to catch Mr. Yazzie?" Mac asks anxiously.

"Get behind me!" I shout, fearing the bird is another monster. I grab Mr. Yazzie and tuck him into the neck of my hoodie. He sputters and hisses.

"Let me go!" he shouts. "The audacity!"

"I'm trying to protect you."

"From what? I assure you, I don't need protecting from the herald of Dibé Nitsaa! She is a noble creature."

"Hello, cheii," the bird says in a melodious voice. "I heard you were on Sisnaajiní this morning, and I had to come see for myself. And you've brought three children with you? How unusual."

"These are no average children. These siblings have inherited the powers of Monsterslayer and Born for Water, and their friend is very wise, surely destined to be a scholar."

His prediction doesn't surprise me. Davery is already a genius.

126

"Do you know this bird?" I ask Mr. Yazzie.

"Yes! I mean, er, I think so. Surely we've met before. I just can't quite recall. . . ."

"Didn't you say she was the herald of Dibé Nitsaa?" Davery prompts.

"Of course!" Mr. Yazzie's spikes pop out of the neck of his fuzzy sweater. "Now I remember. Łizhin. It is an honor." He says her name like *CLEH-zhin*.

"The honor is mine," Łizhin says, ducking her head in a small bow. "I am the herald of Dibé Nitsaa, the Mountain of the Folding Darkness, the northernmost sacred mountain and the home of the Jet Guardians and the Black Bird Heralds."

"Folding Darkness?" Davery murmurs. "I don't like the sound of that."

"And while it is good to see you again, little cheii," Łizhin continues, "I am here for another reason."

"And what is that, Black Mountain Herald?"

"Jet Girl, our guardian, cannot be found. Without her, there's no one to defend the mountain from danger." Łizhin pauses and looks each of us in the eye. "And indeed, danger has come to Dibé Nitsaa."

Mr. Yazzie makes a worried noise.

"What is it?" I ask.

"The four sacred mountains and their guardians keep Dinétah safe," he says. "If one goes missing, all the people, animals, and other beings that live there are at risk."

"That's not good." Mac, the king of understatements, strikes again.

"It's Mr. Charles," I say, sure of it. "You said he would

attack the land, and taking out a guardian seems like his style. He definitely has something to do with this."

"While I never think one should rush to conclusions, I'm afraid you may be right," Mr. Yazzie says. He turns to Łizhin. "What can we do to help?"

"Not you, cheii, but your ward."

Łizhin bows in front of me. I look around and behind me, sure there's been a mistake. "Me?" I squeak.

"Yes, Monsterslayer. You are also a guardian of Dibé Nitsaa."

"I am?" This seems highly improbable, since I didn't even know about the place until about five minutes ago.

"You must come and defend the mountain," Łizhin says adamantly.

"We don't have time," Davery says. He pulls out the flyer and points to the third line of the song. *"Four days to find you are not alone.* I think this means we only have three and a half more days to get everything done. And we still have to find the other three gifts and go see Spider Woman before we even get the map."

"If Dibé Nitsaa falls, there will be no Dinétah, and no Dinétah means no Spider Woman, which means no map, which means no path to the Sun," Mr. Yazzie says solemnly. "It is all interconnected. You cannot let one fall without every-thing else falling with it. I hate to suggest it, but I believe we must split up,"

"I don't think that's a good idea," I say, feeling uneasy. This is hard enough as it is. Without Mac and Davery, it sounds impossible.

"It's the only way," he insists. "Nizhoni will go with Łizhin to Dibé Nitsaa. She will help find the missing guardian and convince her to give us the black jet gift for Spider Woman. Davery, you go to the Dook'o'oosłiid, the western mountain, and retrieve the abalone shell. Mac can go to Tsoodził, the southern mountain, and find the turquoise."

"By myself?" Mac says, his voice climbing an octave.

"I will go with you, if you wish," Mr. Yazzie offers.

"Didn't the song say we're all supposed to stick together?" I ask. It also said we were supposed to beware the friendly toad. . . .

"We don't have a choice," Mr. Yazzie says forcefully. "We weren't given much time to begin with. We will run out of time if we don't split up."

"Even if we agree to split up," Davery says, "how are we going to get to the other mountains?"

"Leave that to me," says Łizhin. She takes a step back, lifts her beak, and begins to sing. Her song is beautiful, a trilling, twisting melody that fills the winter air. It rises into the sky and travels toward the top of the world, beyond Sisnaajiní. We all listen, rapt. When she finishes, Mac claps politely.

"I have called the heralds of Tsoodził and Dook'o'oosłiid," Łizhin explains. "They will be here momentarily. Each herald will take you to their mountain and alert the guardian to your presence, and the guardians will help you find what you need."

"How will the heralds take us?" I ask nervously. "Are . . . are you going to carry us in your talons?"

Łizhin blinks at me and I'm pretty sure she's smiling.

"Talons, no. Carry, yes. You will each ride on one of our backs. Nizhoni, you will ride on mine."

"Well," Davery says, "I certainly didn't see *that* coming."

I eye Łizhin's back, excitement starting to edge out my fear. It seems broad enough to hold me and her feathers look soft, but there's one thing missing.

"I'm all for giant bird riding, but how can I stay on without a saddle?"

"Or a seat belt?" Mac asks. "We always buckle up for safety."

Łizhin laughs. "Are you worried that, as we fly through the clouds hundreds of feet above the earth and you have nothing to hold on to but a handful of feathers, you might plummet to your deaths?"

"Yes," we all say at once.

"Then I guess you'll just have to hold on really tight!"

TWENTY

◆

Warning: May Cause Screaming

We hear the heralds coming before we see them. Great feathery bodies block the sun and the sound of what seems like hundreds of massive wings fills the air. The wind grows stronger, blowing us back so hard we have to dig our feet into the ground to keep from falling over. And above us, two birds appear, both as big as trucks. One blue, one yellow.

The bluebird lands first. The plumage on its back and wings is the brilliant hue of a perfect summer sky, and its belly is a grayish white.

"Yá'át'ééh," it says, its voice a deep rumble. "I am Dólii, the herald of Tsoodził, the Mountain of the Day, the southernmost sacred mountain and the home of the Turquoise Guardians and the Bluebird Heralds." It turns its head to Łizhin. "I heard your call, sister, so I came. How may I help?"

"Dólii, my brother," Łizhin says, "this child, called Mac, is a descendant of one of the Hero Twins. You must take him to Turquoise Boy so he may collect the gift he needs to offer Spider Woman. The tiny cheii will accompany you."

Dólii bows his head to Mac. "I would be honored to take you to my mountain so you can meet my guardian and request your boon." He drops down until his belly rests against the snow. "Climb on my back, child called Mac and tiny cheii, and we will be off!"

Mac gives me big eyes. I know that expression. Those are his chili-cheese-dog-on-the-roller-coaster vomit eyes.

"You'll be okay, Mac," I say firmly. "You can do this. Just think about reuniting with Dad."

"What if there's a test?" he asks morosely as he climbs on Dólii's back. "What if I'm not tough enough to do it by myself?"

"You can do it," I repeat, reminding myself of my basketball coach. Okay, Coach doesn't always have the most original sayings, but I try to make it sound reassuring anyway. "Besides, you'll have Mr. Yazzie to help you." I hand the horned toad up to him, and he tucks him into the neck of his own black hoodie. "He'll make sure you get the turquoise."

Mac nods and puts his brave face on.

"We will meet at the top of the Spider Rock in Canyon de Chelly," Łizhin says to Dólii.

"I will see you there no later than sunrise tomorrow," Dólii says before he gathers his great body and launches himself into the air. I think I hear Mac screaming. Or maybe that's just the wind. Hard to tell.

The second herald, who has been waiting patiently for Dólii to leave, lands in the spot the other bird vacated.

"Yá'át'ééh," it says in a soft laughing voice that sounds like clear water running in a rocky stream. "I am Tsídii, the herald of Dook'o'ooshiid, the Mountain of the Afternoon, the westernmost sacred mountain and the home of the Yellow

Corn Guardians and the Yellow Warbler Heralds." It turns its head to Łizhin. "You rang?"

"Yes, sister." Łizhin introduces Davery and explains his mission, and Tsídii lowers her body to let Davery climb on her back.

"I guess I'll see you at Spider Rock," I tell him, feeling suddenly extra anxious, like maybe I won't see him again.

"Don't worry about me, Nizhoni," he says, guessing what I'm thinking. "I've never ridden on a bird's back before, so this should be fun!"

Did I mention that Davery is the best?

I watch as Tsídii flaps her great wings and takes to the air. This time I'm sure I hear screaming.

"Well, Nizhoni," Łizhin says, "are you ready to go to the Black Mountain?"

Now that the two of us are alone, I can tell her the truth. "I think there's been a mistake," I say. "I know what Mr. Yazzie said, about me being related to the original Monsterslayer and how I'm supposed to be the backup guardian of Dibé Nitsaa and everything. But, and this is hard for me to admit"—I take a deep breath—"I'm no hero."

I squeeze my eyes shut and wait for Łizhin to laugh at me. When I don't hear anything, I open one eye enough to peek. She's standing in the same place, waiting patiently.

"Uh, did you hear me?" I ask. "Zero hero material over here. I wouldn't go so far as to say I'm a loser, but I'm not exactly a winner, if you know what I mean. So maybe you should try someone else."

"I think I've got exactly the right person," Łizhin says. "Why don't you just pretend you're a hero for a while, and let me carry the burden of believing in you?"

"What do you mean?"

"It's scary to have people expect something from you. Sometimes it's so scary we want to run away or give up."

I nod my head vigorously. "Bingo," I whisper under my breath.

"So don't worry about what you're supposed to be. Just be who you are."

"Just . . . Nizhoni Begay?"

"Exactly."

"But what if that's not enough?"

"Who you are is always enough. Now, climb on and we'll go for a ride. I want to show you my beautiful mountain."

I clamber onto Łizhin's back, digging my hands into her thick layer of feathers. "I'm ready!" I shout.

"Then hang on tight!" she says as she takes to the air.

I do as she says, pressing my face against the soft down on her neck and squeezing my eyes shut. My stomach flutters and dips as the earth goes out from under me. But I am proud to say I do not scream. Not even once.

TWENTY-ONE

◆

Black Mountain

Łizhin had said her mountain would be beautiful, but as we descend toward it, I'm not so sure. Rocky black peaks jut up through the clouds like sharp claws, and when we get lower, everything is shrouded in a dark gray fog so thick and heavy I can't see through it.

"We're going to land here?" I ask with a gulp.

"We must," Łizhin says.

The air turns icy, even colder than on the snowy mountain we left behind. Or maybe it's a different kind of cold. This chill doesn't remind me of hot cocoa and Christmas presents and sledding—it feels alive, like it could eat my flesh and gnaw on my bones with its frozen teeth. I huddle closer to Łizhin's back, whimpering quietly.

The currents grow stronger, buffeting us violently, and for a minute, I think I'm going to fall off.

"The wind is trying to throw us against the rocks!" I shout over the howl of the gale.

"I won't let it!" Łizhin growls as she fights with all her might to bring us down safely. When we are close enough, the herald gives one great flap of her massive wings and lands hard, digging her claws into the side of the mountain. I tilt dangerously, almost slipping from her back. The squall pulls greedily at my clothes and hair, but once Łizhin has a hold on solid land, it dies down.

Not just dies down, but totally disappears. The air around us becomes completely still and eerily silent. The heavy mist remains, and it's hard to see much besides the distinctive big black rocky mountaintops. But at least the weather doesn't seem to be trying to kill us anymore.

Points for us.

"Well, that was unexpected," Łizhin says, ruffling her plumage, "and not a good sign." She ducks her head under her wing and straightens a few crooked feathers. "But nothing broken. No worse for wear."

"Is it always like this on Dibé Nitsaa?"

"No," Łizhin says, and I catch the worry in her voice. "This strange weather must be related to Black Jet Girl's disappearance. Without her here to keep the mountain in balance, things have become perilous."

"Great," I mutter.

Łizhin gives me a reassuring look. "Courage!" she says. "You were born for this, and your hero quest is only just beginning. You must be steady." The herald points up the mountain with her beak. "I have done my best to get close to Black Jet Girl's home—now you will have to climb the rest of the way."

I squint through the fog, hoping to spot something that resembles our house back in Albuquerque, or Rock Crystal Boy's hogan back on Sisnaajiní, but I can't see anything. I'm about to say so when something catches my eye. I scramble up the mountain a little ways to get a closer look and Łizhin hops behind me. Sure enough, there's a door built into the side of the peak. It's made of a single piece of smooth black jet that seems to absorb the afternoon light. And I'm not positive from here, but it looks like the mist covering everything is coming from a chimney above the door.

It's creepy, and I get that feeling again, like there's something on this mountain that would eat me if it could. I shudder, rubbing my arms before tucking my hands inside my sleeves.

Łizhin glances up at me knowingly. "That shiver you feel? It's your monster-sensing instincts, Nizhoni. They're warning you that danger is near."

"Do they ever do anything besides that?" I ask. "I mean, Mac has, like, sprinkler powers, and Davery knows everything ever, like a human Google. I think knowing when monsters are near but not being able to do much about it is sort of crummy."

"Don't undervalue good instincts," Łizhin says. "Trusting your gut will keep you safe when others tread recklessly. It's a beginning."

"Yeah, you said that already." I don't mean to sound rude, but I'm starting to get scared. Łizhin wants me to go up the mountain alone, and I don't know if I can do it.

"So I did," she says patiently, ignoring my impoliteness. "Now it's up to you." She lifts her head suddenly, eyes searching the area around us. I follow her gaze, but I don't see anything except rocks and mist. "I must go," she says tensely. "My presence here may attract more monsters. You'll have a better chance of defeating them without me."

I really doubt that. Having a giant talking bird by my side

seems like the distinct kind of advantage I'd like. "But how am I supposed to find Black Jet Girl and fight the monsters, too?"

Łizhin plucks a single feather from her wing. "Take this."

I accept the huge black plume and it immediately shrinks down to normal bird size, small enough to fit in my hand.

"When you are in need, use this and it will become what you require most."

"It's a weapon?"

"It is ingenuity."

"*Ingenuity?* Pretty sure that's one of the vocabulary words I missed on our test last month."

"No more talk," Łizhin says, her voice sharp. "I can feel the monsters searching the mountain for me. They don't know to look for you, and I think your powers may keep you hidden from them, at least for now. But you must hurry. I'll be back at sunset. If you haven't found Black Jet Girl by then, I fear it will be too late."

"Too late?" I squeak. "Too late for who? Me?! You can't just leave me!"

But leave me she does. Without another word, Łizhin leaps into the air. Immediately, the wind comes howling back, even more vicious, more ravenous. The mist closes in, hiding her from view.

As the hungry gusts nip at me, I quickly tuck Łizhin's plume into my pocket to keep it safe. With nothing else to do, I decide I've got to tackle what I came for. Time to find Black Jet Girl and kill some monsters . . . with a feather.

Yeah, great plan, Nizhoni. What could possibly go wrong?

◆

TWENTY-TWO

The Buzzard Bozos

Dilemma: When facing a door made of solid black jet and possibly leading into a dark scary cave where a nonhuman Navajo mountain guardian lives, should one knock? Normally I would, but all things considered, including the fact that my monster instincts are screaming at me something serious now, I decide to go on in.

I push the door open a crack and whisper-shout, "Hellloooo!" in case Black Jet Girl made it back unexpectedly and she's in the shower or something. And then I remember she's Navajo, so I whisper-shout, "Yá'át'ééhhhh!" to cover my bases.

No answer, so I slip inside.

And immediately wish I hadn't.

Black Jet Girl's house is clean, and maybe, at another time, it might be cozy. It's not a cave but an octagonal room, just like Rock Crystal Boy's hogan. In the middle is a pit where a nice bright fire is crackling. But on the other side of the fire are, well . . .

. . . two of the ugliest buzzards I've ever seen.

Once, when Mac and I were small and Dad was taking us trick-or-treating in the neighborhood, we came upon this one house—a big old creaky-looking thing with a heavy wooden eave and a wide front porch with deep shadows filling the corners. On that porch, perched on the edge of a bench, was someone in the spookiest costume ever. A birdman creature, with hunched shoulders, strands of black hair combed over a balding head, and a long, curved, mean-looking beak. It sat in front of a plastic pumpkin bucket brimming with the best candy—all full-size chocolate bars, none of the random gross cinnamon candy or (heaven forbid!) pennies or dental floss like at some of the other houses. But the trick was, if you wanted the good candy, you had to brave the creeptastic birdman. I was willing to try, but Mac was too scared. He took one look and started wailing and screaming about how the monster was going to get us, and Dad made us turn around and leave before I could make my move and potentially score a Hershey bar. I complained, telling my dad it wasn't fair and that Mac was a big baby—which, technically, he was, since he was only five at the time. But secretly I was glad I hadn't had to get too close to the horrible thing.

That Halloween birdman had nothing on the buzzard creatures on the other side of the firepit in Black Jet Girl's house.

There are two of them, both hunchbacked and squatting in the firelight. Their hair is black wire, sticking up in patches from their otherwise bald pates. Between their long pointed beaks, they are playing tug-of-war with something that smells like rotten meat. I gag, covering my mouth with my hand.

But worse than their wire hair and rotten-meat lunch are their eyes. Both creatures have bulging eyeballs. Their irises are bright red, and blue veins crisscross the whites of their eyes like cracks in a boiled egg.

Is this what Mr. Charles looks like under his human costume? Yuck! No wonder he wears a disguise.

So far the two cackling vultures haven't noticed me, too intent on their fight over whatever it is. I definitely don't want to get close enough to know the details.

And then I spot something else. There's a girl lying on the floor right beside the entrance, so close I could have tripped over her. She looks about my age and is wearing a traditional Navajo rug dress with moccasins and leg wraps that come up to her knees. But she's made out of black rock the same way Rock Crystal Boy was made out of white rock. Her skin is smooth and flawless and glimmers in the firelight.

I've found the missing guardian of Dibé Nitsaa. But Black Jet Girl is as unmoving as the material she's named after.

I bend down and try to shake her awake. No luck. She's cold and hard to the touch. Then I see a tiny drop of water fall from the corner of her eye, cascade down her hard cheek, and pool in the corner of her mouth.

Black Jet Girl is frozen and scared, and my guess is those creepy buzzard creatures are to blame.

Łizhin hadn't said anything about what to do if I found Black Jet Girl paralyzed. If the bird had known, surely she would have left me with more than a feather to work with. . . .

A feather! And just like that, I have a brilliant idea. If Black Jet Girl can cry, she's not completely lost in there.

I pull the plume from my pocket and wave it under Black

Jet Girl's nose. Nothing happens at first, and I'm ready to give up on my not-so-brilliant-after-all idea. A moment later, Black Jet Girl sniffles and snuffles and, with one great heave, sneezes herself alive.

I owe Łizhin an apology. Her gift was exactly what I needed.

And then I realize the babbling buzzards have fallen silent. I slowly turn my head to look across the fire, and both monsters are staring directly at me.

Or maybe they aren't, because their gaze seems to go right through me, as if they can't see me at all.

"Who's there?" one of them shouts, its voice a raspy croak.

"I don't see anybody, brother," its companion bleats, sounding annoyed.

"Of course you don't, fool! You're blind, just like me. But I *heard* something." He shuffles a few feet in my direction. I stiffen. Black Jet Girl doesn't seem to be thawed enough to move yet. I gently nudge her with my foot, hoping to help her along. She moans a little but still doesn't open her eyes.

"There it is again!" the first buzzard croaks. "Check the girl!"

"The girl is fine, brother," the other one protests. "We paralyzed her with our stare. Nothing can resist our stare!"

I feel a hand clutch my wrist, and I almost jump out of my skin. I look down and Black Jet Girl is awake. Her eyes are penetrating mine, trying to tell me something. She mouths a word at me.

"Feather?" I ask. I think that's what she said.

"What's that?" one the buzzards squawks. "Did you say 'feather'?"

"No. Someone else did," says his brother.

Black Jet Girl rolls her eyes at the two birdmen and raises herself a little to talk to me again. "Throw the feather into the fire," she manages to whisper before she drops back down, looking exhausted.

"I definitely heard it that time," says a buzzard.

"Speak up, whoever's there! Or we will turn you to stone and then beat on you until you break into a hundred pieces."

"A million!"

"A dozen!"

"What? A million is more than a dozen."

"Is it? Then how 'bout a thousand million?"

"How 'bout you learn to count?"

"How 'bout you shut your beak so I can find out who's come into our new house to steal our prized possession?"

I can't take their squabbling anymore. It's worse than Mac and me on a long trip. Now I know how my dad feels when he tells us to stop it or he's going to pull the car over this minute.

"My name is Nizhoni Begay," I shout, "and I'm here to rescue Black Jet Girl. She is the guardian of this mountain, and you can't have her."

"Oh-ho-ho!" one of the buzzards squawks. "A rescue mission, is it? Who do you think you are that you can take what belongs to us?"

I inhale deeply, and even though my hands are shaking

and my voice doesn't sound all that steady, I tell them, "I am a monsterslayer."

The buzzards stiffen for a second. Then one of them yelps and tries to hide behind the other.

"Don't be an idiot," he says, pushing his brother away. "This Nizhoni person cannot be a real monsterslayer. Where's her lightning sword? She's delusional."

That's insulting. But he does have a point.

The other one peers over his brother's shoulder. "You're right! We'd be able to hear the crack of thunder or smell the lightning if she were a real monsterslayer." He chuckles. "Somebody has lied to her. She's confused."

"Misled."

"Duped!"

"Discomfited!"

"Stop it!" I shout. "Besides, I don't even think 'discomfited' means what you think it does."

They roll their ugly heads on their necks like the world's grossest bobbleheads. "Discombobulated! Discombobulated!" they screech.

"I said, stop!" I shout again, but why should they listen to me? They're right. I don't have a lightning sword, as cool as that sounds. I don't even have any protective clothing. Just a black-and-red Isotopes hoodie from school, and that's not going to stop their sharp talons.

"Look into our eyes," one of the creatures croons at me, his voice a singsong. "Don't be scared, little monsterslayer. If you're a real monsterslayer, we can't hurt you."

"Yeah," his companion cackles. He bulges his eyes, as if looking for me. "Monsterslayers are immune to our powers."

"So look closer," the first one warbles, shuffling forward, eyeballs popping out even farther.

I fight the urge to throw up a little. Eyeballs skeeve me out on the best of days. This bulging thing is taking it to a whole new level.

"Closer!" the other one says, and I realize they're both moving around the fire, trying to get near to me.

My heart speeds up, and I swallow hard. I want to run, but I can't leave Black Jet Girl in here alone. I've got to fight these monsters, but how?

"Little monsterslayer, where did you go?" says the first one, his eyes so big now they're practically hanging out of their sockets.

I clutch Łizhin's feather. It already woke up Black Jet Girl. I wonder if it has a little bit more ingenuity left. Black Jet Girl said I should throw it in the fire, but that would mean getting rid of my only weapon. Yet I don't have a lot of choices here, and maybe the guardian knows something I don't. "Here goes nothing," I say to myself. I hurl the feather into the flames.

It explodes into a million tiny salt crystals that pop and sizzle. Hot granules fly everywhere, and I duck my head under my arm to avoid getting hit. But the buzzard brothers are too close to the fire. The salt strikes their protruding eyes and they stumble around, screeching in pain. One flaps his stubby wings, trying to protect his face. But then the grains light on his oily feathers, and he just shrieks louder. The other tries to fly away and bangs into the ceiling. Rocks come loose, crumbling and falling, and the whole little house-in-the-mountain seems to shake.

"We've got to get out of here!" I say to Black Jet Girl, tugging on her arm. "The roof's going to come down."

TWENTY-THREE

◆

A Sawdust Cookie between Friends

Black Jet Girl is more awake now, as if the salt in the air revived her, and I'm able to help her to her feet. She leans on my shoulder, I wrap my arm around her, and together we stumble toward the door.

I hear a terrible rumbling just as we get outside. I look up, and it seems like the whole top of the mountain is slowly sliding off its foundation. It's heading straight for us!

"An avalanche!" I shout. "We've got to run! Can you manage it?"

Somehow, she does. We rush down the mountain, trying our best to outpace the stream of dirt and rocks and—whoa, was that a tree that just hurled past us? Okay, a small tree, but still.

"Faster!" I yell.

"There!" Black Jet Girl points to one of the claw-shaped rocks that I'd found so scary when I first landed. Now I can see its overhang would make a perfect little shelter. We huddle underneath it as the avalanche passes.

Once we're sure it's over, I peek around the rock. Black Jet Girl's house is completely covered by a ton of debris, with the buzzards still stuck inside. I can't even see the door anymore.

The chimney that was belching out that awful dark fog is gone, too, crushed by the rubble.

We both sit in our hiding spot, panting, until Black Jet Girl finally speaks. "Are we safe?"

I check again, just to make sure. "I don't think the birdbrains are getting out of there for a while, if ever. But your house was destroyed. I'm sorry."

"Don't worry," she says. "I'll just ask the mountain to make me a new home."

Oh. Well, that's handy.

The air is starting to clear, and now I can see that Łizhin was right—Dibé Nitsaa really is beautiful. The great black claw rocks are towering spires set into the side of the mountain like spikes in a crown. Tall pines and aspens surround us, and with the smoke gone, the breeze smells fresh and earthy. It's not exactly warm out, but the temperature feels like the refreshing chill that comes in the evening after you've played outside all day in the summer.

"It's nice here," I tell Black Jet Girl.

"Did you mean what you said back there to the bináá' yee agháni?"

"The bina who?"

"The staring-eye creatures."

Oh, right. I knew that. Mr. Yazzie told us about the vicious bird monsters.

"You claimed to be a monsterslayer," Black Jet Girl says. "Is it true?"

"Umm . . . sort of? I'm working on it. Right now, I'm just Nizhoni. I don't have any of the weapons or training of a true monsterslayer. My brother, my best friend, and I are trying to get to Spider Woman's house to ask her for a map of the Glittering World. Once we have that, we'll follow it to the Sun and get the weapons we need. But we only have a few days. . . ." With a pang, I think about my dad, praying with all my might that he's out of that trunk and getting food and water.

Black Jet Girl smiles, her smooth black skin shining in the waning afternoon light. "Weapons or no, only a brave warrior would not be afraid of the bináá' yee agháni. You were immune to their powerful stare. Maybe you think you are just Nizhoni, but I think you are already becoming more."

Her words fill me with warmth—and hope. "Thank you," I say.

She sways in place, looking like she's going to fall over. She must be hungry, and thirsty, too. Who knows how long she was trapped in there with those nasty creatures?

I dig in my backpack and pull out one of Davery's cookies. "It's not much in the way of dinner, but my best friend's mom made this, and it's super healthy. I'm happy to share."

She takes a bite. "It's . . . different."

"That it is." But I guess it must be okay, because she keeps eating it. I'm so hungry that I have one, too. I wash it down with some lukewarm water and then hand her the bottle, which she takes gratefully.

"Why have you come to Dibé Nitsaa?" she asks me.

"I was hoping you could help me find the jet that I'm supposed to bring to Spider Woman as a gift. Though it looks like there's plenty around here to choose from."

149

"Oh, you can't take just any jet. If it is for Na'ashjéii Asdzáá, it must be the best there is!"

My stomach sinks. Is this going to be like finding the shell on the White Mountain? I don't think I'm up for another five-hour search for just the perfect piece of black rock. Why does everything have to be so hard?

Black Jet Girl coughs.

"What's wrong?" I ask. "Are you okay? It's the cookie, isn't it?" I knew it was a killer.

She shakes her head. "I breathed in some of the bináá' yee aghánís' awful smoke, and when they froze me, it got stuck in my lungs. I will heal, but it will take time."

Time to heal, time to find the jet for Spider Woman. I can almost hear the minutes ticking away. "Um, I don't mean to be rude, but how *much* time?"

"I must sleep now. In the morning, I should be well enough to help you."

I chew on my lip, worried. Łizhin promised to return at sunset. But I can't leave Black Jet Girl here by herself if she's still impaired. Łizhin said other monsters might come, and what kind of backup guardian would I be if I abandoned her?

"If you want to sleep, I can keep watch," I say, making up my mind.

Black Jet Girl gives me a tired and grateful smile and lies down on a bed of leaves, resting her head on her arms. I push my back against the rock, pull up my knees, and wrap my arms around them. I'm not that tired, so it shouldn't be hard to stay alert until Łizhin arrives.

A wave of sadness rolls over me. I miss Davery. If he were here, he would know how to build a makeshift shelter that he'd read about in *101 Survival Tricks*, and probably how to whip up a three-course meal out of wet leaves and dirt. Gluten-free, of course. I even miss Mac, who would be telling jokes and drawing funny pictures of the buzzards to cheer us up. And even though I've only known him for a day, I miss Mr. Yazzie, too. He'd teach us stories about Navajo history or songs about the Black Mountain that would make us all feel like we were special. Most of all, I miss my dad, who would lecture me about going off on dangerous adventures and then still tuck me into bed with a kiss.

But none of my companions are here. It's just me. I sniffle a little bit, feeling sorry for myself.

"From now on, we're staying together," I vow aloud to Mac and Davery, wherever they might be. "And we're coming to save you, Dad," I add quietly. "Don't give up."

It's the last thing I think before I fall asleep.

TWENTY-FOUR

◆

The Earring

I wake to the smell of piñon burning and the sound of a crackling fire. I whip my head up, thinking I'm back in Black Jet Girl's house with the creepy buzzard brothers, but I quickly realize I'm outside, in the shade of the great rock. The exact same place I fell asleep.

There's a small campfire in a hole in the ground about ten feet in front of me, and it's burning merrily, warming the chilly morning air.

Whoa! Morning air! I stifle a yawn, stretch my arms, and look around. Sure enough, the sun is barely coming up on the horizon. I slept through the entire night. So much for keeping watch . . .

Panic hits me and I scramble to my feet. Where's Black Jet Girl? Is she in danger again? And if it's already morning, that means I missed Łizhin!

"Hello?" I shout. "Black Jet Girl? Łizhin? Is anyone there?"

I tell myself to calm down. If there's a campfire, chances are good that I haven't been left all alone out here. But that logic doesn't stop my stomach from bunching up with worry.

"We're here, Nizhoni," comes a musical voice from the

wooded area beyond our sheltering rock. Black Jet Girl walks toward me, a small black bird perched on her shoulder.

"Łizhin?" I ask. I rush forward and give her a . . . uh . . . pat on the head. "Is that you?"

The bird flies to the ground. Within seconds, she has expanded back to riding size. "It's much easier to take a walk through the forest when you aren't as big as a tree," she explains. "Black Jet Girl was just telling me about how you defeated the bináá' yee agháni. I am very proud of you, Nizhoni."

"Thanks," I say, shuffling my feet through the dirt and feeling my face heat up with embarrassment. "Your feather came in handy."

"You had the ingenuity to use it," the bird says with sparkling eyes. "Are you ready to go to Spider Rock and be reunited with your friends? If we leave now, I can have you there before breakfast. Then I'll return to help Black Jet Girl make sure the mountain is cleansed of monsters. For now."

"For now?"

"The deaths of those two will discourage other attacks, but only temporarily. If you fail to stop Mr. Charles by sunrise the day after tomorrow, there will be more monsters on the sacred mountains than we can fight. The threat is still very real."

"And my dad . . . Do you know where he is?" I ask, almost afraid to hear the answer. "How he is?"

"His fate depends on your success."

"Then we better go!"

I rush to grab my backpack. I sling it over my shoulders

and hurry to Łizhin. She lowers her head to allow me to climb onto her back, and I settle against the warm down of her neck.

"Wait!" Black Jet Girl says. "Aren't you forgetting something?"

Backpack? Check. Hoodie? Check. Amazing heroic story to tell Davery and Mac? Check, check. "I think I've got everything."

"The gift for Na'ashjéii Asdzáá," she says.

Duh. I almost neglected the most important thing!

Black Jet Girl reaches up and touches the side of her head. I hadn't noticed before, but she's wearing long beaded loop earrings. She pulls one from her earlobe . . . or *disconnects* it, I should say, since her whole body, including her clothes and jewelry, is one big piece of animated rock. She winces when she does it.

I'm sorry for causing her more pain after all she's been through lately. "Are you sure you're strong enough to give me a part of yourself?"

"I am now, because you allowed me time to rest." The guardian holds out her earring on an open hand. "Take this to Spider Woman so she may refashion it as she wishes. It's a part of the mountain, just as I am. A worthy gift for a Holy Person from a warrior."

I get the Holy Person part, and at first I think she's calling herself a warrior, but then I catch on—she means me. I gulp, feeling sort of undeserving but also really proud.

"It's important to always give your best," she explains to me with a soft smile. "Do not hold back, and do not be afraid to sacrifice. The things that mean the most to us often have the most power. If my part of the gift cost me nothing, then it would mean nothing."

She shakes her palm, gesturing for me to take the earring. So I do, tucking it into the padded pocket in my backpack along with the white shell from Sisnaajiní. Two down and two to go. I can't wait to see what Mac and Davery got from their mountains.

"Thank you," I whisper to Black Jet Girl. "I mean, ahéhee'," I add hastily. Got to remember to speak Navajo when I know the right words, and it never hurts to double up the thank-yous.

"Come back and visit." She says it so sadly I'm not sure she really means it. Maybe she thinks I'll never return, since my first visit wasn't exactly a relaxing vacation. Or maybe she thinks I'm not going to live long enough to see her again. That's not terrifying or anything.

Łizhin pumps her powerful wings and launches us into the sky. I dig my hands into her feathers and hold on tight. I watch Black Jet Girl waving at us until she becomes a tiny speck, and soon the entire mountain fades behind us.

"How long until we get to Spider Rock?" I shout loud enough to be heard over the wind.

"I didn't want to say anything in front of Black Jet Girl, but I have some bad news, Nizhoni."

My stomach dives. Mac! Davery! I knew we shouldn't have split up!

"What is it?"

"I'm afraid there's been an accident."

TWENTY-FIVE

◆

On Top of Ole Spider Rock

Łizhin won't say more about what happened, so I spend the entire journey to Spider Rock imagining the worst. What if Mac and Davery had walked right into a monster ambush?

Up until this point, the land below has been all high mesas—tall, flat-topped mountains sprinkled with sage shrubs, creosote bushes, and cedar trees. But now we're flying over a lush valley. I can see cornstalks growing in tidy rows near a stream, and the smooth red-rock walls are decorated with drawings. They don't look like much this high up, but I know they must be petroglyphs. We learned about them last year in Mr. Lee's social studies class. I really want to get up close and take a better look.

"Where are we?" I ask Łizhin. "This isn't the Grand Canyon, is it?"

"No. This is Canyon de Chelly. We are in Dinétah now, the heart of Navajo Nation."

"I've only ever been to shimásání's house," I explain. "This is beautiful!"

We swoop down, skimming over the river that cuts through the canyon.

"Whoa, what is that?" I ask. In front of us is the tallest,

skinniest rock I've ever seen. It's standing all by itself in the middle of the canyon, looking like the Empire State Building but made from red rock.

"That is our destination—Spider Rock. It marks the home of Na'ashjéii Asdzáá."

"Is she nice?" I ask tentatively. With a name like Spider Woman, it is highly possible that nice is not one of her qualities. I should have asked Mr. Yazzie earlier, but I was distracted by too many other things. Now, as we're approaching Spider Rock, it seems very important.

"Well," Łizhin says, sounding thoughtful, "there *are* stories. . . . See those white streaks near the top of the rock? Some say those are the bones of the children she has eaten."

"What?!" Mr. Yazzie never said anything about Spider Woman eating kids.

"I wouldn't worry about it. It's only the naughty ones."

"Pretty sure eating children of any kind is frowned upon! Somebody could have mentioned it, you know?"

"You'll be fine," the herald says.

She circles the rock as we come in for a landing. We're close enough now that I can see figures on top—two massive birds, one blue and one yellow, and two humans. Mac and Davery!

After what Łizhin said about an accident, I was worried that one of them was hurt, or worse. But they look okay to me. Mac has his hair hanging down in his face and his hands stuffed in his pockets, as usual. Davery waves calmly as Łizhin settles next to Dólii and Tsídii.

Once we've landed, I jump from Łizhin's back and rush over to Davery and Mac. Unthinking, I go to give Davery a hug, but he looks startled and holds out a fist instead. "Oh," I say, embarrassed. "Sorry." We fist-bump, ending with our three-part secret handshake. I mean, it's not like we can't hug each other. We've hugged before. But it's already getting a little awkward being boy/girl best friends, and hugging reminds us of that, so fist-bump secret handshake it is.

I punch Mac in the shoulder, which is pretty much the same thing as a hug. Besides, it's payback for that earlier punch-not-pinch he gave me. I hope he knows it's because I'm happy to see him, but he sort of stumbles away from me, head down with his face still hidden behind his black hair.

"What's wrong with you?" I can't imagine why Mac's being a party pooper. But little brothers are moody, especially artsy-fartsy ones, so I don't worry about it too much.

"You want to see the black jet I got for Spider Woman?" I take off my backpack and reach into the pocket. I carefully pull out the tissue containing the perfect white shell and Black Jet Girl's earring and open it on the ground. "Let me see what you got!"

Davery comes over and removes a folded leaf from his back. He unwraps it to reveal an abalone shell, perfectly shaped and as bright and glimmering as a pearl.

"It's beautiful!" I whisper, running a finger over the edge.

"It came from the shoulder of the guardian, Abalone Shell Boy. He said it was important to give Na'ashjéii Asdzáá the best."

"Black Jet Girl said the same thing," I say.

"Mac?" I look up at my brother. "Let's see your turquoise."

He flicks his hair back and crosses his arms. "This quest is a waste of time," he mutters. "Like rocks and shells are going to get us anything good. We need swords or guns or something to fight the monsters. Not a bunch of junk."

I frown, surprised by Mac's words. "We're taking these as gifts to Spider Woman in exchange for a map, not using them against Mr. Charles and his monster crew directly."

"It's still stupid," he grumbles, kicking at some loose rocks. The three heralds flutter nervously.

"I think you should tell them, Mac, child Born for Water."

It's Mr. Yazzie. In my excitement, I'd forgotten about him. He emerges from the neck of Mac's hoodie and looks up at him, his face sympathetic.

I plant my hands on my hips. "What's going on? Mac, you better stop moping and start talking. Łizhin said there was an accident. Is that why you're upset? Did you have a . . . bathroom accident? Like that time at sleepaway camp? Dad said it's nothing to be ashamed of."

My brother rolls his eyes so hard I'm surprised they don't fall out of his head and bounce off the top of Spider Rock.

"If I may," Mr. Yazzie says, clearing his throat. He climbs down Mac's torso and leg and makes his way over to where Davery and I laid out the gifts. "I'm afraid young Mac failed to secure the turquoise from Tsoodził, and he feels just terrible about it."

"Oh no!" I whisper. "What happened?"

"Nothing happened!" Mac stomps his foot, and eight hundred feet below us, the river that cuts through Canyon de Chelly suddenly rushes faster, whitecaps rippling across the previously calm surface.

"Watch your anger, Mac," Mr. Yazzie says. "The water responds to it."

Mac looks both abashed and pleased. And then a little scared. Ancestral powers are definitely cool, but it's not ideal when you cause a minor flood by throwing a temper tantrum.

We move back from the edge, and Mac flops himself down next to Davery, who has been sitting and watching calmly this whole time. Mac picks up the black jet earring, turning it over in his hand. "Sorry," he mumbles.

"What happened?"

"I tried, Z," he says finally, sounding like he feels crummy. "But at first we couldn't find the guardian of the mountain, and then, by the time we did, a storm was coming in. We got the turquoise and I was holding it in my hand, but it was raining and Dólii's feathers were slippery. When he made a sharp turn, I lost my balance and Mr. Yazzie fell out of my hoodie. I couldn't grab him and hold on at the same time with only one hand. I had to catch Mr. Yazzie or save the turquoise. I chose Mr. Yazzie."

"And many blessings that you did, Mac," Mr. Yazzie says. "I am a very resilient horned toad, but even I have limits. One of them is not being able to survive a fall like that."

"It was my fault," Dólii says, sticking his large head in between us. "I should have warned Mac I was turning."

"No, no, it was my fault," Mr. Yazzie says. "If I hadn't lost my grip . . ."

"It sounds like it was no one's fault," Łizhin says, joining us. "Accidents happen."

"But what do we do now?" Mac wails. "We still need the

turquoise if we want Spider Woman to give us the map! Dad should never have made us do this alone!"

Davery frowns and opens his mouth like he's about to say something about Dad's kidnapping, but I shake my head and mouth, *He doesn't know.*

You have to tell him.

Not yet.

But—

I gesture to my miserable little brother. Now's not the time to lay something as scary as that on him. Davery looks at Mac, too, and his face softens. *You're right,* he mouths.

"Hey, Mac, I have some turquoise," I say, clutching my pendant, the one I wear all the time. The gift from my mom, who I now know was a monsterslayer. Or at least had monsterslayer heritage that she passed down to me. But she's gone, so it's up to me to fight the monsters and save our dad.

"Are you sure?" Davery asks me. "I know how much that necklace means to you. Maybe we can go back to Tsoodził tomorrow and try again."

"We don't have time for that," I say. "Besides, according to Black Jet Girl, I shouldn't be afraid to make a sacrifice. She said the things that mean the most to us have the most power. My necklace must be super powerful, because it means everything."

The heralds all make chirping sounds of approval. I hug Mac, who smiles weakly with relief (or is it guilt?). Davery gives me another fist bump.

"Okay, so we've got the gifts from all four sacred mountains," I say to Łizhin. "What's next?"

Łizhin says, "Our work as heralds is done. We must return to our mountains in case our guardians need us. Na'ashjéii Asdzáá's house is just across the canyon. We will take you there, but then you must continue your journey without us."

I stand up and give Łizhin a hug around her neck. "I think I already miss you."

"And I you, little hero. Now, hop on my back for one last ride. The sun is getting higher and you are running out of time."

The heralds take us across the gap to the rim of the canyon beyond and there they say their good-byes. After they're gone, we head up the road they said would take us to our destination.

"There's something you should know before we get there," I say as we walk. "Łizhin told me the Spider Woman used to eat children."

"What?!" Mac says.

"That would have been good information to know beforehand," Davery observes.

"That's what I said!"

"Nonsense," Mr. Yazzie scoffs. "That's a story from long ago. You'll all be quite safe." He cocks his head and eyeballs my brother. "But just in case, maybe Mac should stay close to me."

TWENTY-SIX

◆

Spider Woman and Dr. Thunder

"Are you sure this is it?" Mac asks as we make our way up the dusty road. The lushness of Canyon de Chelly is behind us, and if we turn around, we can still see Spider Rock. But up here, on the lip of the canyon, there's just a trailer home with an old pickup truck in front. I didn't know what I expected Spider Woman's house to look like. Maybe a massive web, or a dark cave where you can't see your hand in front of your face, but there's nothing like that around here.

We reach the driveway and pause. A sign on top of an old tin mailbox reads THE NA'ASHJÉII. RUG WEAVERS EXTRAORDINAIRE! in red and black letters.

"This must be the place. Mr. Yazzie?" I ask, peeking down into the neckline of my hoodie, where our guide is sound asleep again.

"Perhaps you shouldn't wake him," Davery says. "He's probably traumatized after what he went through with Mac."

"I'm traumatized, too!" Mac mutters. "You don't see me napping."

"Don't be rude. He's old." Then, eyeing the trailer door, I say, "Well, we didn't collect all these gifts just to stand here and not find out whether this is her. Let's go knock." I pat the backpack pocket holding our three precious items, touch my mom's necklace (which I'm wearing for as long as I can) for bravery, and march forward.

I look at the area around the trailer. Besides the truck, there's a small fenced-in yard with a massive satellite dish and a little toolshed. Thick green extension cords run from the shed to the trailer, and as we get closer, I can hear a television blasting from the home, the laugh track echoing. Seems normal enough. No piles of children's bones out here. Of course, who knows what's hiding in that toolshed.

I square my shoulders, take a deep breath, and let it out, reminding myself that I'm a descendant of a Hero Twin. I can do this. I think?

I climb the three front stairs and raise my fist. Knock three times, firm and heavy. I hold my breath and wait for the door to open, but nothing happens. Just more fake laughing.

"Do you think maybe she can't hear us over the TV?" I whisper to Davery.

He shrugs. "I didn't know spiders liked sitcoms."

I knock harder. "Hello?" I yell, just in case. "Is anyone home?"

The television shuts off, leaving the yard suddenly quiet. Footsteps clomp across the floor inside as someone comes to the door. I wring my hands nervously.

"Who's there?" comes a woman's voice. She doesn't sound mean, but maybe a little irritated, like we just interrupted her favorite show.

"Sorry to bother you," I shout, cupping my mouth and

leaning close to the door, "but we're looking for . . ." I hadn't thought this through. I can't say Spider Woman—that would be too weird. Because what if this is the wrong house? Then we'd really have some explaining to do. But I can't just stand here. I clear my throat and try again. "We're looking . . ." And then inspiration hits. "To buy a rug!" Genius, if I do say so myself. If Mrs. Na'ashjéii is just a regular weaver, we won't seem completely loony showing up at her door.

The door creaks open slowly. I half expect spiders to scuttle out and crawl up my legs, but instead, a beautiful Navajo woman stands there. She's wearing a black-and-red robe that trails all the way down to her feet, and her long black hair is tied back in a messy bun like one an artist might wear. Small gold-framed glasses perch at the tip of her nose, and she squints down at us. She holds a remote control in one hand, and she props the other on a hip. "You kids want to buy a rug?" she asks skeptically.

"Yes!" I say enthusiastically. Maybe too enthusiastically, because her eyes narrow, and it looks like she might not let us in.

"We would love to see what you have for sale," Davery adds helpfully, and I sigh with relief. He always knows the right thing to say.

"You would?" she asks, sounding surprised. "Well, come on in, then." She pushes the door open wide enough to allow us in and walks back into the trailer. The three of us and the sleeping Mr. Yazzie, still tucked in my hoodie, follow her inside.

"You kids want some pop or something?" she asks over her shoulder. "I got Dr. Thunder. That's it. We're not fancy in this house."

The trailer is small and cluttered. The walls are covered with rugs of all sizes and colors. A large weaving loom sits in the middle of the living room, surrounded by three smaller ones, and behind them, attached to the wall, is the biggest TV I've ever seen.

"Nice!" Mac says. "That TV has got to be at least seventy inches!"

"Seventy-*five*," the woman says, smiling. "You like TV?"

"I prefer YouTube."

"Too bad," she says. "There's some real good shows, especially the telenovelas. So you want some pop, or not?"

Davery and I exchange a look, and Mac nods vigorously, but I'm thinking of the whole eating-children thing. What better way to trap kids for a cook-up than by offering them poisoned Dr. Thunder?

As if she knows what I'm thinking, the woman turns around to fix me with a stare. "I've never known a kid to say no to pop, so what's the problem?"

"We're watching our sugar," Davery says quickly.

"We are?" asks Mac, seriously disappointed.

The woman eyes us suspiciously, but I give her a thumbs-up.

"Suit yourself," she says with a shrug.

"You wove all these rugs yourself?" I ask. "They're beautiful."

"Thank you." She gestures toward the looms. "These are the rugs I'm working on right now. There's more in the shed, but you'd have to wait until my husband comes back to take a look at those. He has the only key. So maybe you can pick one you like now, and I'll finish it for you."

"How long will that take?"

The woman taps the remote control against her cheek as she calculates. "Year and a half? Maybe two."

"Two years!" I yelp. "We can't wait that long for the map!"

"Map?" the woman asks. "I thought you said you were here for a rug."

"We are!" I say.

"We're not," Davery admits at the same time.

"I really want a soda pop," Mac whines.

"You all better tell me the truth," she says. "I don't like naughty kids."

I gulp.

"Don't eat us!" Mac says, lifting his hands in the air. "I'm innocent! It was Nizhoni's idea."

Once again, Mac fails to play it cool. "Okay, we might have lied just a little bit," I say. "We're here to get a map of the Glittering World. But I couldn't just come to your door and ask for Spider Woman!"

"Why not? I'm not exactly in hiding. The mailbox says 'spider' on it."

"So you are Spider Woman?"

"Depends who's asking."

I introduce myself in the proper Navajo way, and Davery and Mac follow suit.

"We have something for you." I walk to her kitchen table and open my backpack. I pull out the carefully wrapped treasures inside and spread them in front of her. The white shell, the black jet, and the abalone shell.

She looks at our gifts, mouth pursed. "I see," she says thoughtfully, running a hand over them. She picks up each one in turn and studies it. "These are lovely."

I sigh with relief. We brought the right stuff!

"But it seems you're missing something," she adds.

What? Oh! The turquoise.

I lift the leather cord with the pendant from around my neck and hand it to her, trying hard not to feel any regret. "Will this do?"

She examines it the longest, frowning now. It's probably not perfect enough for her. It has become a little worn on one side over the years, from my constant touching. And it didn't even come from the mountain. . . .

"It's not from Tsoodził," I say, figuring I shouldn't hide that fact. "It was my mother's."

"Was she a monsterslayer?" she asks, eyes still on the blue-green stone.

"Uh, I think so. . . ." Why would she ask?

"I never forget a face, and you look just like her," she says, her chin tilted as she studies me. "Yeah. She came this way once. Owes me."

She's met my mother! Before I can recover from my shock

to beg her to tell me more, Spider Woman pockets the pendant and asks, "Now what was that about Tsoodził?"

"We couldn't get the turquoise from there," I explain. "There was an accident, and Mac had to choose between holding on to the stone or saving Mr. Yazzie's life." I reach into my neckline and lift the still-sleeping horned toad from his warm little bed. He paddles his feet and grunts like he's having an excellent dream. I pet him gently across the back with one finger. I don't know if horned toads like to be stroked, but it seems like a good idea, and he settles down and starts snoring. I put him back in my hoodie.

"Now there's an old face I haven't seen in a while," Spider Woman says, light dancing in her eyes. "How is the little cheii?"

"He's the one who told us to come here for the map of the Rainbow Road that will take us to the Sun. He said you would help us."

Spider Woman pulls a wooden toothpick from her sleeve and picks at her teeth, studying me. "Hmm. Map, you say?"

I nod. "Something that shows us how to cross through the Glittering World."

"I see," she says in a voice that makes it sound like she doesn't see at all. "Come, sit, everyone." She sets herself down on the far side of the kitchen table, and I slide into the empty seat across from her. Mac and Davery take the two remaining chairs.

"You've brought me some powerful gifts. I will use them to make tools for my weaving," Spider Woman says, her long delicate fingers brushing the white shell. "They are proof that you climbed the sacred mountains and engaged with their guardians, who are good but not always kind—they don't like strangers much. Particularly the human variety. You were brave to face them at all."

We all sit up a little straighter at being called brave, but we slump down again when Spider Woman shakes her head.

"That's why I'm so sorry about what I have to tell you. There is no map."

◆

TWENTY-SEVEN

The Glittering World

"No map?" I moan. "That can't be right. We came all this way. We spent all that time going to the mountains. . . ."

"If we don't have a map, how will we find the Rainbow Road that leads to the Sun?" Davery asks.

"And if we don't get to the Sun, we won't get the weapons we need to fight the monsters," Mac says.

The corners of Spider Woman's eyes crinkle. I feel like she's trying to decide something.

My stomach tightens and I feel my cheeks heating up. I'm pretty sure I know how this is going to go.

"It's okay if you can't help us," I say quietly. "We'll just leave—"

"Cheii's older now," Spider Woman says. "It's been a while since he trained anyone, and he's forgotten." She waves a hand. "You don't need a map of the Glittering World. You're already here."

I frown, looking around the trailer. The fading couch, the heaps of wool and assortment of looms, the dishes piled next to the sink. "Uh, no offense, but if this is the Glittering World, it isn't very big on the glitter part."

"I honestly thought there would be unicorns," Mac adds, echoing my own views on the matter.

"Okay," Spider Woman says with a slightly insulted sniff. "Maybe not in my house. Come with me, all of you."

We follow her to the back door. She opens it to reveal the canyon beyond. The bright sun is setting, and the landscape is bathed in glowing light. Raindrops from an afternoon shower cling to the pine trees' needles, sparkling like crystal ornaments on a Christmas tree. The horizon pulses with pinks and oranges and reds before fading into a dark purple. And everywhere around us, the air smells of fresh pinecones. It's magical, and I hadn't even noticed.

"Do you see it now?" she asks me, her voice soft.

"Yes," I say, feeling breathless. "It *is* a Glittering World!"

She wraps an arm around my shoulders and pulls me to her side for a brief hug. "Our world is full of beauty, Nizhoni. Just like your name says. You only need to look around to see it."

"But how do we find the Rainbow Road?" Davery asks.

"That I can show you. There's a trailhead just across the canyon. But it's only safe to travel during the day," she says. "At night it is too unpredictable and has been known to lose people."

"Lose people?"

"Yes. I'll take you there tomorrow, when the sun rises."

Worry squeezes my chest again. Mr. Yazzie said we had four days to rescue Dad, and tomorrow would be the third already. We only have one day left to reach the Sun and convince him to give us weapons. What if we don't make it?

"Is it far to the Sun?" I ask. "We don't have much time, and I was really hoping we could go sooner."

"It is not a long distance," she says, "but the road is hard. You must endure four trials in order to reach the Sun."

"Trials?"

"But since you were able to defeat the monsters on Black Mountain, I'm sure you will be able to pass the Rainbow Road's tests."

I groan. "Why is everything a test?"

"All good things come through hard work," she says. "If something is too easy to get, it isn't worth much, is it?"

I don't know about that. I once got a coupon for a free popcorn and bag of gummy bears at the movie theater and that was pretty good. But I don't think that's what Spider Woman is talking about.

"Come inside now," she says. "You can help me make dinner."

My stomach growls at the mention of food. I haven't eaten anything since I had a sugar-free cookie with Black Jet Girl.

"Do you know how to make bread?" Spider Woman asks me.

"Is this another test?"

She laughs. It's a really nice laugh, nothing like what I expected a spider to sound like. Especially one known for eating children.

"No, but it's good to help out when you're visiting family."

I feel a little brightness spark inside me. "Are we family?"

"All Diné are related in one way or another, so we should always be helping one another."

I can't help smiling as the spark inside me expands. RC said we were extended family, too.

"Okay, I'll try. I've never made bread before," I admit.

"Not even frybread?"

"My dad never showed me. He said it was 'struggle food.'" Then I'm embarrassed that I said something bad about him.

But she only nods. "Your dad is right. Frybread is not traditional, but there's no shame in it. Your ancestors created food out of nothing, like magic. Flour, water, and baking soda were all they had, and they made something delicious. Now come inside and I'll show you."

We go back in and get to work. Spider Woman tells Davery to check on the beans she already has soaking on the stove and then get the cheese, lettuce, and tomatoes out of the refrigerator. She gives Mac a knife, along with a warning not to cut his fingers off, and he grins and grabs a tomato. Within seconds, he's nicked himself, and Davery takes over the slicing while Spider Woman finds Mac a Band-Aid and demotes him to stirring the beans. Davery grates the cheese and chops the lettuce while Spider Woman and I work on the bread. She helps me mix the flour and baking soda and supervises as I add warm water a little at a time until the dough is sticky and elastic in my hands. We stretch it into flat circles about the size of a small plate and then plop them, one by one, into the hot oil. The bread sizzles as it puffs slightly into perfectly round golden deliciousness. Spider Woman has me grab each piece with tongs and set it on a paper towel to drain. When she says so, we pile on all our ingredients and sit around the table.

"This is so good," Mac says as he stuffs his mouth. "I can't believe Nizhoni made the bread."

"Hey!" I protest as I take my own bite. The beans have soaked through the bread just enough to make it soft in the middle but not soggy, and the edges are still crisp. The cheese is melty and perfect. I can't believe I made it, either, but I'd never admit that to Mac.

"I think your sister has more talents than she realizes," Spider Woman says as she eats her own Navajo taco.

"Oh, yeah, she's also really good at catching basketballs with her face!"

"Mac!" I throw a bean at his head, which he narrowly avoids.

"And what are you good at, Mac?" Spider Woman asks.

"I'm an artist," he says proudly. "I can draw anything, and I make my own designs, too. I'm also handy with a water sprinkler."

"And you, Davery?" she asks.

"I know things."

"He knows *every*thing," I add.

He grins. "Not everything, but I am curious about stuff, and I have a good memory."

"Quite a formidable team," Spider Woman says, giving us all a nod of approval. And we all sit up a little straighter, feeling powerful under her praise.

Afterward, we take our dishes to the sink and wash them, putting them on the plastic rack to dry. Then I wander over to look at one of the looms. The rug in progress is a combination of browns and tans. It reminds me of the desert.

"Would you like me to teach you how to weave?" Spider Woman asks as she joins me.

"Maybe another time," I say. "I kind of have a lot going on right now, what with the monster-killing duties and all."

"I understand. But weaving can soothe the mind as well as the soul. There is beauty and harmony in it."

"This one's my favorite." I brush a hand across another rug, red and black, with a white zigzag lightning pattern.

"Your mother liked that one, too."

My hand freezes. In fact, my whole body does.

Spider Woman nods. "That's right. Your mother loved this color combination, too. I suppose I shouldn't be surprised you like the same rug."

"When was she here? Recently?" I try to keep my voice calm.

"No, no," she says. "She saw another version of this rug years ago. Like I said, she came though this way once."

"What for?"

"She was seeking the way to the Rainbow Road. Same as you."

"When was this?"

"Oh gosh." Spider Woman pushes her reading glasses up on her forehead and scratches her nose. "That must have been . . . hmm, ten years ago, maybe?"

"My mom left us when I was three. . . ."

"About the same time, then," says Spider Woman.

I've always thought Mom just abandoned us. But if she came here seeking the Rainbow Road, she must have been going off to fight a monster just like we are. Maybe she'd been trying to *protect* us.

"You might be the only person I've ever met who knew her," I say. "I mean, besides my family."

Spider Woman frowns. "Well, she seemed like a very nice lady. For a monsterslayer. They can be a little rough around the edges. But your mother, if I'm recalling correctly, was quite lovely."

"I wouldn't know. She never came back." I drop into the weaving stool next to the loom.

She tilts her head to look at me. "Are you having a moment?"

"You have no idea." I want to hear more about my mother, but a wave of exhaustion comes over me. Against my will, my jaw cracks open in a huge yawn. I cover my mouth, embarrassed, but Spider Woman only laughs.

"I think it's time you got some sleep," she says.

"It has been a pretty busy day," I admit. "And last night I slept on a rock."

She laughs. "I think I can do better than a rock."

Spider Woman has an old trunk full of blankets and sleeping bags. Mac immediately goes for the Spider-Man one. I look over at our host and she winks at me. "Peter Parker is a total fave," she says.

Davery and I pick plain old sleeping bags in a green camping color with a red plaid lining, and we roll them out and hunker down on the floor. It's like a sleepover. I take the still-snoozing Mr. Yazzie from my hoodie and lay him next to me on my pillow.

"He sure is sleeping a lot," I say, a bit worried.

"Horned lizards are reptiles and need the sun to warm their bodies so they can move around. It's totally normal," Spider Woman assures me.

After she says good night, we all lie on our backs, looking at the ceiling and talking quietly. "I miss Dad," Mac says wistfully. "I wish he'd at least call and let us know where he is."

Davery looks at me and clears his throat loudly with an *Ahem!*

I roll my eyes at his obviousness, but he's right. It's time I told my brother the truth.

"So, Mac," I start, "I don't want you to worry, but Dad hasn't called us because, well . . ." I take a deep breath. "Because I think Mr. Charles is holding him against his will."

Mac sits bolt upright, his face twisted with worry. "What does that mean? He's been . . . kidnapped?!"

"But he's alive," I assure him. "I heard Mr. Charles talking, and he said he needed Dad to help convince us to do something. So as long as we're out here fighting, Dad will be okay." I don't tell him what Łizhin had said: *His fate depends on your success.*

"You don't know that for sure," Mac practically wails.

"I know we can't let him down, and Dad will be fighting,

178

too. I have to believe he's going to be okay. And we have Mr. Yazzie, and the heralds and the guardians, and now Spider Woman helping us. We can't lose."

He sniffs and swipes at his teary eyes. "Okay," he says morosely. "As long as we stay together . . ."

Mac flops down and buries himself in his Spider-Man sleeping bag. I can tell this is all too much for him, because soon enough, he's fast asleep and a thin trail of drool is leaking out of his open mouth. So gross. But I still lean over and give him a pat on the shoulder, careful not to wake him.

"Nizhoni," Davery whispers, "you know that line from the song, *Four days to find you are not alone*? You just said it. We have each other, Mr. Yazzie, the beings from the Four Sacred Mountains, Spider Woman, and the Diyin Dine'é."

"Yeah, and . . . ?"

"I think the song is reminding us that this is a team effort."

I fold my hands behind my head and gaze up at the ceiling. "I like that," I tell him.

Davery says, "I do, too. I think you're right and we're going to win."

But after he falls asleep and I'm alone with my thoughts, I can't help but think about my mom.

She never came back.

And that means she lost.

◆

TWENTY-EIGHT

The Rainbow Road

Spider Woman wakes us up bright and early. So early that when she opens the blinds to let the morning sunlight in, there's no sunlight. Even worse, I can hear the soft patter of rain.

"Why are we awake if the sun isn't even awake?" I ask, groaning and pulling the sleeping bag over my head.

"If you want to catch the Rainbow Road, you must be there in time to greet the dawn. That's when the Diyin Dine'é will see you and open the road to you. Not just anyone can travel on it, you know."

I pull the cover off my face. "Why do the Diyin Dine'é have to see us?"

"Well, they want to make sure you're the right ones. It would do no good to show monsters the way to the Sun."

"Can they refuse us?" Davery asks, sitting up with a jaw-cracking yawn. "The Holy People, I mean."

Spider Woman taps her cheek, thinking. "Technically, I suppose so. But they usually don't."

"But they could?"

"Well, of course. They can do anything they want."

I reach over to check on our horned toad friend. I'm

worried that he hasn't woken up yet, but his chest is rising and falling, so I know he's alive, at least. "What should we do about Mr. Yazzie?"

Spider Woman lifts his sleeping form in her cupped hands and peers at his face. "I think this little cheii should stay with me a bit longer. I'll send him along to meet you at the House of the Sun when he feels better."

"Wait, you can get to the Sun without going through the trials?" Mac asks incredulously.

"Mr. Yazzie can, yes. But you can't."

"Why not?"

She laughs. "Hey, I don't make the rules. All wannabe heroes have to go through four trials. I suppose the Sun wants to make sure you're worthy of wielding his weapons." Spider Woman looks at the clock on her kitchen wall. "We better hurry up! Sunrise won't wait for anyone. You can eat breakfast on the walk across the canyon."

Breakfast turns out to be Spam and scrambled eggs wrapped in a fluffy tortilla. Spider Woman offers us a green chile pepper to go with it, and we each take one, munching on the hot pepper between bites of the salty goodness of canned meat. Rain clouds keep the sky heavy and a light mist falls around us. Not enough to soak us, just enough to make my hair fall flat around my face. Despite the delicious breakfast, walking through the rain in the dark is no fun.

Spider Woman leads the way, and it's a good thing, because she seems to know every twist and turn of the narrow dirt path. It must have rained heavily during the night, because the red dirt has turned into red mud that sticks to the sides of our sneakers and makes a sucking sound when we walk. Spider Woman is wearing big brown lace-up hiking boots, so she doesn't have the same problem.

"This Rainbow Road better be worth it," Mac mutters as a fat raindrop lands on his burrito. He sighs and chews a soggy bite.

"Water in the desert is a blessing," Spider Woman says cheerfully, slowing down a bit so we can keep pace. She's wearing a headband with a cave explorer light on it, and the beam bobs and weaves through the darkness, a beacon for us to follow.

After a while, she pulls up abruptly. "Here we are!' she exclaims. "The start of the Rainbow Road!" She holds her arms out wide, the big smile on her face illuminated by the headlamp.

We look around. It's still dark, but I can tell in the lightening morning that there's nothing here. No cool tower like Spider Rock, no petroglyphs like I saw while flying in on Łizhin's back, and definitely nothing that looks like a rainbow.

"How do you know?" I ask.

"What, you can't see it?" she asks us, dropping her hands to her hips.

"No," I say.

"Not really," Davery admits.

"See what?" Mac asks.

"Huh." She shrugs, looking unconcerned. "Anyway, this is as far as I go. Good luck!" She turns like she's going to go back down the path we just came from.

"Wait!" I shout. "You can't just leave us in the middle of nowhere in the dark."

"You're not in the middle of nowhere. You're in the middle of everything. Now just . . ." She looks up at the sky. The rain has started to dissipate, and the gray clouds look thin and wispy as the sun starts to rise. "And here it is."

"Look!" Mac shouts, pointing to the ground at our feet. And just like that, as the sun breaks through the clouds and catches the puddles, a bright path banded in the colors of the rainbow appears under our feet.

"Whoa!" I say. I jump up and down a few times, and the rainbow road stays in place.

"See?" Spider Woman says, laughing. "You'll be fine! And now you're ready to go. Just remember to stay on the path."

"What happens if we don't?" Davery asks.

"Best if you do," Spider Woman says. "There's danger all around, and people have been known to disappear after going astray."

I bite my lip, wondering if that's what happened to my mom.

Spider Woman's still talking. "Monsters are going to try to stop you from reaching the Sun," she says. "But as long as you stick to the Rainbow Road, they can't touch you."

"And what about the four trials?" I ask. "How will we know what they are and when we've passed them?"

"Look to the song the Diyin Dine'é gave you. It's a map, in a way. Showing you not where to go, but what to wonder."

"You mean 'wander'?" Davery asks.

183

"I meant what I said. Now"—she makes a shooing motion with her hands—"walk in beauty, my darlings."

And with that she turns and disappears down the path, leaving us alone on the Rainbow Road.

"Well, at least she didn't eat us," Mac says, looking at the place where Spider Woman was standing moments ago. "Hey, are you going to finish your burrito?"

I hand Mac my uneaten half. "I wish Mr. Yazzie were here," I say, suddenly feeling like maybe this isn't such a good idea. "I didn't realize how much I was starting to rely on a horned toad to get me through the day."

"I miss him, too," Davery says. "But following the road should be easy enough, especially with the song to guide us. I think I get what Spider Woman meant when she said it's like a map of wonder."

"That makes one of us," I mutter. But I trust Davery knows what he's talking about. After all, Mr. Yazzie said he was destined to be someone wise, like a scholar or a hataɫii, which means he can probably understand things that I can't. Like that song. "Could I see it again?"

He digs the fair flyer out of his pocket and hands it to me. I read aloud the lines about the trials.

A talking stone, a field of knives, a prom of thorns, a seethe of sand.

Thoughts take form, form becomes true.

To defeat the trials, you must know you.

"Okay, so we'll meet some talking rocks first," Davery says, stepping forward. "That could be interesting."

"Yeah, talking rocks don't sound so bad. Maybe they'll ask

us a riddle, like a Sphinx or something." Beneath my feet, the rainbow road spreads about twenty feet in front of us as we walk, the stripes of color a steady glow in the morning sun. "But a field of knives can't be good."

"And I'm too young to go to prom," Mac says. "Besides, I can't dance."

"And I don't know what a seethe is, exactly," Davery admits. "But it sounds like it could be dangerous."

"That song will only make sense *after* we've done all the things it talks about," I say, putting it in my backpack. "What's the point of even having it if it can't tell us where to go?"

"Maybe we should focus less on the destination and enjoy the journey," Mac says as he stuffs the last of my burrito in his mouth.

Davery and I turn to stare.

"What?" he asks, wiping his cheek. "Do I have Spam on my face?"

"You sound like a Hallmark card," I say, rolling my eyes a little. "We can't enjoy the journey when we only have until tomorrow's sunrise to get to the Sun!"

"Hey, don't yell at me. It works when Oprah says it."

"You are definitely not Oprah."

"Dream crusher."

I turn back to Davery. "What do you think we should do?"

"I think we should pick up the pace," he says, "or our road might disappear."

I look down at my feet and sure enough, the rainbow stripes that were perfectly solid just seconds ago are fading, like pastel watercolors with too much water added.

"If I had to guess," Davery says, walking a little faster, "I would say that as the sun rises and the rain dries out, the rainbow disappears. Just like a real rainbow would. We have to hurry!"

We start fast-walking and then running as the colors dwindle to Easter-egg versions of themselves. I look back once and the spot where we started is plain red mud again, the road having completely disappeared.

"Faster!" I say as we rush forward.

I'm going so fast, looking over my shoulders as I run, that I don't even see what's in front of us.

"Nizhoni, stop!" Davery yells, but it's too late.

Feet scrambling for purchase, arms flailing wildly, I fall off the edge of a cliff.

◆

TWENTY-NINE

Rock Concert

Luckily, the cliff drops off to a small muddy hill, which I slide down on my heels, like I'm skiing. I skid to a stop at the bottom and try to stay upright, but the ground is so slippery, I end up sitting in a puddle.

"Are you hurt?" Davery asks as he scrambles down to join me.

"Ow!" I exclaim. "My butt!"

Davery giggles, and I guess it is pretty funny, but it also hurts.

"I landed on my tailbone."

"Good thing the mud cushioned your fall, or it could have been worse." He puts out a hand to pull me up.

Once I'm on my feet, I try to wipe mud from the back of my pants. It comes off thick and red in my hands. Seems like the humiliations never end. "I can't believe the Rainbow Road led us off the side of a cliff!"

"Speaking of rainbows, where did the road go?" Mac asks as he climbs down.

We all look around, and yup, there's no more road to be seen. I groan in disappointment. We went to all that trouble to find it, and we've already lost it?

"There!" Davery says, pointing across the gorge. Squinting, I think I can just barely see glowing colors on the far side, picking up again on the top of a hill like the one we just slid down. It's as if the road used to be connected but these two hills were pulled apart, the space between them forming the valley we're in now, which is divided by a wide rushing river. We have to get across, but how?

"I guess we should take that?" Davery says, pointing at a dry narrow path that winds between two tall rock walls about twenty yards away. The early morning sunlight hasn't risen over the walls yet, and the trail looks dark and creepy. But it's the only way through.

"It's not part of the Rainbow Road," I point out. "And Spider Woman warned us we could get lost if we—"

"What's that noise?" Mac asks, sounding scared.

An eerie sound is coming from the dark path, sort of like a low moan. I shudder as chills run up and down my spine.

"Is that a ghost?" Mac whispers. "I hate ghosts."

"No," says Davery. "When wind blows through a narrow canyon, it can sound like a supernatural phenomenon, but it's really quite natural."

"Promise?" Mac asks as the groaning picks up. It sounds like wind blowing through a narrow canyon, sure, but it also sounds like a dozen voices in some kind of awful pain. A pain way worse than what my butt is feeling right now.

Davery blinks. "I guess I can't exactly promise. . . ."

I try to peer into the corridor, but I can't see a thing. It's darker between the walls than it was back at Spider Woman's before the sun came up.

"I vote ghosts, then," Mac says. "And that means we need to find another way to get to the road."

"There is none," I say. "Unless we want to try climbing back up that slippery hill and going the long way around. It could take hours—hours we don't have."

Another moan emanates from the valley path, and this time I swear it's saying something. "I think that's a voice," I say.

"Is it saying, *This way, children?*" Davery asks.

I hear it, too. *Thissss wayyyyy . . .*

"Welp!" Mac says, throwing up his hands. "Definitely haunted."

"Or," Davery says, "remember the song? The talking rocks? Well, these rocks are talking."

"Yeah," Mac says, "and they're saying, *Run away, we're haunted!*"

"No, I think we're meant to go through them. I think this is the first trial."

Of course the first trial would have to involve a haunted canyon. Why couldn't it just be a math test or something? I'd rather try to divide fractions than fight ghosts, and I really, really hate fractions.

"Okay, then," I say, squaring my shoulders, "let's do it. But everyone stay close together."

"I wish Mr. Yazzie was here," Mac says mournfully. "He would know what to do."

Davery pats Mac's shoulder. "Yeah, he—"

"There he is!" Mac shouts. And miraculously, there's a horned toad sitting right at the entrance to the corridor.

"Hurry, little heroes!" he shouts, waving us forward.

"The path is only open for a few more minutes. You must get through before it closes."

"But how did Mr. Yazzie get here?" Davery asks, a puzzled look on his face. "Last we saw him, he was—"

"Who cares how he got here?" Mac says. "Let's go!" And just like that, he takes off.

It *is* really strange. The lizard couldn't have gotten here first, could he? And there's another thing. "Where's his sweater?" I ask.

Mac is almost to Mr. Yazzie, when Davery exclaims, "The song!"

"What about it?"

"*Beware, beware the friendly toad.* We skipped that part, because I didn't know what it meant!"

I'd totally forgotten, but the meaning seems pretty clear now. "It's a trap!"

"Mac!" we both shout, running after my little brother.

"Hurry, children!" the fake Mr. Yazzie says. "This way! Right through here. You're almost there." And as he turns to wave Mac forward, I can see his eyes. They're red, just like the fake Adrien Cuttlebush's at the train station, and the buzzard bozos at Black Mountain. Which means . . . monster!

"No, Mac! Stop! That's not really Mr. Yazzie!" But he's not listening. And as the horned toad scuttles down the path and disappears into the dark, Mac follows him.

The canyon rumbles. The whole ground shakes like we're having an earthquake. Debris showers down as the rock walls start to move. I rub my eyes. Move? That's impossible.

Davery skids to a stop and grabs my arm. "Are you seeing what I'm seeing?"

"The canyon walls are moving closer together, aren't they?"

"Yes, and if we don't get Mac out," Davery says, "they're going to squish him like a grape!"

"We have to follow him!"

"And then *we'll* get squished like grapes! No, there has to be another way."

"Did the song have any ideas about how to win the trials?"

Davery purses his lips, thinking. *"To defeat the trial, you must know you."*

"How am I supposed to know myself? I mean, I already do. That makes no sense and is entirely unhelpful." I look around the valley, feeling frantic, searching for something we could use to get Mac back. There's a pile of stones nearby, a few scrubby plants growing in the sandy wash, and a small grove of cottonwood trees. Rocks, mud, and trees—that's all there is.

And then I have an idea. I run over to a cottonwood. I jump up and grab on to a long branch that's sticking out at about eye level. I haul myself up, like I'm doing a pull-up in gym class, and then let my weight drop. The branch wobbles and starts to crack. I do it again. Up, then drop. And the crack gets bigger. On the third try, when I come down, the branch breaks off. I land on my feet, now holding a branch longer than I am.

I rush back over to Davery. "That was really impressive," he says. "You're strong."

"For a girl?" I say sarcastically.

"No. For anyone. It was . . . cool."

I hadn't really thought about it, but I guess I am strong. Maybe that's part of my ancestral powers, or maybe I'm just naturally that way and never had the chance to try it out. Either way, I'm glad it worked.

"Watch this!" I exclaim. The canyon trail is getting narrower by the minute. When we first got here, it was wide enough for Mac, Davery, and me to walk through side by side without even touching shoulders. Now it's only wide enough for Davery and me, and that might be a tight fit.

I step forward, just a little way into the corridor. The wind still howls like it's full of ghosts, and when I look down into the darkness, Mac and the fake Mr. Yazzie are nowhere to be seen. I gulp nervously. What if something's happened to Mac?

No, I can't think that way. This is going to work, and I'm going to rescue him.

I thrust my branch into the opening and turn it horizontally so it's jammed between the two rock walls. The canyon rumbles and the sides keep trying to move closer, but this time, the branch stops them. The moaning wind picks up a notch. But my branch doesn't break.

"It's working!" Davery exclaims.

I turn to my best friend and mimic his voice. "Well, if you understood the science behind it, it's actually quite—"

A groaning sound, like an animal in pain, comes from behind me. I whirl back around to see my stick bending and buckling as the canyon walls heave together again, refusing to just stop already.

"Uh, Nizhoni?" Davery says worriedly. "I think you'd better move out of the way."

I take a big step back, and then another, and we watch as my brilliant plan shatters under the pressure of the closing rock walls and a hundred splinters come flying right at us.

THIRTY

◆

The Coolest Moment Ever

"I thought it would work," I moan as I pick myself up off the ground. Once again, there's a fine coating of mud on my rear end. The only upside is that this time Davery has a mud butt, too.

"It was a good idea," he says generously. "But now we're back to square one." He leans over to pick a twig out of my hair.

The walls are still closing in, and the corridor is now only wide enough for one person to pass. And it's still dark and spooky in there, but it's clear what we have to do.

"I have to go in and find Mac."

"I knew you were going to say that," Davery says, sighing.

"You did?" Maybe foretelling the future is Davery's ancestral power. That could be handy.

"Not in a magic way or anything. Just because it's what we have to do."

Oh. Disappointing. "You don't have to come."

"Don't be ridiculous. I'm not letting you go in there by yourself. Besides, you might need me."

Might? Most definitely. I breathe a sigh of relief and tighten my backpack straps. "Ready?"

Davery adjusts his backpack, too, and his glasses so they're tight against his face, and then nods. "Let's do this!" he shouts, and takes off.

My friend has a lot of enthusiasm, but there's no way he's faster than me. I catch up to him before we've even entered the corridor, and I go in first. The darkness closes around me immediately, but I keep running. After a few seconds in the pitch-black, I glance behind me. I can't even see the light from the opening where we came in. It's like we dropped into another dimension. The only way I know Davery is still back there is because I can hear his feet as they slap the ground, as well as his heavy panting. He really has to work on his cardio if he's going to fight monsters with me.

And then, over the rumble of the canyon walls and Davery's breathing, I hear something else. Faint, but I'd recognize Mac's voice anywhere.

I shift into another gear, asking my legs to really move, and they answer me with a burst of speed. I'm racing through the passage almost like I can see in the dark. And then I realize I *can*! Things aren't as sharp as if I were in daylight, more like a sketch. The walls are outlines that I instinctively know to keep away from, and I can see the curves of rock up ahead.

"I think I have X-ray vision!" I shout over my shoulder.

Davery doesn't say anything, so I turn to repeat this amazing information, but he's too far back.

I must have superspeed, too! Probably inherited from my monster-fighting ancestors. Clearly, this is the coolest moment ever.

"Nizhoooooniiiiii!"

It's Mac. His voice is a wavery, hollow-sounding moan, but

it's definitely him, and he's in trouble. I accelerate even more, trying to get to my brother as quickly as possible, and trusting that Davery will catch up.

Finally, I see Mac. He's slumped against the wall, his head tucked between his knees and his arms wrapped around his legs. He's crying.

"Mac!" I grab his shoulder and shake him gently. "Are you okay? Did that fake Mr. Yazzie hurt you? Where'd he go?"

He won't look at me, just keeps sobbing with his head down.

"You've got to snap out of it!" I tell him. "The walls are closing in, and we can't stay here."

He sniffles, but he still won't look up. And suddenly, the hairs on the back of my neck rise. I whip around, expecting a monster to be sneaking up on me. But no one's there.

And then I realize Mac's crying has stopped. With a feeling of dread, I slowly turn to face my brother.

He's staring right at me. With big red eyes.

I scream and stumble away. He bares sharp teeth and hisses. Climbs slowly to his feet.

The walls seem to have stopped moving. I could go back the way I came. I'm fast and could probably outrun him if he tried to chase me. But Davery's coming up behind me, and I don't want him to smack into the monster. Besides, I need to find out what happened to my little brother.

Monster Mac takes a swipe at me, and I see that besides having long, pointy teeth, he has long, pointy claws, too.

"What did you do with my brother?" I shout.

"Nizhonee baloney," the monster hisses. "Nizhonee's a phony!"

"I am not!" I say. What in the world is going on? This monster is just like Adrien Cuttlebush with its weird insults.

"Nizhonee pepperoni, Nizhonee rigatoni, Nizhonee macaroni!"

That's it! I can take a lot, but mocking me with my favorite Italian foods is going one step too far. I turn and launch a swinging kick right at the monster's stomach. It lands with an *Oomph!* I elbow him in the chest and he doubles over. One more kick—this time to his ribs—and he's down. He's on all fours, panting.

"Come at me, bro!" I shout, because I'm ready to dish out more, and the monster still looks like Mac, who is, in fact, my bro, so it makes sense. Plus, I heard the line on a commercial once.

But the monster doesn't attack. Instead, it makes this horrible wail that forces me to cover my ears. It's the same sound I heard earlier and mistook for ghosts. And then the monster shudders, and right before my eyes, it gets blurry and turns into Mr. Yazzie. Then it shudders and blurs again, and this time it becomes a cockroach. It scuttles off into the darkness before I can squish it with my shoe.

"Nizhoni!"

I whirl around, ready to fight again, but it's just Davery, huffing as he finally catches up to me.

"Why . . . did . . . you . . . stop . . . running?" he asks, between gasps for air.

"Mac!" I cry. "They turned him into a monster!"

Just then, the canyon rumbles, and tiny rocks slide down the walls as they start their trash-compacting routine again.

Davery looks panicked, and I know we can't stay in here any longer. There's no sign of the real Mac anywhere anyway.

Mr. Charles got him.

At that thought, my knees buckle and I almost fall to the ground. But Davery, even though he's barely caught his breath, grabs my arm and hauls me forward.

THIRTY-ONE

♦

Avoid the Pointy End

By the time we stumble out of the corridor exit, the walls are so close together we have to squeeze out sideways. It's a tight fit, but we do it, and just in time. Not two minutes after we're clear, the canyon closes with a mighty *bang*. Behind us now is a solid wall, the path we followed less than a crack in the rocks.

And stretching to the left, running parallel to the riverbed and extending all the way across the valley floor, is the Rainbow Road. It's no longer a faraway glimmer, but an up-close ribbon of bright colors.

It makes me want to cry. It's like a taunt. Because I flunked the first test.

"How could I lose Mac?" I wail. "I was supposed to protect him! Some hero I am." I sink to the ground and put my head in my hands.

Davery sits down next to me and puts an arm around my shoulders. "You were totally heroic back there. You ran faster than I thought was humanly possible, without stumbling in the dark, and you fought off the Mac monster."

I know he's trying to make me feel better, but all I keep thinking is that I'm a complete failure. "I should never have let Mac out of my sight," I say between sniffles. "I should have run after him right away, and—"

"Mac acted impulsively, as usual," Davery says. "He didn't listen to Spider Woman, or to you. It sucks that he's gone, but he did it to himself."

"He's just a kid!" I protest, pushing Davery away in frustration.

"A kid with ancestral powers, remember?" Davery says. "He's related to Born for Water. Don't underestimate what he can do against an enemy."

"But Mr. Charles—"

"If it's true that Mr. Charles got him," Davery cuts in, "then he's probably in the same place your dad is now. We've got to keep going. If we find one of them, we'll find the other."

I nod and wipe away my tears, feeling a little better. "At least maybe he's not alone, then."

"We'll rescue them both. But first we have to get through these trials and get the weapons we need. Mac would understand. We need to stay focused."

"But how can we keep going if I failed the first trial? Aren't I disqualified?"

"Doesn't look like it to me," Davery says, pointing at the ground. "The Rainbow Road is your proof."

"I hope you're right," I say, standing up and trying to pull myself together. My legs feel shaky, and I feel a tension headache coming on. What's worse, I'm going to have to do like a month's worth of Mac's chores for this. "We thought the talking rocks weren't going to be so bad. What's our next trial?"

"Knives," Davery says. "A field of knives."

"Great," I say, sighing heavily. "Something else trying to kill us."

"Knives shouldn't be too hard," Davery says optimistically. "We just need to avoid the pointy end."

That sounds like it's going to be easier said than done, but we don't have much choice but to move forward, since the rock wall has cut off our access to anything behind us. We walk on the rainbow. Slowly the landscape changes, the desert cliffs and sandy dunes giving way to a scrubbier green with low mountains squatting on the horizon. The sun keeps rising in the sky, and in the distance, light glints off a small lake. It's pretty here—different from Canyon de Chelly, but pretty all the same. The rainbow at our feet stays steady, but soon the solid ground turns into swampy marshland, and before we know it, we're wading through ankle-deep water. The lake extends farther than I expected. All around us are tall thin reeds, and eventually they become so thick it's hard to push our way through.

"Wish we had a knife of our own about now to cut through these reeds," Davery says. He swats at the gnats that have started to swarm around our heads in annoying clouds.

"Ouch!" I say as something pokes me in the calf. I look down, figuring there'll be a bug bite, but all I see are more knee-high stalks of brown reeds.

"Hey," Davery says, reaching for his own calf. "These reeds are sharp."

"And getting sharper," I exclaim as one cuts me on the back of the hand.

"Uh-oh," Davery says. "I think we found our field of knives."

"What do we do?" I say as another reed slices my leg.

"Maybe we should turn back."

We stop in the middle of the swamp. Davery and I stand back-to-back and survey our little patch of land. We're surrounded on all sides by reeds tipped with razor-sharp cattails. We've only made it about halfway across the valley, and the Rainbow Road behind us is already fading. Ahead of us, the colors are still strong.

"I don't think we can turn back."

Davery swallows nervously. "I'm fresh out of ideas."

I shift, the mud sucking at my sneakers. And suddenly I have an idea.

"Grab some mud," I tell Davery.

"What now? I'm already dirty enough."

"No, you're not! If we cover our skin and clothes in mud, it will protect us from the reeds."

Davery's eyes light up. "Genius!" he says.

"I think that's the first time you've ever called me that."

"Well, it's the first time you've had a really genius idea." He scoops up a handful of swampy mud and starts coating his arms with it.

"Whatever," I say, doing the same thing. The seat of my jeans is still pretty much covered in mud, so I concentrate on covering my legs and arms. "I have genius ideas all the time. How 'bout that time we had to share that vanilla shake and you said get two straws but I said no, get an extra cup and then we can each have our own?"

"That's a pretty low bar for genius."

"How do I look?" I ask, holding out my muddy arms and hands and doing a little spin. I am covered in mud up to my neck.

"Terrible," Davery says as he pats the last of the mud onto the backs of his own hands. "But I think beauty is a secondary concern at the moment."

"Counting my basketball uniform, this is the second set of clothes I've ruined this week."

Staying close together, we start walking forward slowly, careful to stay on the rainbow road. I can feel the sharp reeds brushing against my legs, but this time, they don't cut. It's working!

"I think it's even keeping the gnats away," I say.

"Uh-oh," Davery says. "I know what's keeping the gnats away, and it's not the mud. Look up!"

Above us, dark thunderclouds have started to gather. They're rolling in heavy with rain, just like the ones we woke up to this morning.

"If the rain washes us off, we're done for!" says Davery.

I feel the first big drop of water hit my face. Another splats on my nose. And then the whole sky opens up, as if someone turned on a faucet, and the rain falls in a drenching Super Soaker–like downpour.

"Hurry!" I say. "We need to get through this field!"

I take off, but it's hard to run on the swampy ground, and my legs are stiff with mud, and the rain is blinding, so it's more like I stagger through the reeds.

"I can see the edge," Davery says from behind me. "Keep going. Stay on the Rainbow Road."

I do as he says, stumbling forward as best as I can. When I start to fall, I reach out to steady myself and a reed slices my palm. I look down. The rain has washed all the mud off me. Oh no! I can see the end of the marsh now, too, but we still have a way to go and all my protection is gone.

I tuck my hands inside the sleeves of my hoodie and keep going. The reeds whip me and it feels like I'm being cut by tiny razor blades. I'm sure my legs are bleeding, and my favorite jeans are getting shredded.

Finally, I stagger out of the reeds and into the clearing on the other side of the swamp. I drop to my knees. Davery lurches out behind me. His jeans are also torn, and his hands are bloody. He falls to his knees beside me, soaked and exhausted.

"We made it!" I say triumphantly. "Trial two, in the dust!"

"Not only did we make it," he says, wheezing, "but we definitely became more stylish." He lifts one leg in the air, showing off his ripped jeans.

"Pretty cool," I admit. "This story is definitely going on my YouTube channel."

"You don't have a YouTube channel," he says.

"Not yet! Goals, Davery. I have goals."

He rolls his eyes and gets to his feet. Puts a hand up to shade his face. "It's stopped raining," he observes. He swats the air. "And the gnats are back."

The timing of the rain is suspicious, or maybe just unlucky, but I definitely don't want to stick around the swamp and get eaten alive by gnats. "Let's keep going," I say. Thankfully, the Rainbow Road still stretches before us. "What's next?"

"A prom of thorns."

I groan. "I don't think I can take any more nature trying to make us bleed."

"Maybe it isn't literally thorns . . ." Davery says thoughtfully. "A prom . . . What could that mean?"

I look around. We're still in the middle of nowhere, basically. I can't see any houses, and we haven't met any people since we left Spider Woman. "Well, I'll tell you one thing—I don't think we're going to come across a school dance out here."

"Then what's that?" Davery asks, pointing into the distance.

Maybe I need glasses, too. I squint to see better. Sure enough, there's some kind of building ahead. It's one story and square, and it looks a lot like the gym back at our school. We start walking toward it, and eventually I can hear music wafting our way, something catchy with a lot of bass and a woman singing, but we're too far away for me to make out the words.

"You've got to be kidding me," I say.

"Not kidding," Davery says.

Because I see now that the Rainbow Road is leading right up to the doors of the gym. If we want to stay on the road, we have to go inside.

"Well, you said you didn't want any more nature. I guess the Holy People heard you."

"Yeah, but I didn't think they'd make us go to high school."

◆

THIRTY-TWO

Last Night a DJ Saved My Life

"Well," Davery says. "Who's going in first?"

"Not me." This close to the gym, we can feel the dance music thumping under our feet and hear voices inside, laughing and shouting.

"You know," Davery says, "we've survived red-eyed monsters, rocks that want to crush us, and reeds that want to slice us into deli meat, but I think I'm more afraid of what's behind these doors."

"High school kids," we both say at the same time.

"At least it sounds like they're having a good time." I stick out a leg. "And we do look fashionable."

He shakes his head. "Remember what the song says—*a prom of thorns. Thorns*, Nizhoni. This is not going to be good."

I swallow nervously. "We have to go anyway."

"I know."

"On three. One, two . . ." And before I can say *three*, the double doors swing open.

"Welcome!" shouts a friendly voice. It's a boy in an honest-to-goodness tuxedo—black pants and jacket, and he's even wearing a black bow tie speckled with tiny fake diamonds. He's Navajo, with short black hair and dark brown eyes. Brown eyes are a relief. I was half expecting them to be red. The boy looks a little like my cousin Freddie, except Freddie's not as cute as this guy. He gives me a big grin and holds the door open so we can enter. "Come on in!"

"Might as well," Davery says with a sigh.

Not surprisingly, the gym is decorated for a school dance. Rainbow-striped crepe-paper streamers hang tastefully from the beams and are taped up in flowerlike clusters along the walls. Giant poster-board picture frames, hand-painted and liberally sprinkled with glitter, invite kids to pose for photos with their friends. On the stage is a huge video monitor playing short clips of what look to be the best moments of the school year—sports events, science fairs, plays, and class trips. Spotlights hit the disco ball that hangs from the ceiling, making the room twinkle. Round tables that seat at least eight people each line the dance floor. The centerpieces are colorful balloon arrangements, accented with ribbons and confetti. Loose balloons float lazily around the room, drifting around the dancers' feet.

A DJ spins beats, earphones pressed between her shoulder and right ear as she works her deck. I recognize the song she's playing. It's the newest radio hit, the one my dad always turns off because he says the lyrics are not appropriate for kids our age. But nobody here seems to care that we are too young. I look around and realize there are no adult chaperones. Only teenagers. And they all seem to be having fun.

"Would you like some punch?" another voice says. We turn, and a girl is holding out two red plastic cups. She has on a beautiful silver dress that sparkles and stands out against her brown skin. Her black hair is tied back with a matching ribbon.

"Thank you," I say, taking the cup. I'm actually pretty thirsty and the punch looks delicious.

"Don't drink it," Davery warns me.

I stop, the cup already halfway to my lips. "Why not?"

"In all the stories, the heroes go somewhere and drink or eat something that's been enchanted and then they get stuck there."

"If the heroes never eat or drink anything, how do they survive?" I whine. "They would die of dehydration."

Davery frowns, shrugs off his backpack, and digs around inside it. "Remember how you didn't want Mac to drink soda pop at Spider Woman's house? It's the same thing." He hands me his water bottle. "Have this instead," he says. "Let's not take any chances until we figure out this trial."

Disappointed, but seeing how he might be right about not ingesting food or drink from strangers, I set the cup down on a nearby table and take a swig from his bottle instead. The water is warm, and there's no way it tastes as good as that punch. But I swallow it anyway.

We make our way around the gym, looking for signs of monsters or anything that might resemble the thorns the song warned us about. To my surprise, everyone is friendly. They greet us with smiles and seem to know our names. A couple of kids ask us to join them at their table, but Davery says we shouldn't, so we keep moving.

"Don't accept any gifts, either," he warns me tersely.

"Why not?"

"That's another trick they use to trap you."

I sigh and take another drink of boring water. "I don't think anyone's trying to trap us. Maybe this isn't a trial at all. It could just be a chance to relax, like we did at Spider Woman's. Maybe the Rainbow Road knows we need a break."

Davery gives me a *Don't be naive* look.

"Whatever," I say.

I watch a boy and girl skip by, headed to the dance floor. The DJ starts up a new track, and everyone cheers.

"Hey, isn't this your favorite song?" I ask Davery.

He pauses to listen. "It is," he says, surprised. "I know all the words." He sings a little, and his voice is perfectly in tune.

"Since when did you learn how to sing on-key?"

He presses a hand to his throat. "What's going on? Why do I sound so good?"

A girl comes up next to us. It's the same girl who offered us punch earlier, the one in the shiny silver dress. "Do you want to dance?" she asks Davery.

His eyes get really big, and he looks at me for help.

"He can't dance."

"Oh, come on," she says, laughing and grabbing his hand. "One dance won't hurt. I'll show you some steps."

"How 'bout you?" asks a voice behind me. "Care to join me?" I turn to see the cute boy in the tuxedo standing behind me, his hand extended.

I glance at Davery and he shrugs. We haven't had anything to eat or drink in this place, so maybe dancing is okay?

"Sure," I say. The four of us walk to the middle of the floor just as the DJ starts a new song, and this time, it's *my* favorite.

And I decide that, after everything we've been through, I'm going to have some fun and dance with this cute boy.

After the song is over, a new one starts, and I can't believe it, but it's my second-favorite song, so we keep dancing. And then some new kids join in, and there's one big group on the floor, and everyone is super nice. Unlike my classmates back at ICCS, these kids like me!

When we take a break and sit down, the high schoolers want to know all about us, so we tell them about Mr. Charles and the buzzards and the trials we've been through.

"At first I thought Abalone Shell Boy was going to crush me with his fist," Davery says, "but then I impressed him with my knowledge of sea snails. Next thing I knew, he was handing me a chunk of his shoulder."

The girls surrounding him ooh and aah.

"And when the rock walls were closing in, I tore down that corridor with superspeed. The night vision really helped," I say.

"Night vision?" says the boy in the tux. "That's so cool!"

Davery and I exchange grins. We feel like superstars. I thought having ancestral powers was the best thing in the world, but this might be even better.

There's a break in the music and I lean over to Davery. "We're popular!" I whisper. "I've always wanted to be popular!"

"Yeah, these kids are pretty decent," he admits. He looks longingly at the punch bowl. Next to it someone has put out a tray of cookies—chocolate chunk and even some sugar-free vegan oatmeal ones. "I suppose it would be okay to have some refreshments. . . ."

"I was hoping you'd say that!" I say. Laughing, we rush over to the snack table, load up a plate of cookies, and grab two cups of punch.

"This is the best party I've ever been to," I say, stuffing a whole cookie into my mouth at once. I wash it down with the punch, which is cold, sparkling, and delicious. "I only wish Mac were here with us."

"Who?" Davery asks, taking a more restrained bite of his oatmeal cookie.

And for a second, I can't remember who Mac is, either. The name is so familiar, though. "I'm not sure. . . ."

"Hey, beautiful girl," the boy in the tuxedo says, coming up beside me. "Ready to dance again?"

"I . . . Does the name Mac mean anything to you?" I feel like I should know who Mac is, but it's just out of my reach.

"Come on," the cute boy says, taking my plate from me and setting it on the table. "Let's dance our cares away. No need to worry about Mac or anything else."

The next song comes on, and the boy starts singing along to it.

"Beautiful girl, lovely dress . . ."

It sounds so familiar, but I can't recall the name of it.

"'Cause it's gone, daddy, gone . . ."

Daddy . . . gone . . .

I stop in my tracks. "My dad . . ." I say. "I . . . I think he's in trouble."

The tuxedo boy grabs my hand and pulls. "Forget about that," he says.

I tug my arm away. "My dad . . . and Mac!" Mac is my little brother. How could I have forgotten?

Oh no. Davery was right. This place isn't good at all.

I follow Tuxedo Boy to the dance floor and edge my way over to Davery, who is swaying in place, happily munching on another cookie.

"Davery," I whisper when Tuxedo Boy looks lost in the music, "we've got to get out of here."

"What's the rush?" he asks. "I thought you said everything was great."

"Maybe it's a little *too* great," I say. "Like, no way am I this likable. This whole prom is fake. It's a trap, just like you thought it was going to be. A prom of *thorns*."

"I don't even see any roses in here," says Davery with a shake of his head, "much less thorns. Only crepe-paper flowers."

The boy in the tuxedo grabs at my hand again, his smile fixed, white teeth gleaming in the disco ball light. "Come on, pretty girl," he says again, insistent.

He and I dance together again for a few minutes, and suddenly it all makes sense. I twirl over to my best friend.

"Davery! I get it. The people with their fancy clothes and perfect looks? They're the roses—because they're beautiful, like flowers. And we're trapped, like we're tangled in thorns. I think getting out of here is our third trial."

He considers this for a moment, and I'm worried he may not agree and we'll be stuck in this gym forever.

Finally he says, "You may be right," taking another bite of the cookie. "There's an easy way to find out. Let's head for the back door, where the Rainbow Road probably picks up again, and see what happens." He takes two more cookies from the table and slides them into his pants pocket.

I give him a look, and he grins sheepishly. "I don't think the food's poisoned after all," he admits. "And these cookies are really good. We may not get a chance to eat anything else until we get to the House of the Sun."

I want to roll my eyes, but he has a point, so I pocket a few cookies myself. We walk shoulder to shoulder toward the door, but immediately, partygoers start blocking our path.

"Don't you want to dance with me, pretty girl?" the boy in the tuxedo asks, frowning in confusion.

"Tell me another monster story," says an enthusiastic girl in a pink dress.

"Isn't this your favorite song?" asks another girl with short hair and diamonds on her black pants.

They swarm around us, asking us questions, trying to make us stay, but Davery and I push forward, mouthing apologies, not stopping. Someone grabs at my shoulder, pulls my hoodie, but I slip by them. The crowd is getting so thick now that it's hard to move. They back us up against a wall.

"What do we do?" Davery asks. I see a boy reach for his arm, but he manages to brush him off.

I look to my right and my left, trying to find any empty space. And then I see it—a familiar red box on the wall.

"I think it might be time to water these roses."

I pull the fire alarm, which sets off a horrible *whoop whoop* sound. The kids move back, hands over their ears. Then the ceiling sprinklers kick in, spraying the entire room. People start to scream and run in all directions, and Davery and I take off, breaking through the crowd. A boy in a powder-blue jacket steps in front of me, but I raise my hands and push through him like a running back. He goes skidding across the slick floor. "Almost there!" I shout, and as soon as I'm close enough, I lower my shoulder and hit the exit door full force.

Lucky for me, it's not locked, and Davery and I go through at top speed. We spill out into the fresh air, while hands still grasp for our clothes. Davery slams the door behind us, muffling the alarm and the shrieks. Then, in an instant, the whole gym shimmers and disappears.

"What . . . just . . . happened?" I ask in between gasps.

"It . . . was . . . all . . . an illusion!"

"Good," I say. "That means . . . I won't get . . . arrested for . . . pulling the . . . alarm."

That gets a laugh from Davery, who's the biggest rule follower I know.

As we catch our breath, I peer around. We're back in the middle of nowhere. But at least our feet are solidly planted on the Rainbow Road, so we're where we're supposed to be. Wherever that is.

"How long were we in there?" I ask. It was no later than lunchtime when we went in, but now the sun is setting and the sky overhead is darkening quickly.

"Too long," Davery says. "And we have one more trial to get through."

"But we still have to get the weapons, and find my dad

and Mac, and defeat Mr. Charles. . . ." I slump to the ground. "How are we ever going to do all that before sunrise?"

"Just one more, Nizhoni," Davery says. "It can't be that much farther. And we have all night. . . ."

"But what if it takes a long time to even find the next trial? What was it? *A seethe of sand?* We still don't know what a 'seethe' is."

"I don't think it matters," Davery says, his voice sounding anxious, "because I think the trial has found us."

THIRTY-THREE

◆

Sandcastles

"What are those?" I ask.

"They look like . . . mirrors?"

Davery's right. As we walk closer, I see that the field of yellow-green desert grass in front of us is dotted with mirrors—the old-fashioned kind that stand on two legs. I think they're called dressing mirrors. Some of them have carved wooden frames and look like they belong in an old English mansion. Then there are modern ones with metal frames in black or silver. There's even a bright pink one that looks like it's from a child's room.

"What are they all for?" I wonder aloud. "And what do they have to do with the fourth trial?"

"Well . . ." Davery says, tapping a finger thoughtfully against his chin. "Mirrors are made of sand."

"They are?"

"You really don't pay attention in science class, do you?"

"Sorry."

"Glass is made by heating sand until it's boiling and then shaping and cooling it. And a mirror is made by painting the back of a sheet of glass with silver nitrate. So"—he waves his hand toward the field of mirrors—"this looks like our fourth trial."

"Well, let's get this over with," I say, marching forward. I reach the first mirror, a nice tall glass in a dark mahogany frame with elaborate curlicues carved into the wood. I check out my reflection. Despite what the prom kids said, I'm not looking too hot. I've been covered in mud not just once but twice today, been rained on, and my jeans have a big rip in the knee from the knifelike reeds.

"Wow," I say to Davery. "Why didn't you tell me I look like day-old garbage?" I press a hand to my hair, trying to make it a little more presentable, but who am I kidding? I'm going to need professional help.

Davery's gazing into a mirror a few feet away and brushing flakes of dried mud from his shoulders. "We aren't looking our best," he agrees.

I turn to the side, assessing myself. "When you said sand, I expected quicksand or something."

"I—I think the trials adapt to our wonderings, our thoughts. Just like Spider Woman said. We're following a map of wondering."

"Huh. So when I said I didn't want any more nature challenges, it took me seriously and gave us an actual prom? And now it's giving us mirrors?"

"I bet the other monsterslayers who went through the trials had different challenges," he says. "Like, their trials made sense for their time, just like ours are contemporary and make sense for us."

"Cool," I say. It makes me wonder what kind of trials my mom faced. "But what are we supposed to do with a field of mirrors?"

"Well, the song did say that in order to defeat the trials we have to know ourselves."

"*You must know you,*" I quote. "I remember."

"So maybe this is somehow helping us to get to know ourselves."

"All I know from looking in this mirror is that I need a serious shower."

"Let's try different ones."

We each move on to another mirror. The one I pick is wider than it is tall, and it looks like it belongs above a girl's dresser. Its frame is white, and there are small stickers of daisies in the corners, pretty bursts of yellow petals on green stems. "This one's nice."

"See anything different in it?"

"No." I start to move on, but then something catches my eye. I turn back and there's a woman's reflection next to mine.

I yelp in surprise and whip around, but there's no one behind me. I look back at the mirror, and she's still there. Standing in the high yellow grassy field, a soft breeze ruffling her hair.

"Davery . . ." I say slowly, "there's someone in my mirror."

The woman looks about thirty, and she's wearing blue jeans and a motorcycle jacket over a white T-shirt. She has a beautiful squash blossom necklace made of silver and turquoise. Her long black hair blows around her face so that I can't get a good look at her features.

She seems so familiar. I reach out my hand, almost touching the mirror. If only I could see her clearly.

She waves—at me?—and beckons. . . .

"Do I know you?" I ask.

"Who are you talking to?" Davery asks.

"This woman. I can see her. I—I think I know her. . . ."

I dig in my pocket and pull out the picture of my family—the one Mr. Charles tried to steal. I know it by heart. I'm a toddler, no more than two years old. Mac is a baby, wrapped up tight on a cradleboard. Dad is standing behind the woman in front, who is holding Mac with one arm and has me on her knee.

I hold up the picture so I can look at it and the mirror at the same time. And for a second, I can't catch my breath. When I can breathe again, only one word comes out of my mouth.

"Mom?"

THIRTY-FOUR

◆

Snow

I lean forward to press my hand against the mirror, and suddenly the surface is not there anymore. Or at least it's not solid. I go plummeting into the glass. I squeeze my eyes shut and try to scream, but no sound comes out. After a dizzying tumble, I finally land on my feet.

When I open my eyes again, I'm alone in a clearing. Not the field that was in the mirror, all scrub grass and sage-brushes, but somewhere else. This glade is surrounded by high pines and other trees. And it's winter here. It looks a bit like the first sacred mountain, Sisnaajiní. But this snow is a lot deeper, almost up to my knees. And snowflakes are falling fast and heavy, the wind whipping them around like I'm in the middle of a blizzard.

I instinctively try to wrap my hoodie tighter around my body to stay warm before I realize that I'm not cold. Wait. How's that possible? I'm in the middle of a snowstorm and I can't feel anything?

I hear the crunch of footsteps behind me and whip around to see who it is. A figure, bundled up against the cold, is trudg-ing determinedly toward me. Davery?

The person is wearing a shapeless coat and has a wool

hat pulled down over their face and a thick patterned scarf wrapped around their neck.

They are carrying a large bundle in their arms, something wrapped tightly in layers of blankets. Then I hear a weak and tired whimper. A human whimper. The bundle is a baby—a baby who can definitely feel the cold.

"Hello?" I say as the person gets closer, but they totally ignore me. They walk right past, close enough to brush my shoulder, and I realize they can't hear me or see me. It's like a scene from a movie is playing, and I can only watch.

The figure keeps walking, fighting the snowstorm, making their way to a bare patch of ground under a pine tree two dozen feet away. I follow, curious to see what they're doing and wondering why I'm here. If the mirror is trying to show me something, I want to know what it is.

Under the trees, there's a little bit of shelter from the elements. The snow has abated and the wind has calmed and there's almost a warm welcoming glow where the moonlight cuts through the pines.

The person sets the bundled child down gently on a bed of needles and then pulls off their own scarf, unwinding it bit by bit. Then they remove their gloves and hat and shake out their black ponytail. A smile breaks across a beautiful face.

I know that face.

"Mom?" I whisper.

She looks fierce, and maybe a little intimidating, with an undercut beneath her long tresses. A tattoo peeks out of the gap at her collar and trails a few inches up her neck. Her brown eyes are accentuated with black eyeliner and thick mascara, and her fingernails are painted blue and bitten down to the quick. But as she gazes lovingly at the toddler, still wrapped in a bundle of blankets, I can tell she has a good heart.

"Hello, Nizhoni," she whispers to the child.

My breath catches in my throat, and I feel a little dizzy again. This vision is a memory—Mom's memory, because I was too young when it happened to remember it.

I don't have a chance to wonder how it is that I'm seeing this, because my mom is talking. "I know this is really hard, baby," she says to little me, "but I'm going to need you to be a warrior."

Little me doesn't answer, because, well, I can't be more than two years old. And it looks like my lips have started to turn blue and my teeth are chattering in my toddler-size head, so even if I could talk, I would probably just ask to go home. I mean, I knew my mom wasn't the greatest mother in the world, but why would she take me out here in the middle of a snowstorm? It makes my chest feel heavy.

I watch with disbelief as my mom unwraps little me from the layers of blankets until I'm just wearing one-piece pajamas. Not much protection from the cold at all! She lays me on my back directly on the snow. I sink in a bit. And then, very gently, my mom pushes me back and forth. And then she turns me all the way over, back to tummy, the same way I rolled out the dough for bread at Spider Woman's house. Until there's snow clinging to my onesie and soaking me through to the skin.

I totally expect little me to start wailing at any moment. I mean, it's freezing, and my wacky mother just made it ten times worse! But to my surprise, I don't cry at all. I just stare at her with huge baby eyes and shiver a little.

She smiles at me. "Already a warrior," she says, sounding proud. "Already so brave."

My mom called me brave? The thought spreads warmth through my veins.

After a minute, my mom wraps me up again in the original blankets and dusts the remaining snow from my head. She leans down and kisses my forehead.

"That was to make you tough," she explains to me, even though there's no way I could have understood her. "I'll be gone soon, and you will need to be strong."

Little me makes a happy laughing sound, but real me is starting to feel sick. My stomach hurts deep down, and I wrap my arms around myself. I knew my mom left us, but the mirror is showing me the actual moment when she said good-bye, and I don't want to see any more. I don't think I can take it.

I try to turn away, get out of here, but I can't move. The scene plays out before me, and I have no choice but to watch.

"If the day comes when the monsters rise again, you will be the first to see them. It will be scary, and you'll feel overwhelmed, but I'll be there with you. In spirit, if not in body . . ." Mom's voice trails off, and her eyes get distant, as if she's remembering something painful. Then she shakes her head like she's flicking the memories away, and she keeps talking. "So don't be afraid, okay? You won't be alone."

The wind picks up her words and tosses them around the trees. They seem to twist back to my ears in echoes. *Alone,*

alone, alone. And I can't tell if her words feel like a blessing or a curse.

I watch as my mom reaches into her pocket and takes out a necklace. I swallow past the hard lump in my throat. My hand automatically reaches for the place where the turquoise hung on my chest for eleven years, before I gave it to Spider Woman.

My mom slips the loop of brown suede with the pendant around my tiny neck. "This is to keep you safe," she says. "Whenever you wear this necklace, the ancestors can find you. Even when I'm gone, you will be protected."

The necklace is way too big for little me, so the pendant rests against the baby's tummy. I watch, wide-eyed, as the turquoise seems to glow bright blue, like a tiny, perfect star. My mom touches it with one finger and bows her head like she's saying a silent prayer.

Crack! Something breaks in the distance, making me flinch.

My mom looks up and peers into the dark and swirling snow. I can't see anything, but she does, and whatever it is isn't good. Fear tightens her mouth and narrows her eyes.

"So soon?" she murmurs.

She gets to her feet, gathering baby me up in the blankets and tucking me close to her chest inside her worn coat. She pulls her hat and gloves back on, wraps the scarf tight around her neck, and starts running through the snow, back the way she came.

Real me chases after her. The snowfall seems to have gotten even heavier while we were in her little shelter. I glide through the storm, because I'm not really there, but my mom stumbles as she tries to avoid ever-growing snowdrifts. I can see where she's headed now—a house not too far away. Warm golden light shines from the windows, driving back the darkness like the beacon from a lighthouse.

Another booming *crack* comes from the woods. Something is definitely out there. Something big and scary.

My mom speeds up, still holding little me tight. It seems like the snow is actively trying to drag her down. I can see ice forming around the tops of her boots, and I imagine that her feet are freezing. She trips and falls to her knees, but she's back up in seconds.

I feel a presence behind me, something shadowy that seems to grow. My mom must feel it, too, because she turns to look over her shoulder and lets out a soft cry. She reaches the front door of the house, and I accompany her as she barrels through, slamming it shut behind her. Not a second later, something hits the door from the outside. A spine-shaking *boom* rattles the house.

My mom slowly backs away, staring at the front door to see if it will hold or if whatever is out there will break it down.

"What is it?" I whisper, afraid, even though I know she won't answer.

There's another *boom*, and now little me stirs and lets out a scared whimper.

"Shhhh," my mom says, patting my head.

"Bethany?"

We both turn at the voice coming from down the hallway.

"Bethany, is that you? Is everything okay with Nizhoni? I woke up and the two of you were gone." Soft footsteps pad toward us. It's my dad, sounding a lot younger than he does now.

"Mac wouldn't sleep, either," he calls, yawning. "I thought I'd make him some warm milk. . . ."

My mom's gaze whips between the front door and the hallway, and it's clear that she's struggling. And then I see her face shut down, her expression go cold, and I know she has made her decision. She drops to her knees and lays little me gently on the floor. Gives me one last kiss on the forehead and murmurs something I can't quite hear. And then she's up on her feet. She shrugs off her coat and pulls something from a holster on her back. It's a bow, but not like the kind you see in old movies. This one has a complicated drawing mechanism and a place where you can slot arrows, and it has a black metal grip like a gun.

She readies an arrow and steps toward the door. Her hand hesitates on the knob, and she looks over her shoulder. My dad is still talking to her, something about Mac being colicky, but he hasn't turned the corner and can't see us yet. I focus on the spot where he will appear any second now.

Then my eyes flick back to my mom, but the front door is already closing behind her. I missed her leaving, and she is no longer part of this vision.

I hear a fierce cry outside, like a challenge, and the roar of a monster in response. There's a flash of light and a heavy *thump* that feels like it could take the house down. My dad doesn't even seem to notice. Can he not see the monsters? Does he not know that my mom is fighting for her life?

I want to scream in frustration, but I'm just a helpless, invisible observer.

"Bethany?" my dad says as he finally comes around the corner. "Honey?"

But he's too late.

Little me, still lying on the floor, starts to wail for the first time.

My dad peers down at the baby with a sleepy and confused expression. And then he looks up at the door, bewilderment on his face.

"No, no, no!" I murmur. "This can't be how it happened." I try to back away from my dad and Mac and little me, but the memory has me trapped.

"I want out of here," I say, my voice quiet at first, then getting louder, until I'm yelling. "Let me out! Let me out!" I don't know who or what I'm screaming at, but if the trials are aware enough to change depending on how we imagine them, then they should be able to stop this.

"This is too much. Let me out! Please!"

And suddenly I'm back in the field of mirrors, staring into the white-framed one, my hand pressed against the glass.

I gulp air, as if I've been holding my breath. I feel like sobbing.

"Nizhoni? Are you okay?" Somebody shakes me by the shoulder and I turn, blinking back tears.

"What happened?" Davery asks, voice concerned. "You disappeared for a minute. And then, when I turned around again, you were back."

"I was in there," I say, pointing at the glass, my hand

shaking a little. "I fell into the mirror, or a memory or some-thing. I saw my mom. The day she left."

"Wow, that's wild," Davery says with wide eyes. "What happened?"

"She left to fight a monster, Davery. She knew what she was doing, and she left."

"I'm sorry," he says quietly.

"Me too," I say, sniffling. "I can't believe she chose to fight the monster over staying with her family."

Davery's brow crinkles like it does when he's thinking hard. "Maybe she didn't have a choice. Maybe if she didn't kill the monster, it would have killed you and everybody else, too."

"But she *didn't* kill the monster!" I shout at him.

He takes a step back, surprised at my anger.

I'm surprised by how angry I feel, too, but I can't help it. It's like lava inside me, bubbling up from my stomach and rising to fill my head. The pressure of it makes me want to scream, to hit something. It's worse than when I got into a fight at school, worse than when I attacked Mr. Charles. And it comes out of my mouth as words I wish I never said.

"The monsters are still alive, which means my mom failed, and she's probably . . . she's probably dead! Or she might as well be dead! And now we have to fight the monsters all over again, so what good did she do, anyway?"

"She did her best."

"Maybe she did, maybe she didn't. All I know is that I didn't get to have a mom and IT'S ALL HER FAULT!" And the anger still boiling inside me, the part that didn't come out as words, now comes out as a kick. I strike the mirror with my heel as hard as I can. It cracks down the middle. I kick it again, slapping my whole foot into it. I want it to shatter. To look the way I feel inside. But no matter how many times I hit it, it won't break any further.

After a dozen kicks and a few screams of frustration, I'm tired. The anger has drained away. I slump to the ground, exhausted. "I hate this place," I say, my throat raw and my eyes wet. "I want these trials to be over. What else can it show me that's worse than this?"

Davery's been really patient, not saying a word while waiting for me to let out all my rage. I owe him a serious apology for throwing a tantrum, but it's not every day you see your mom leave you as a baby to fend for yourself. It hurts, and it feels like it won't stop hurting for a long time. Maybe ever.

"Promise me you'll go back to that anger management class when this is over?" he asks.

I sniffle, feeling embarrassed. "I promise."

"Good. Because I can't handle another freak-out like that."

"That's fair."

Davery holds out a hand to pull me to my feet. "Okay, then let's focus on getting through this trial and to the House of the Sun. We can deal with your feelings about your mom later."

The Sun. He's supposed to give me weapons so I can save my brother and my dad. I'd almost forgotten why we were doing all this.

"What did you see in your mirror?" I ask.

"Nothing like you did. I mean, I just saw me. It was a normal mirror."

I take a deep breath. "Well, we better try another. I'm sure this trial has something else to throw at us."

Davery points to a mirror a few dozen feet away. It's faceted around the edges, the sunlight bouncing off the diamond shapes and making it sparkle. "How 'bout that one?"

"Okay," I say, "but let's look at this one together. I don't want to do that alone again."

"Sure," Davery says. He grips my hand in his, and we both walk to the mirror. "Close your eyes, and then we'll open them at the same time."

"Okay." I close my eyes, squeeze his hand, and say, "On three. One, two . . ."

On "three," I take a look.

The reflection shows only me, and my hand is empty.

Davery is gone.

◆

THIRTY-FIVE

Worst-Case Scenario

"Davery?"

I whirl around wildly, but I don't see him anywhere. I'm alone.

I run from mirror to mirror, looking into and banging on the glass, praying one of them will let me back in. Not to the snowy past with my mom, but to wherever Davery went.

I can feel my breath getting short and my heart beating too loud in my ears as panic starts to creep in. First Mac, now Davery. I lost them both. I knew I wasn't cut out for this hero business!

Why me? I want to wail. Is this what I get for wanting to be someone special? Stuck in the middle of I-don't-even-know-where with all my friends and family gone?

I plop down onto the Rainbow Road and sob. Big, fat tears stream down my face and I can't stop them. I'm exhausted and starving and dirty, and I feel lonelier than I've ever been.

After a while, when all the tears are spent, I look up and see something amazing: A herd of deer is coming my way. No, scratch that—it's just one, a doe, reflected in many mirrors. She cautiously picks her way over, ears flapping. When she's a few feet from me, she stops and stares. She must wonder what kind of creature I am, hunched over and sniffling.

"Hello," I say quietly, not wanting to frighten her off. "Are you lost and alone, too?"

She doesn't move, just considers me curiously with her liquid brown eyes.

Then I get it. "Don't tell me. You're one of the Holy People, right?" Mr. Yazzie did say they were everywhere, and a talking deer is no weirder than a horned toad advisor.

But the doe doesn't answer.

"Well, go ahead. Impart your wisdom or whatever."

The deer turns her head and gazes at the horizon.

"You think I should keep going," I say, filling in the silence. I stand up and wipe off the back of my pants. "Well, you have a point. I've come this far and risked everything to get here. If not for myself, I should do it for Mac, and Davery, and my dad."

The deer paws the ground with one hoof.

"And yes, my mom. Maybe her most of all." I touch my chest automatically, wishing my turquoise necklace were there.

I look toward the mirror I cracked with my foot. Its surface looks black now. The boiling anger I felt toward my mom before has been replaced with a clawing sorrow. Leaving us wasn't something she'd done on a whim. She had to sacrifice everything to try to keep us safe. She was being self*less*, not selfish. And so strong . . .

She wanted me to be strong, too. She called me brave, a warrior, just before she went off to save the world.

"It's time to show her I *am* a warrior," I say, turning back to the deer.

The doe flicks her tail and bounds away.

"Thanks for your advice!" I call after her.

I'm not sure whether the deer was sent to help me or not, but either way, I feel better. I wipe the tears from my face and hoist my backpack onto my shoulders. "I'm going to do this, Mom," I declare. "And I'm going to make you proud."

Next stop: the House of the Sun.

◆

THIRTY-SIX

The House of the Sun

The Rainbow Road ends at the top of a hill. And on top of
that hill, spread out across the horizon, is a massive house. Well,
"house" doesn't quite do the place justice. This is a mansion.
Maybe a castle. Definitely the home of someone important.

The mansion/castle was built in a pueblo style, like a lot
of the houses in Albuquerque. Only this one isn't made out
of the adobe mud so popular back home. It was constructed
with chunks of turquoise. The blue-green surface glimmers
in the predawn light, the tiny veins in the rocks shining like
diamonds. The building is at least three stories, with tall
windows in the top level, and a long flat roof. As I walk up
the front path of finely crushed white shells, my footsteps
crunching, I hope the Sun, or whoever answers the door, is
expecting me.

To the side of the entrance is a bench carved out of a log,
and it is set off from the path by a red velvet rope—the kind
you see in movie theaters. Judging from the plastic water
bottles and foil sandwich wrappers piled in a nearby trash bin,
I'm guessing it's some kind of waiting area, and visitors have
used it recently.

Above the front door is a neon sign that says YÁ'ÁT'ÉÉH. PLEASE TAKE A NUMBER AND THE MERCILESS ONE WILL SEE YOU SHORTLY. FIRST COME, FIRST SERVED. Beside the velvet rope stands a round red ticket dispenser, and a piece of paper flutters at its mouth, the edges of a black digit showing. It seems a little strange to take a number, especially when I don't see anyone else around. But it seems just as strange to simply walk up and knock on the door.

Standing at either side of the door are two giant bear statues. They are very lifelike—black and shaggy, and at least ten feet tall, with muscled bodies and oversize paws tipped with sharp claws. As I get closer, I swear one of them is staring at me with its dark beady eyes.

And then it turns its head and roars, "Who goes there?"

I freeze in my tracks. The bear's fangs glisten, looking extra sharp under the entrance lights. "Be brave," I remind myself, and step forward.

"Yá'át'ééh," I say loudly to the sharp-toothed bear. I hope I'm doing this right. "My name is Nizhoni Begay. My mother's clan is Towering House. My father's clan is Bitter Water. My maternal grandfather's clan is the Mud People clan, and my paternal grandfather's clan is the Crystal Rock people." There. Perfect!

The other bear, who has a notch in its ear, turns his head to look at me. "Where's your number?"

"What?"

"You need a number."

"Oh." I reach over and pull a ticket from the dispenser.

Number 4444. I hold it up to the bear and he leans over to look.

"What business do you have with the Sun?" the bear demands.

"I'm here to ask for his help."

"Help?" The bear with the piece missing from one ear laughs, a big belly-shaking chortle. "Everyone comes to Jóhonaa'éí for help! What makes your case so special?"

"Jo who?"

"You don't even know his name? Jóhonaa'éí is his Navajo name."

"Oh, I'm sorry," I say, embarrassed. "I'm still learning. But I have come a long way and been though the four trials on the Rainbow Road, and I lost my brother and my best friend and my trainer, and if I don't see Jóhonaa'éí, I may lose my dad and maybe the whole world, so could you at least let him know I'm here?"

"No."

"Why not?" I ask, incredulous. "I asked nicely."

"And I said no nicely, so we're even."

I've been trying to control my anger, really trying, but I can feel it rising again at these very rude bears. "Tell Jóhonaa'éí that I faced some serious danger to get here, and the least he can do is see me! It says he will!" I point to the neon sign above us.

"He doesn't have to see anybody!" the bear counters. "Read the sign!" It points, and as we watch, the letters morph to spell out THE MERCILESS ONE DOESN'T HAVE TO SEE ANYBODY.

"You made it do that!"

"Did not! Well, maybe I did. But you can't prove it!"

"Are you kidding me?" I say, exasperated.

The words on the sign morph again, and now it reads TOTALLY NOT KIDDING.

I throw my hands up. I don't know what I was expecting when I got here, but this wasn't it.

"You can see him," the other bear, the one with the fangs, says. "But you'll have to wait."

"I don't really have a lot of time."

"Sorry, those are the rules."

"I don't care about your rules!" I shout, my frustration boiling over, just like it did in the sand trial. "I've done everything I was supposed to and now I want—no, I *demand* to see the Sun! This minute!" I hold up my ticket and very deliberately tear it in half. I let the pieces float to the ground. But then I feel a little guilty about littering and hastily pick them up and drop them into the nearby trash bin. I hurry back to the entrance, plant my hands on my hips, and say, "Now!"

The bears lean in to talk to one another, their murmuring voices a low grumble. I can't hear exactly what they're saying, but I catch the words "highly unusual" and "fierce cub girl" and "not really doing anything anyway" before they turn back to me.

"Very well," the bear with the notch says. "I'll ask if he can see you now."

"Ahéhee'," I say. "And tell him I can't wait long. Mr. Charles plans to release the monsters at sunrise."

Fangs turns to me. "Did you say monsters?"

"Yes. I'm here to ask for the weapon I need to fight them. Spider Woman sent me."

"Oh," the bear says, eyes wide, "why didn't you say so?" It hurries to push the door open. "Right this way! Hurry, hurry. Time is of the essence. We never keep a hero waiting! Your friend is already here. He arrived a while ago, just in time for supper. We've been expecting you!"

Expecting me? They sure didn't act like they were expecting me. But I'm more surprised by the other thing they said. "Did you say my friend was here?"

"Yes." It reaches around and pushes me through the door with a paw as big as my head. "He's in with Jóhonaa'éí right now."

My steps pick up and my heart races. Did Davery somehow get here before me? The bear rushes me down the halls of the great house. We're almost running now, and while I'm glad we're hurrying, I barely have time to look around. The inside of Jóhonaa'éí's house is what I would call bright, and by bright, I mean blinding. Every surface is a shining unblemished white, like my auntie's plastic-covered couch that we're not allowed to sit on. Pictures of the sun cover the walls—sunrises in the desert, the sun at high noon over a mountain range, sunsets on a beach. One is just a huge photo of the sun, big and glowing and centered in a solid gold frame.

"He sure must think a lot of himself," I murmur as we fast-walk down a long corridor.

"Well, he *is* a star," the bear explains. "People like to take his picture. And here we are."

We've reached a tall wooden door with a carving of a sun in it. Not surprising. The surprise comes when the bear pushes the door open and there, seated at a round table in the middle of the room, is a distinguished-looking Navajo man, and on the tabletop is someone I wasn't sure I'd ever see again.

"Mr. Yazzie!" I exclaim, a huge smile breaking across my face. "Is that really you?" His white turtleneck tells me it is.

The Navajo man turns toward me. He's wearing a traditional yellow velvet shirt over blue jeans, more Navajo jewelry than I've ever seen on one person, and a fancy silver-and-coral concho belt at his waist. His dark eyes burn with intensity and I stutter to a stop under that frightening gaze.

"Who are you," he demands, "who dares to enter the House of the Sun?"

I swallow, my mouth suddenly dry, and try to form words, but nothing comes out. I even start my deep breathing exercises, but I'm so nervous I can't get enough air in my lungs.

"Please," I manage to squeak. I've never met anybody famous before, but I imagine this is a thousand times more intimidating. It's much scarier than when I got sent to the principal's office for hitting Elora Huffstratter that time.

"Jóhonaa'éí," Mr. Yazzie says hurriedly, "this is my ward, the young one I was telling you about. She endured the trials of the Rainbow Road to get here."

Jóhonaa'éí glares at me. "Prove it."

"What?" I blurt.

He leans forward and beckons me closer. Somehow I get

my feet to move until I'm across the table from him. "If you completed the trials, prove it."

"How?"

"Tell us about each trial and what you learned, child," Mr. Yazzie says encouragingly. "Just a little, so Jóhonaa'éí can get to know you."

"And know that you are worthy to stand in my house," he adds with a deep rumble.

I clear my throat and, to calm my nerves, try to think of it like a book report I'm giving in front of the class. I can do this. No way Jóhonaa'éí is worse than the mean kids at ICCS, no matter how much he scowls at me.

"The first trial was the Talking Rocks. There were these moving rocks that tried to crush us, and—"

"Us?" Jóhonaa'éí asks. He spreads his hands. "And where are the others?"

I feel a lump in my throat. "I—I lost them. On the Rainbow Road."

"And yet you continued here alone?" he asks. He sounds like he doesn't believe me.

I nod, not sure I can trust my voice to work.

"Drink some water, child," Mr. Yazzie says gently, motioning to a glass on the table. I gulp it gratefully and then Jóhonaa'éí motions for me to continue.

"A monster at the Talking Rocks pretended to be Mr. Yazzie and—"

"Me? Really? How unusual." The lizard puffs up with pride until the Sun shoots him a glare.

"Yeah. He lured Mac— my brother—inside, and I ran after

him as fast as I could, but by the time I caught up, he'd been replaced by the shape-shifter."

"You ran into the closing rocks . . ." Jóhonaa'éí echoes. "And what did you do when you encountered the monster?"

"I fought it and it escaped, but the rocks closed before I could catch it and find out what happened to Mac." Despite my vow to be brave, I feel my chin begin to quiver. "I . . . failed. . . ."

"That is for Jóhonaa'éí to decide," says Mr. Yazzie.

The Sun leans back, thinking. But he delivers no verdict. Instead, he asks, "What about the second trial?"

I take a deep breath and continue. "That was the Field of Knives. Davery—he's my best friend—and I were getting cut up by these really sharp reeds, so I said we should cover ourselves with mud to protect our skin, and we made it through."

"You didn't consider turning back?" the Sun asks, that same skeptical tone in his voice.

"I knew we had to get through the trial, even if it did mean ruining my favorite jeans." I point to my cut-up pants and smile sheepishly. "I'm sorry I don't look more presentable."

Mr. Yazzie *tsk-tsk*s, as though he's a little embarrassed on my behalf.

But Jóhonaa'éí doesn't seem to care about my pants. After a minute, he says, "Tell me of the third trial."

"It was hard," I admit. "It was the Prom of Thorns, which turned out to be a real prom."

"A school dance," Mr. Yazzie explains.

"And everyone was so nice, and there were punch and cookies and a DJ, and a really cute boy asked me to dance.

241

I could have stayed there forever. But if I had, I would have forgotten my family, and I didn't want to do that. So I got us out."

The Sun crosses his arms. "You got out. . . ."

I don't confess that I did it by pulling a fire alarm, but by the suspicious way he's looking at me, it's like he's already guessed.

"And the fourth trial?"

I take another drink of water. "I went into a mirror and saw a vision of my mother," I say simply.

Now Jóhonaa'éí leans so close I can feel his heat against my skin. "And what did you learn from your vision, Nizhoni?"

"I learned I was wrong about my mom," I whisper. "I thought she left us because she just didn't want to have a family anymore, like maybe she was tired of raising me and my brother. But it turns out she loved us and she had a good reason for leaving."

"And what was that?"

"She left to fight her own monsters. She was a monster-slayer, too."

"Ahhh," Jóhonaa'éí says. "And is that what you are, then? A monsterslayer? Someone who is willing to face danger to save her family? Someone who thinks on her feet? Someone who never gives up?"

He waits expectantly for my answer. My first impulse is to deny it, but then I think about all the trials I went through, and how they each made me do something brave. . . .

"Yes," I say, standing up straight. "I am a monsterslayer, just like my mom."

His brown eyes pierce mine. "Then we must go about procuring you your weapons."

I beam with pride, relief flooding through my body.

Mr. Yazzie claps his claws together. "Now we're talking!"

◆

THIRTY-SEVEN

Sacrifices

I rush forward to give Mr. Yazzie a hug, which is kind of hard 'cause he's so small, but I manage.

"Oh goodness, child!" the horned toad says, fussing. "Gently, please. I'm not quite in the boat. . . . No, I'm not floating in the sea. . . . No, no that's not it. . . . Oh! I'm not quite shipshape! Yes, that's it!"

I giggle. This is definitely the real Mr. Yazzie.

"When did you get here?" I ask him. "*How* did you get here?"

"I took a shortcut."

"There's a shortcut?" I ask incredulously.

"Not for heroes," he adds hastily. "You needed to face the trials, to learn about yourself. I am old and have seen many a trainee through this adventure. I don't need to face any trial harder than getting out of bed in the morning."

"Speaking of heroes," I say, my voice catching in sadness, "you heard that I lost Mac and Davery."

"And yet you continued on the Rainbow Road."

"I didn't know what else to do. I knew everyone was counting on me to finish the trials and come here so I could fight Mr. Charles."

"I'm very proud of you," Mr. Yazzie says, his voice quiet and serious. "You made it to the House of the Sun, which is more than many monsterslayers-to-be have accomplished, so I think you did quite well."

"But what about my friends?"

Jóhonaa'éí, who has been listening, says callously, "Sacrifices must be made."

"All I've done is make sacrifices!" I shout at the Sun.

"Nizhoni," Mr. Yazzie whispers out of the side of his mouth. "The Merciless One, remember?"

"Listen to the horned toad," Jóhonaa'éí growls. "Don't anger me, child, when you still need my help. I can get quite heated."

"Sorry," I mumble, chastised. "But all these losses don't seem fair. . . ."

"Victory comes at a price," he says.

A phrase comes to me—*Who will pay the lost ones' price?* "That sounds like the song of wonder," I say, reaching for my backpack to take out the flyer. "From the cart lady."

"Cart lady?" Jóhonaa'éí asks.

"One of the Diyin Dine'é, to be sure," Mr. Yazzie explains. "In clever disguise."

"Likely Nilch'i," says the Sun. "He does like to help out, and his songs are sometimes obscure but always wise. What did it say?"

I read aloud. *"Blood and flesh will not suffice. A dream must be the sacrifice."*

"Well," Jóhonaa'éí says, rubbing a hand across his chin, "then you see the truth in my words."

"But do not fear, Nizhoni," Mr. Yazzie says quickly. "If your friends disappeared on the Rainbow Road, they weren't sacrificed. They are most likely just stuck in the Lost and Found."

Surely I didn't hear that right. "Did you say 'lost and found'?"

"People vanish from the Rainbow Road quite frequently," Jóhonaa'éí confirms. "Things, too. Ideas. Thoughts. I have my bear sentinels collect them all and keep them in the Lost and Found."

My heart speeds up. "Can we go there now?"

Jóhonaa'éí makes a sound like he's annoyed. "I must remind you that you only have until sunrise to stop the monsters. You should visit the weapons room and arm yourself first. Perhaps even get in some practice, so you aren't immediately slaughtered. It would be a shame for you to have come all this way only to die."

I blanch, but I'm not backing down. "Didn't you say one of my hero traits is caring about my family? Well, Mac is my brother and Davery is my best friend, who is just like family. So they come first."

The Sun frowns but doesn't argue.

"Can you at least tell me if they're okay? I mean, they aren't hurt, are they?"

He folds his arms like he's not going to tell me, then finally gives in. "If they are in the Lost and Found, they might be a bit uncomfortable," he acknowledges. "But otherwise they are fine for now."

"For now?"

"Yes." And he doesn't explain further.

I chew my lip, unsure. As much as I hate to admit it, the Sun has a point. I'm desperate to have Mac and Davery back, and Jóhonaa'éí knows where they are. On the other hand, maybe they *can* wait a little longer. What's the point of saving them now if doing so would mean the world is overrun with monsters?

I thought I'd be more excited to finally be able to pick out weapons. Without Mac and Davery here to share the experience, this hero business feels overrated. I know I have to be responsible, but it makes my stomach ache. Dad says there are always things we don't want to do, like clean our rooms or do math homework, but we have to do them anyway—that's part of growing up. This feels ten times worse, though, and I really wish I had someone with me to tell me what I should do.

"It's a heavy responsibility, being a monsterslayer," Mr. Yazzie says, his face sympathetic.

"Way heavier than I thought," I confess.

I turn to Jóhonaa'éí. "I'll get the weapons first," I say. "As long as you promise me that Davery and Mac are safe and I can go see them right after."

"As you wish," he says, looking more amused than angry. "You know," he adds, "most people don't dare argue with the Sun. Even though you annoy me, I am impressed."

"Thank you," I say with a sniff. Point for me.

"Follow me!" Mr. Yazzie says, hopping off the table to trundle down the hallway. "And behold the weapons of a true monsterslayer!"

THIRTY-EIGHT

◆

Made-to-Order Weapons

Jóhonaa'éí leads us down the corridor. Mr. Yazzie and I follow, the horned toad back in his favorite riding spot right inside my hoodie. Once again I'm struck by how many pictures of the sun cover the walls.

"Someone thinks he's the center of the universe, doesn't he?" I murmur.

"No," Jóhonaa'éí says, looking over his shoulder at me. "Just the solar system." He smirks.

I flush. "They're very nice," I add quickly. Gotta say he's not my favorite Diyin Dine'é.

"Here we are," he says, stopping in front of a huge wooden door. It's tall enough to allow in those bear sentinels while standing on each other's shoulders. A pair of lightning bolts is carved into the center, adding to its intimidating look.

I'm starting to get that feeling again—that I'm in over my head. But all of a sudden, I remember what Łizhin told me: *Don't worry about what you're supposed to be. Just be who you are.* I can almost hear her voice saying it, and it reassures me.

Jóhonaa'éí pushes and the door swings open. The three of us enter.

Once, Dad took us to this museum that had an ancient

weapons room. The gallery was filled with ten-foot-long spears pinned to the walls and arrowheads and knives under glass cases. I guess I was expecting something like that. Boy, was I wrong.

Entering the weapons room is like stepping into a roiling ball of electricity. Light and fire seem to flash all around me, and my instinct is to cover my head and get out of the way. Lightning shoots out in a jagged line, headed straight for Mr. Yazzie.

"Duck!" I yell, reaching for my horned toad friend. But I shouldn't have worried. The lightning strike stops short by at least a yard, and I realize the fiery mass is somehow staying in the center of the room, as if surrounded by an invisible shield.

"You are quite safe," Jóhonaa'éí says from behind me. "The lightning is contained and will not harm you."

The lightning continues to flash and flare, close enough to reach out and touch. I sure hope Jóhonaa'éí's right, or we're going to end up very crispy.

"What do you think?" Jóhonaa'éí asks.

"Very impressive," I say, "but I thought there would be weapons."

He sweeps a hand across the room. "Is this not a weapon?"

I remember what the buzzard bozos said about a true monsterslayer wielding a lightning sword, so I shouldn't be surprised. I mean, I knew there would be lightning. But I guess I wasn't thinking of it as *actual* lightning, more like metaphorical lightning. "It definitely is. I was just expecting . . ."

"A gun?" He sounds disappointed.

"No," I say hastily. "Something more old-timey. Maybe a

knife, some swords, a bow and arrow in the shape of lightning? Does that even make sense?"

He smiles warmly now, for the first time since I got here. "I control lightning, and from it I can forge any weapon of your choosing. Tell me what you and your friends require and I will shape them for you."

Awesome! "Anything I want? Anything Mac and Davery want, too?" My mind reels.

And then it crashes back to earth, because what are we going to do with a bunch of deadly weapons? Davery spends most of his time reading, and while I have definitely improved over my gym humiliation days, what with the superfast running and the night vision, I'm not sure either of those things are going to help me wield a weapon. Mac is the only one who seems to have a direct attack power, but unless Jóhonaa'éí can turn the lightning into a water sprinkler, there's nothing here for him, either.

"Go on, Nizhoni," Mr. Yazzie says encouragingly. "Tell him what you need."

"Well . . ." I hesitate, worried I'm going to blow this. "Do they have to be, like, weapons weapons?"

"What do you mean?" Jóhonaa'éí asks.

"It's just . . . Davery's never needed anything more than internet access or a book. His ancestral power seems to be extra smartness or something. So maybe he could just use a . . . lightning book?"

Mr. Yazzie groans and smacks his forehead with a tiny claw, but Jóhonaa'éí looks thoughtful. "A weapon of knowledge . . ."

he says. "I like it. For what is knowledge but a weapon against ignorance?"

Jóhonaa'éí steps forward. He rolls up his sleeves and reaches into the center of the room. Lightning flashes and crackles around us, like we're inside one of those plasma balls at the science museum. Thunder booms in the distance as the room fills with light. It's so bright I have to shield my eyes and turn away. The flare fades, and when I look back, Jóhonaa'éí is holding something in his hands.

A book about the size of a regular novel but not very thick. On its gold cover are two lightning bolts, just like on the door to the weapons room.

"What does it do?" I ask.

"It contains the secrets to defeating your enemies," says Jóhonaa'éí. "When the right person reads from it, it shall tell them everything they need to know to beat the monsters."

"Not to be rude, but if the Holy People already know how to defeat the monsters, why don't they do it themselves?"

"HOW DARE YOU?" Jóhonaa'éí erupts, his voice echoing through the chamber.

"It's just a question," I insist, ignoring his bluster.

"The monsters threaten humans," Mr. Yazzie explains. "They don't bother the Holy People. While they may provide some assistance, it's up to the humans to fight their own battles."

Jóhonaa'éí nods, his face still dark.

"Okay, okay, I get it now," I murmur. "Sorry I offended you."

In a sign that he accepts my apology, he hands me the golden book, and I slide it into my backpack.

"A book of lightning is all well and good, but shouldn't our heroes also have something sharp and pointy?" Mr. Yazzie asks the Sun. "Not that I don't trust your judgment," he adds hastily. "It's just . . . it's never been done quite like this."

"Each monsterslayer will have the weapon most appropriate for them," Jóhonaa'éí chides. "You know this." He looks back to me. "Though forged in the fire, each weapon is simply a part of the bearer, made solid in the Glittering World. Now, for your brother?"

"Well, his ancestral powers have something to do with water."

"Ah, yes, he is related to Born for Water. I remember now. I have just the thing." Jóhonaa'éí reaches back into the tumult of white fire, and again I have to shut my eyes at the flare of bright light. When I open them, Jóhonaa'éí has a small bottle in his hand. It's attached to a loop of leather cord, just like the one my piece of turquoise used to hang from.

"What is it?"

"Liquid lightning," he explains. "For the boy who can control things in a fluid state. But he must be careful. It is very unstable and can only be used once."

"Whoa! He's gonna love this!"

He hands Mac's weapon to me, and I carefully put it in the padded pocket of my backpack.

Mr. Yazzie makes an unhappy noise behind me.

"What's wrong?" I ask.

"I don't mean to complain, but how can I be a weapons

252

master if I don't even recognize the weapon?" he huffs. "Books? Liquid lightning? Bah! Maybe I'm getting too old for this after all."

"We all must change with the times," Jóhonaa'éí says, not unkindly. "These children are different from their ancestors. Just as the trials changed to fit Nizhoni's imagination, so must the weapons adapt. The ways of the Diné are not static but alive and ever-changing."

Mr. Yazzie sighs, but it's a satisfied sound, like he understands.

The Sun regards me with expectant eyes. "And for you, Nizhoni?"

"I took an archery class at summer camp once," I say in a rush, remembering the weight of the bow, the feeling of the taut string close to my cheek, the whip of the arrow as I loosed it at the target. "And I was good at it." I hit a bull's-eye that day. My instructor called it beginner's luck, and maybe it was, or maybe I was a natural and the teacher didn't recognize it. I believed her because she was an adult and I thought she knew better, but now I'm not so sure.

"And there's something else," I add. "When I saw my mom in the vision, she had a crossbow. So I'd like to try a bow and arrow."

Jóhonaa'éí studies me for a moment before nodding. "I think a more traditional weapon would suit you well. 'A pointy one,' as your weapons master called it. Yes, it should suit very well indeed." He does the whole hand-in-the-fire/ blazing-light thing again, and this time he pulls out a glowing bow and a quiver full of arrows.

"Well, thank goodness," Mr. Yazzie says. "Finally, a weapon I know."

The bow and arrows are beautiful, made of a fine golden wood that seems to pulse with shadow and flame. The bow is just my size, not too big, and there are four perfectly formed arrows in the long thin quiver, which has a strap for wearing on your back. He hands them to me.

"Carry these proudly, Monsterslayer. You have earned them."

A feeling of deep satisfaction fills me, as if the fire from the lightning forge is flowing through my veins. But it's more than just the weapons. It's knowing for a fact that this is my destiny.

"They're beautiful," I whisper. "Thank you. Ahéhee'."

I sling my backpack onto one shoulder and pull the quiver over the other. Not a perfect solution, but it will have to do.

"And now we must go," Mr. Yazzie says. "Before we lose any more time."

"You two go ahead," Jóhonaa'éí says. "There is one more weapon I must forge before sunrise. I will join you when I am done."

I want to ask who the other weapon is for, but Mr. Yazzie is already pushing at my ankles, trying to hurry me out of the room.

I pull the big wooden door open, and Mr. Yazzie and I spill back out into the hallway.

"Can we get Mac and Davery from the Lost and Found now?" I ask. I can't wait to show them the weapons Jóhonaa'éí made especially for us.

"I suppose so, if we don't dally," Mr. Yazzie says. "Hmm, which is the door to the Lost and Found department again . . . ?"

I groan at his forgetfulness as we rush down the hall, past a row of similar doors, each marked with a different symbol. A geometric basket on a red, white, and black door . . . a sand-painting figure in browns and tans on a door that looks like solid turquoise . . . But nothing that says LOST AND FOUND.

When we are almost at the end of the hallway, I ask, "Did we miss it?"

"No. I'm sure it's here somewhere. . . ."

The last door on the right is bigger than the rest, with a drawing of a sheep on it. It looks just like the sheep Davery made for Ancestor Club, except sadder. Like maybe the little guy got separated from his flock. Like maybe he's . . . *lost!*

"This is it!" I push on the door, flinging it wide open.

But I don't see Mac and Davery.

Instead, I see her.

My mom.

THIRTY-NINE

♦

Lost and Found

"Nizhoni, wait!" Mr. Yazzie calls.

But I'm not listening, and definitely not waiting.

My throat is suddenly dry, and my legs are shaking, but I make myself go through the Lost and Found door. Standing all around the room are strange glasslike cases, transparent but solid, and more amber-colored than clear. And inside the cases, frozen in place, are people. People like my mom.

I walk over to her case and peer at it closely. It's definitely her. She looks the same as she did in my mirror vision. The punk rock hair, the leather jacket, the motorcycle boots. The sad eyes.

"What's she doing here, Mr. Yazzie?" I ask, my voice quiet. I press one hand against the side of the amber and reach for my turquoise with the other. But, of course, my pendant is no longer there.

"Oh dear," he says. "I didn't know she would be in the Lost and Found, but now that I think about it, it does make sense." He lets out a heavy sigh. "If I could, I would spare you this sorrow, child."

"Why?" I stare down at him, incredulous. "Were you trying to hide my mother from me?"

"She failed, Nizhoni. She is here because she failed to kill the monsters of her generation, and with her failure, the threat grew stronger, the evil bigger. She is not a role model for you now. In fact, she's a distraction we can't afford."

"She's not 'a distraction.' She's my mom! Whose side are you on?"

Mr. Yazzie crawls up my leg and torso, settling on my arm so he can look me in the eye. "I am on the side of the monster-slayers, as always. It's my job to help you save the world."

"Even if that means losing my friends?" I turn back to my mom. "My family?"

"Your mother did not succeed," he says again. "You need to move on. Our hopes are riding on you now."

"Maybe it wasn't her fault," I argue. "She must have followed the same path we did, but she didn't have any companions to help her. She had to fight the monsters all alone. . . ."

"Your mother was one of my most promising students, but she could not pass the trial of the sand."

My eyes widen. "The mirrors? The trial of the sand manifested as mirrors for me. Is that why I saw her there? She's stuck there?"

"In a way," he says. "Her body is here, in the Lost and Found. But her consciousness, her soul, is still in the trial. That must be what you saw—the moment of her life that haunts her the most. It seems she could not let you go after all."

I shiver. "Is that what happens when you fail a trial? Is that what would have happened to me?"

He nods gravely.

"But wait—you left her there?"

"It is not in my power to free her."

"Then how do we get her out?" I spin around, and Mr. Yazzie clings to my sleeve for dear life. There are other slayers here, too—all Navajo, but clearly from different eras in time. A man to my right is wearing blue jeans with the cuffs rolled up and a plain white T-shirt. His hair is slicked back, and he looks like someone out of a movie from the 1950s, like Elvis. Another wears a three-piece suit, a fancy bowler hat, and carries a cane. A woman in velvet skirts and a huge squash blossom necklace is in a case farther back in the room. And just beyond her, I see someone I know.

"Mac!" I rush to the case he is in. He appears to be sleeping, which is less creepy-looking than some of the other slayers, who are frozen in mid-action. I put a hand on the glass. "We have to save him." I look around wildly. "Is Davery here, too?" There he is, just a few cases down. He's sitting cross-legged, hunched over a book, but completely still. "I have to get him out," I cry. "I have to get them *all* out!"

Mr. Yazzie's face scrunches up, and I get the feeling he's about to say something really bad. "You know the song, Nizhoni," he says sadly. "What does it tell you?"

"*Who will pay the lost ones' price?* These are the lost ones, aren't they?"

"Yes."

"And I'm guessing the price to pay is not spare change in my pocket."

"What are the next lines?" he prompts.

I know them by heart. *"Blood and flesh will not suffice. A dream must be the sacrifice."*

Mr. Yazzie nods.

"A dream . . ." I say. "Something stronger than blood and flesh, whatever that means."

"Think about it," Mr. Yazzie urges. "Dreams are our hopes for the future, and as such they are more powerful than anything in the physical world."

"But how do I get a dream to free them?"

"You already have it. What is your heart's true desire?"

I gulp, thinking furiously. I want so many different things. But surely—

"It is up to you, Nizhoni," comes a voice from behind me. I whirl to see Jóhonaa'éí standing in the doorway. He's been listening to our conversation. Mr. Yazzie leaves his perch on my arm and makes the long trek up to the Sun's shoulder.

"Me?" I ask, not liking this at all.

"Yes," he says resolutely. "You are the monsterslayer of this generation. It is you who must make the sacrifice."

I clutch my stomach, suddenly feeling sick. My mouth tastes sour, like I just drank old milk, as it fully hits me what he and Mr. Yazzie are saying. If I want Mom, Mac, and Davery back, I have to give up my dream of being a hero. Even though I completed the trials and worked so hard to get here, I must step aside and let someone else finish the battle.

I think about the silly dreams I used to have, too embarrassed to say them out loud. It seems like a lifetime ago that the thing I craved most was internet fame. Then I wanted to be good at sports so the kids at ICCS would respect me. It had felt so great at the Prom of Thorns when I was popular. But now that I've discovered my ancestral powers and I have my lightning weapons, I could be a real hero in the old-fashioned sense, like something out of a storybook. Like the original Monsterslayer.

I look over my shoulder at Mac, and next to him, Davery, frozen in amber. Their lives have barely begun. I can't leave them stuck in there forever.

Then my eyes turn to my mother and I recall the vision, the sacrifice she made to keep us safe, even though there was no guarantee of success. And my dad's confused face when she left . . . If I miss having her in my life, I can't imagine how devastated he must feel.

So maybe it isn't much of a choice after all.

"I'll do it," I say firmly, trying my best to be brave. "I'll give up my dream of being a hero to set them free. All of them. It's worth it. Then they can fight the monsters." I square my shoulders, ball my hands into fists, squeeze my eyes shut, and yell, "Take it! Take my dream!"

I hold my breath, waiting. When nothing happens, I crack an eyelid open. Mr. Yazzie is staring at me, and the Sun is trying not to laugh.

"What?"

"That's not how it works," Jóhonaa'éí says.

I relax, feeling a little silly. "Well, then why didn't you say so?"

"I would have, if I'd known you were going to do something so dramatic."

Okay, so it was a little dramatic. "Then how *does* it work?"

Mr. Yazzie looks at Jóhonaa'éí. "Actually, I'm actually not quite certain about the application of—"

Before he can finish his sentence, the ground begins to shake—a low rattle at first, but then it grows to a great rumble. The amber cases totter on their platforms.

Aha! It *did* work!

"Move back!" Mr. Yazzie yells, and I plaster myself against a trembling wall. I watch in awe as cracks form in the cases, and with a shriek, they all shatter.

I duck as shards fly around me. And when I look up, Mac is standing on a platform, yawning and stretching his arms over his head.

"Mac!" I dash over, pull him down, and give him a big hug.

"Ow!" he grumbles, pushing me away. "Don't mess up the hair."

I laugh, because he's still the same old Mac. I missed him so much. And to think, in the trial of thorns, I almost forgot he existed!

"Where am I?" he asks, looking around. "Last thing I remember, I was running through some kind of maze, but it was too dark to see and I got all confused. I must have walked around forever, yelling for you and Davery, but nobody answered. After a while, I got so tired I lay down for a quick snooze and—"

"Nizhoni?" says another voice behind me.

"Davery!" I run to my best friend and hug him, too. And this time it's not awkward at all.

"What happened?" he asks, brushing amber dust from his

261

hair. "How did we get here? Is this the House of the Sun? How did we get through the mirrors?"

"You didn't," I tell him. "You went into one of them and never came back. I had to keep going, hoping I could find help."

"It was like I was stuck in a vision," he says. "I was in the biggest library I'd ever seen, and I kept looking for the answer to how to beat Mr. Charles, but there were so many books. . . . I could hear you and Mac somewhere, crying for me, but I couldn't help, because I couldn't find the right book." He shivers. "It was not a good feeling."

Trust Davery to do research even in his nightmares.

"Speaking of books, I have something for you." I reach into my backpack and take out the monster-fighting manual. It shines and shimmers like it holds something alive and powerful in its pages.

"Whoa!" As he takes it, the light reflects off his glasses. "What is it?"

"It's a weapon of knowledge from the Sun." I motion toward Jóhonaa'éí. He is helping other freed warriors step down off their platforms while Mr. Yazzie, still on his shoulder, hails each one.

"Is that him?" Davery asks.

"Yep."

Jóhonaa'éí spies us with the lightning book and strides over. Mr. Yazzie raises a tiny claw in greeting. "Ah, our scholar has returned. Welcome, Davery."

"Good," the Sun says to me. "You are distributing the weapons. We have no time to waste." Then he turns to

262

Davery. "If you open this book in your time of need, it will tell you how to defeat the monsters."

"This must have been what I was searching for in my dream," Davery whispers, awed. "Thank you. I mean, ahéhee'."

"And this is for you, Mac," I say, dangling the vial attached to the leather cord. The liquid inside looks like quicksilver, thick and viscous and hinting at the colors of the rainbow. "You have to be really careful with it."

"Sweet!" Mac exclaims, taking it gingerly. "Uh, what is it?"

"Lightning in a bottle," Jóhonaa'éí explains. "You, related to Born for Water, should be able to direct it just as you direct the waters of the earth. But do not use it lightly. There is only this vial and then it is gone."

Mac pumps his fist in the air. "Eat your heart out, X-Men!" he shouts as he slips the cord over his neck.

"Did you get a weapon, Nizhoni?" Davery asks.

I slip the bow off my shoulder, nock an arrow, and point it toward the ceiling.

"Can you shoot that?" he asks.

"She better," Mac says. "Because we've got monster butt to kick!"

Jóhonaa'éí raises his eyebrows, but he's soon distracted by an older warrior who is having trouble getting to his feet. He leaves us to help him up.

This would probably be a good time for me to let Mac and Davery know I won't be fighting alongside them. "Uh, guys, there's something I need to tell you—"

"Umm . . . who's the lady in the leather jacket?" Mac asks. "And why is she staring at us and crying?"

FORTY

◆

One Step at a Time

A lump in my throat makes it hard for me to swallow.
"That," I tell my little brother, "is our mom."

"Whoa," says Davery.

"It can't be. She's dead," Mac says flatly. "And definitely not someone who would wear a leather jacket and motorcycle boots."

"No, she's not dead. She got stuck in a trial, just like you did. And she couldn't come back to us until now."

"Is that really . . . ?" he starts, his voice a shaky whisper.

I don't have to answer, because she's walking over. Davery slips away to give us some private time.

"Nizhoni's right. That's what happened, Marcus," my mom says, standing awkwardly a few feet away. "I'm so, so sorry. For leaving you, for failing you. For putting you both in danger now. This wasn't how it was supposed to . . ." She puts a hand over her mouth, and tears run down her face.

"You did what you thought was best," I say quietly. I sound grown-up, but inside I feel like a confused and hurt little girl. Even though I know why my mom did what she did, a selfish part of me still wishes she hadn't.

"Who cares why you left," Mac says. "You're back now!"

He rushes forward and our mom opens her arms. Mac falls into her embrace, giving her a huge hug. I can hear him sniffling a little. She looks up at me, trails of black mascara scoring her cheeks. She opens her arms a little more, clearly inviting me into the big old group-hug reunion, but I cross my arms and give her a weak smile. Mac may be ready to forgive and forget, but I'm not quite there yet.

"Would you like to meet more relatives?" Jóhonaa'éí asks, coming up beside us. He gestures to the other slayers who've been freed from their amber prisons.

I look around, eyes wide. There are at least a dozen people stumbling around, gazing at each other in wonder. Navajo and English words fill the room as people talk rapidly, asking questions. One man sits on the floor, sobbing quietly. It must be pretty shocking to wake up here, especially for the older ones.

"These people were all monsterslayers?" I ask.

"Yes, child," says Mr. Yazzie from his perch on the Sun's shoulder. "That's your great-great-great auntie." He gestures toward the woman in the velvet skirts. "And that's . . ." He points to the man in the bowler hat. "Oh dear, it's been so long, I can't quite remember. Well," he says brightly, "let's just say he's one of your distant ancestors."

"And this is your great-uncle," Mom says, disentangling herself from Mac. She beckons to the man who looks like a Navajo Elvis. "Yá'át'ééh, análí."

"Bethany?" he says in a soft Navajo accent. "Is that you?"

They hug, too, and there are more tears. But all I can think is: Half my ancestors ended up leaving their kids to fight monsters. That doesn't seem like the greatest sort of lineage to have. I mean, fighting monsters sounded cool when Mr. Yazzie first told us about it, but now that I see how many people in my family went missing because of it, I'm not so convinced. Or maybe my family is just not very good at it.

"What are you thinking, Nizhoni?" Mr. Yazzie asks. "You look upset. Wasn't this what you wanted?"

"It is," I admit with a heavy sigh. "But it seems unfair that so many of my relatives had to bear the burden of fighting the monsters. Why not somebody else's family?"

"A good question, Nizhoni," Jóhonaa'éí says. "The Diné have always been warriors, have always fought against the monsters who would seek to destroy us and our way of life. But the monsters are many, and warriors like the ones in your family are fewer than they were before."

"We don't always win," Mr. Yazzie says, "but we always, always try our best."

"I guess I just wish that sometimes they would have loved their kids a little more and fought monsters a little less. Is that selfish?"

Mom turns to look at me and I flush, embarrassed. Everyone gets really quiet, and I can feel their disapproving stares. My heart is beating super fast, and I know I definitely shouldn't have said that. But it's true, isn't it?

"Oh, Nizhoni." Mom comes to stand in front of me and tentatively places her hands on my shoulders—shoulders she hasn't touched in more than a decade. Part of me wants to shake them off, and part of me wants her to hug me like she did Mac. "Don't you see? I tried to save you from all this. I thought that if I could kill the monsters, you wouldn't have to. You would be free to grow up and become whoever you wanted to be."

"But all I ever wanted was you." Now I'm the one who's crying.

My mom tries to embrace me, but I wrap my arms around my chest. She steps back. "I'm sorry about the way things worked out."

"And what if 'sorry' isn't good enough?"

"Chill pill, Nizhoni," Mac mutters.

I'm not sure why I'm acting this way. I should be happy my mom is back. What's wrong with me?

"Words probably seem pretty empty to you," Mom says gently. "How about I work on earning your forgiveness, hmm?"

I blink. I didn't see that coming. "So, like, actions speak louder than words?"

She nods. "One step at a time?" She looks around the room. "For Nizhoni's sake."

Everyone murmurs their agreement, and I feel that awful hot anger inside me dissipating a little. "Thank you," I say, and then remember my Navajo. "Ahéhee'."

Davery rejoins us, sensing that I've cooled off. After being my friend for so many years, he's an expert at reading my feelings.

Jóhonaa'éí clears his throat. We all turn to him. "I have something for you, Bethany Begay. Something you're missing."

"My crossbow?" Mom asks, breathless.

"No, something else." He pulls a sword from behind his back. It's at least three feet long, and I swear it makes a low rumbling sound like distant thunder.

Mom holds it up, letting it catch the light. It shimmers with the power of a storm.

"I—I'm not sure I deserve this," Mom murmurs.

"I wasn't sure myself, when I fashioned the weapon a few minutes ago," the Sun admits. "But I have decided to give you a second chance. Your children braved many dangers to get here, your husband's life is at risk, and your aid will be needed to defeat the monsters. This is my gift to you."

"Ahéhee', Jóhonaa'éí. It is a powerful weapon."

"It's forged from lightning and not steel," says the Sun. "It will strike true." He can't disguise his pride of craftsmanship.

"Excellent," says Mr. Yazzie. "Now we can—"

We hear a great flapping sound outside, like a hundred giant birds flying by at once. It fills the air, and Mac throws his hands over his ears.

"What is that?" Jóhonaa'éí asks, alarmed.

He may not recognize the sound, but I would know it anywhere. "It's Łizhin, the herald of Dibé Nitsaa. Come on!"

Grasping my bow tightly, I run out of the Lost and Found and head for the main gates of the House of the Sun. I can hear everyone following me. I stop on the front stairs outside, and the bird herald lands in the courtyard, Black Jet Girl on her back. One of the bear guards shouts in dismay as the velvet rope is knocked over and crushed under Łizhin's massive claws, but Jóhonaa'éí says, "Leave it. I never liked the VIP section much anyway. Too Hollywood."

Łizhin settles her massive black wings, and Black Jet Girl waves at us frantically.

"What is it?" I ask her. "Why are you here?"

"Why is *everybody* here?" Davery asks, looking up at the sky.

The other great heralds of the four mountains circle above us. I recognize the great bluebird, Dólii, of Tsoodził, the Blue Mountain. Flying next to him is Tsídii, the yellow warbler and herald of Dook'o'oosłiid. I don't know the great grayish-white bird beside them, but it must be from Sisnaajiní. And on each bird's back, I can just make out the form of its guardian—Blue Turquoise Boy, Yellow Corn Girl, and Rock Crystal Boy.

"Nizhoni," Black Jet Girl cries in a strained voice, "what are you still doing here? Why are you not at the mesa with Jóhonaa'éí's weapons of lightning? The sun has risen on the fourth day."

Sure enough, the sky has begun to lighten noticeably, and we watch as, one by one, the lamps in the courtyard flicker off.

"We found the missing monsterslayers," I explain. "Including my mom. They are ready to fight Mr. Charles!"

"It's too late now," Black Jet Girl says, her voice anguished. "The sun is up, and all the monsters are already free!"

◆

FORTY-ONE

Rise

"That can't be right!" I protest. "There's no sunrise without Jóhonaa'éí, and he's right here." I turn to point out the Sun, but he's gone.

"Look!" Davery shouts. And there, just on the edge of the horizon, where the sky is getting lighter by the second, we can see Jóhonaa'éí. Before, he was dressed sort of Navajo casual with an extra helping of fancy jewelry. Now he's wearing blindingly bright armor and carrying a golden shield. And step-by-step on an invisible set of stairs, he appears to be climbing into the sky.

Mr. Yazzie appears at our feet. "Always a stunning sight," he says.

"The Sun could have at least warned us he was leaving," Mac says, picking up the lizard and putting him on his shoulder. "Holy People. They're always coming and going as they please without even a BRB."

"What other Holy People have you met?" I ask.

"You don't have to meet them all to know a type, amirite?" Mr. Yazzie tsk-tsks.

"What do we do now?" Davery asks.

As if in answer, a wild wailing breaks across the land. At

first I think it's the wind, but it quickly becomes clear that it's something much more ominous. It sounds like the horrible ghostly moaning from the Talking Rocks trial, and it makes my blood run cold. Mac throws his hands over his ears again, and Mom lifts her head like she's sniffing the air.

"Monsters!" Black Jet Girl cries. "They're breaking from their ancient cages as we speak! Hurry! We must stop them!"

Mom steps forward. "Where are they gathering?"

"In the shadow of Tsé Bit'a'í, the great rock with wings."

"Shiprock," Mom says grimly.

"It was the throat of a volcano long ago," Mr. Yazzie tells us, "and it's the legendary home of the bináá' yee agháni."

"Why are they after us?" asks Mac, his face pale.

"The very first monsterslayer, your ancestor Nayéé Neizghani, fought and defeated them, turning some into harmless creatures that could help the Diné, and imprisoning the rest," explains Mr. Yazzie. "Over the years, some have broken free and sought revenge."

"They have tried many times, and they've always been held back," says Mom. "This time we have to beat them once and for all."

"How do we get to Shiprock?" Davery asks.

"On our backs," Łizhin says. "I can take, you, Nizhoni."

"I'll ride Tsídii again," Davery offers. "Mac, can you hop on Dólii?"

"And I'll ride with the Rock Crystal Boy, if his herald will have me," Mom says.

"It would be my honor, Monsterslayer," the white bird says in an ancient windy voice. "You may call me Łigai."

271

"I will lead the rest of the slayers across the land," my great-uncle, Navajo Elvis, says. "It is not so far if we take the Rainbow Road, and we have not forgotten how to fight!"

Everyone hurries to climb on their heralds' backs. Everyone but me.

"What are you waiting for, Nizhoni?" Davery asks as he secures himself with the rope harness on Tsídii's back. All the heralds are sporting combat gear now.

"I'm not going," I say mournfully. "I wanted to tell you sooner, but I didn't get the chance."

"What are you talking about?" That's Mac, already up on Dólii.

"Remember the cart lady's song? The line where a dream must be the sacrifice? I had to give up my dream of being a hero in order to free you all from the Lost and Found. That means I can't go fight the monsters. I'll be cheering for you all from the sidelines, but now you're the monsterslayers."

"Oh dear, Nizhoni," Mr. Yazzie says, peeking out from the collar of Mac's hoodie. "I believe you've misunderstood. You're still fighting the monsters."

I look up. "I am?"

"Of course. You are a descendant of Monsterslayer. You passed the trials. We need you."

"But what about giving up my dream?"

"It's enough that you were willing to make the sacrifice," the horned toad explains. "You had to believe you were giving up that which mattered most. True intent was enough to break the amber cases. But things are much too dire for you not to fight!"

I grin. "So I'm in?"

"Most assuredly!"

I yelp with joy and run to Łizhin. I climb onto her back with a quick hug for Black Jet Girl, adjust my bow and quiver, and tie the rope harness around my waist.

"Have your arrows ready, Nizhoni," the guardian warns me. "The bináá' yee agháni in my house on Black Mountain were but children of the red-eyed birds, blind and foolish. The newly freed ones will be adults, and they will be able to see . . . and fly."

Fly? And it hits me all at once—we're actually going to be fighting monsters that want to kill us.

"We don't know how many or what other kinds of monsters your Mr. Charles will raise, but your ancestors will fight the ones on the ground and we will handle whatever comes at us through the air."

"Are you ready, Nizhoni?" Black Jet Girl asks, sounding grim.

"Never more ready!"

Łizhin smiles over her shoulder. "Then let's go be heroes!" she shouts as she launches into the sky. Behind us, the other heralds rise and follow us to war.

◆

FORTY-TWO

Sky Wars

Łizhin leads us over the Chuska Mountains, great sheer peaks that run north and south down the spine of the Navajo Nation. The rest of the heralds fly with us in tight formation, yellow on our right and white on our left, with blue bringing up the rear.

The wind whips around me, blowing my hair away from my face and burning my cheeks. There, in the distance, is Tsé Bit'a'í. It's a huge mountain, standing all alone in the desert. I wouldn't even call it a mountain. More like a big rock boat stranded in the middle of nowhere. We fly right for it.

"Look!" Łizhin shouts. "There, at the ledge."

Dozens of buzzards stream out of the mouth of a cave near the top of the mountain. These birds are much bigger and scarier than the ones at Dibé Nitsaa. Their wingspan is the length of a school bus, and their glowing red eyes are visible even from here. They must see us, too, because an awful shriek goes up, and they immediately bank to make a beeline for us.

"Remember, only a monsterslayer can look into their eyes," Black Jet Girl reminds me. "Their gaze freezes everyone else. We're relying on you."

"Got it!" I say, hoping Davery and Mac are warned in time.

"Scatter!" Black Jet Girl shouts to the guardians, and Łizhin echoes the sentiment with a piercing call.

The other heralds spread out, banking left and right, respectively. Dólii drops below us. I peer down and see Davery behind Yellow Corn Girl on Tsídii's back. He's holding his lightning book and frantically turning the pages as he looks up how to defeat the monsters.

Davery gazes up, as if he senses me watching. "I can't find anything yet," he says, "but if I had to guess, I'd say aim for the eyes so they can't use their freeze powers. And then the heralds should go for the heart!"

All the heralds answer with battle cries.

"Eyes, then heart," I mutter. Easy enough. If I weren't a hundred feet in the air on the back of a giant bird.

"Are you ready?" Black Jet Girl asks me.

"Sure. Who doesn't like a challenge?"

Łizhin suddenly rears, and I try to grab hold of Black Jet Girl's slick surface to keep from falling. The Black Mountain herald lets loose a skin-tingling scream and thrusts her claws forward just as a huge bináá' yee agháni comes at us, its moldy beak open wide.

"Nizhoni, your arrows! Now!" Black Jet Girl shouts.

I lift my bow, nock an arrow, and take aim. I exhale, just like they taught us at archery camp, and on the next breath, I release. The arrow flies true, a streak of white lightning that hits the bináá' yee agháni in its veiny red eyeball. The monster screeches and veers away. Łizhin's claws rip oily feathers from its chest as it passes, tearing a bloody gash across its body. It screeches again, and we watch as the creature spirals to the earth below. I hold my breath as it strikes the ground and doesn't move.

"We got him!" I shout. Łizhin must have pierced its heart.

"No time to celebrate," Black Jet Girl says. "There's more coming."

A fierce cry to my left draws my attention. I look over, and Mom is standing on Łigai's back, holding up her lightning sword. Rock Crystal Boy is steering, but he's having to do it with his head down to avoid being frozen by the buzzards' gaze.

"Aim for the eyes!" I yell. At first I think she's too far away to hear me, but she turns briefly and gives me a thumbs-up. I watch as a bináá' yee agháni closes in. Mom waits until the buzzard is practically on top of her, and then she swings the sword. Lightning crackles from its tip, slashing the monster's face. Łigai drops, almost too quickly, streaking under the buzzard and dragging its beak across the monster's underside, tearing it open. Mom has to squat and grab her herald's feathers to keep her balance. She barely avoids a disgusting rain of buzzard intestines as the bináá' yee agháni falls from the sky.

And then Black Jet Girl is shouting at me, and I can't watch Mom anymore, because two more bináá' yee agháni are coming for us.

I raise my bow, nock another arrow, and try to figure out which to shoot first. They're both coming in so fast, I won't have time to hit both.

"Nizhoni! Shoot!" Black Jet Girl yells.

I steady my breath, exhale, and release. Another perfect

shot right in the eye! The bináá' yee agháni shrieks in pain and spins away. I turn as quickly as I can, but the other buzzard is so close there's no way I can draw an arrow before it hits us. I can smell its hot, fetid breath and see the rows of rotted teeth inside its mouth.

"Duck!" someone shouts. I drop flat against Łizhin's back and something streaks over my head. I catch a flash of blue out of the corner of my eye. It's Dólii, head down, wings tucked against his body, as he barrel-rolls past us. And there's Mac, legs strapped to his back, arm outstretched as he sends liquid fire directly over my head and into the bináá' yee agháni's face. I smell burned feathers—and is that fried chicken?—and then the buzzard's carcass is plummeting toward the ground below. Black Jet Girl and I let out a cheer, and Mac raises his fist in victory.

He's so distracted, he doesn't see what's coming behind him.

And by the time he does, it's too late.

FORTY-THREE

◆

Out of the Frying Pan

"Mac!" I scream as a huge bináá' yee agháni strikes Dólii from behind, sending the blue herald's controlled barrel roll into an out-of-control spiral. I watch in horror as my brother falls out of his harness and somersaults off Dólii's back into the open sky. Turquoise Boy reaches for him, but he's too far away.

"Noooo!" I slap my palm against Łizhin's back to get her attention. I look around frantically for help, but Mom is too busy fighting off buzzards, and Davery is ducking for cover under his book.

"I see him," Łizhin says, voice grim. "Hold on! I'm going to try to catch him before he hits the ground."

She banks, taking the turn at top speed, and goes straight into a dive. The wind blows me back, and I twist my fingers through the rope, holding on tight. Black Jet Girl does the same, leaning forward as close as she can to Łizhin's back. We don't get far before something hits us from the side, throwing Łizhin off course and bringing our pursuit up short.

"Mac!" I search frantically for his figure and spot him, still falling toward the hard earth below. And then I see it. A shimmery substance unfurls in the air underneath him like a silver net. He falls into the glimmering stuff, and it completely envelops his body, rolling him into what looks like a giant burrito. Then it retracts toward the side of the canyon until it gently bumps the side and comes to a safe stop no more than a few feet above the ground.

That was close. "What just happened?" I ask aloud.

"Looks like we had some help," Black Jet Girl says, gesturing toward a cliff. Probably a dozen feet above cocoon Mac, hanging from the sheer rock wall, is a woman wearing rock-climbing gear—a harness, helmet, nylon pants, and a windbreaker with a black-and-red rug pattern on it. Her hair is tied up in a traditional tsiiyéél, and she's wearing sunglasses. She sees us and waves happily.

It's Spider Woman! Which means Mac is wrapped in . . . a web! Oh boy, he's gonna hate that. Of course, if I tell him that his options were spiderweb or death, he might be grateful. Or not. It's definitely going to be a close call.

Spider Woman is waving more frantically now. She's gesturing to something behind me, and I turn to see what it is. And then I almost wish I hadn't. Coming up fast is the biggest bináá' yee agháni I've seen yet. Twice as big as Łizhin. In fact, I think it could swallow her in a single bite. If the bináá' yee agháni have a king, this guy is it. And I know for sure we are about to be its lunch. The hairs on my neck rise, and I feel a terrible chill.

But the giant buzzard doesn't try to attack. Instead, it curves wide, avoiding us altogether, and tapers into a dive.

Heading for Mac, hanging helplessly against the cliffside.

But why would it go for Mac instead of the four guardians in the sky?

Then I see it—there's a rider on its back. I recognize him immediately. Blond hair. Still wearing a black suit. The head monster.

"It's him!" I shout. "Mr. Charles!"

He looks over his shoulder and stares right at me, as if he heard me. His lips spread into an ugly smirk. But he doesn't turn his buzzard mount—he shoots straight for Mac.

No way I'm letting that monster take my little brother. I may not have been able to protect him from Adrien Cuttlebush, but I'm going to save him from the biggest bully of all or die trying.

"Follow him!" I shout to Łizhin.

I barely get the words out before we're jolted to the side by another buzzard attack. Łizhin cries out, dazed, and we start to drop. I clutch at Black Jet Girl, and she throws her arms around the herald's neck. We freefall, my heart rushing up to my throat, before Łizhin evens out again.

"Are you okay?" I shout.

"My wing. I think it's hurt. I'm going to have to land."

"What about Mac?"

"I can't get to him. They're blocking me. Look!"

Sure enough, two more buzzards have taken positions below us. They aren't attacking, just preventing Łizhin from following Mr. Charles. Each one has a rider on their back—the infamous bodyguards, Mr. Rock and Ms. Bird.

"Nizhoni!" It's Davery, still on Tsídii's back with Yellow Corn Girl. They hover next to us, almost close enough to touch.

"Łizhin is hurt!" I shout over the wind. "She has to land."

"I know, but I found what I needed in the lightning book. It's going to seem a little nuts. Do you trust me?"

That doesn't sound good, but I do trust him. "As long as it gets me to Mac!"

"Okay!" He grins. "Jump!"

"Come again?" Surely I didn't hear that right. We're a hundred feet up in the air. No way I'm getting off this bird on purpose.

"I told you it seems nuts, but it's the only way." He lifts the lightning book and shakes it in my direction. "I read it in here. I know it'll work."

I glance below me. Mr. Rock and Ms. Bird hover there, ready to snap me up like a bug. And if I somehow made it through their blockade in one piece, I'd fall and break my neck against the rock floor below.

"Is Spider Woman going to catch me, too?" I ask. Maybe she'll wrap me in a web. But then how will I fight Mr. Charles?

"No," Davery says. "The book doesn't say anything about Spider Woman." He glances over his shoulder, like there's something behind him, but I don't see anything. Just a big fluffy white cloud. "But you've got to jump. Now!"

"You can do it," Łizhin says, sounding like Coach. "Go get him, Nizhoni!"

I remove the rope around my waist and swing my legs

281

over so they're both dangling off the same side. I tighten the strap of my arrow quiver, painfully aware that I only have two precious arrows left. I pin my bow to my side.

"Good luck!" Black Jet Girl says, and I give her a terrified smile, definitely reconsidering this hero business. It really is for the birds!

"Here goes nothing," I say. I take one last deep breath and push myself off the safety of Łizhin's back. Immediately my stomach falls out from under me like on the worst part of the Cyclone ride. The wind snatches me and throws me earthward, and I go plummeting through blue sky with no idea where or how I'm going to land.

FORTY-FOUR

◆

The Last Arrow

I don't even have time to scream before I smack into some-thing, or someone. I open my eyes to see my mom's face. She's grinning big, one arm holding me tightly. Somehow she managed to catch me while her other hand was wrapped around the hilt of her lightning sword.

"Nice jump!" she shouts as she sets me on my feet. We're both standing on the back of the White Mountain herald. Rock Crystal Boy is hunched over Łigai's neck, steering the bird, but he looks back over his shoulder and gives me a friendly wave.

"Put your feet in here." Mom points to the footholds she engineered in the harness that allow her to stand while in flight. I slip my feet underneath the ropes and immediately feel more balanced, but I'm still freaking out a little, because I'm standing on a bird's back with only some rope loops to secure me, and we're going really fast.

"Ready your bow, Nizhoni!" Mom shouts. "I'll take right and you take left."

"Take left what?"

She gestures ahead, and I see we're closing in fast on the buzzard blockade. We're near enough that I can see the shine on Mr. Rock's bald head, as well as the gleam on the black gun barrel that is pointed directly at us.

"Oh, no you don't," Mom says between gritted teeth. She slips her feet out of the holds and runs down the herald's back. I watch as she launches herself into the air, her sword slashing downward, and Mr. Rock's gun goes flying—while still attached to his hand. Which is no longer attached to his arm. Yuck! But also, whoa! Mom really is a badass.

I watch as she lands safely on Tsídii's back as the herald passes below with Davery and Yellow Corn Girl.

We speed past them, the sound of Mr. Rock's scream ringing through the air. Ms. Bird, on the back of her oily-winged buzzard, is coming up fast on my left. I don't wait. I loose my arrow, not aiming for her, but for her mount. Again, bull's-eye! Or, rather, buzzard's-eye.

The bináá' yee agháni emits an ear-piercing shriek and falls out of the sky. Ms. Bird goes down with it, still straddling the buzzard's back.

Our way is clear. But I can see that Mr. Charles has almost reached Mac. There's no way we can outrun him now.

"Hold on, Nizhoni!" Rock Crystal Boy says, his voice taut as a bowstring. "We're going down."

I crouch as Łigai folds his wings close to his body and dives.

The next few seconds feel like minutes. There is a rush of air and sound and movement. I squint against the wind while trying to keep an eye on our primary enemy. He brings his king buzzard alongside Mac, where it hovers while Mr. Charles makes his way to the top of the monster's head. Soon he is parallel to Mac, who is motionless and hanging within easy reach. I hope Mac is still breathing in there.

I frantically scan the cliff wall for Spider Woman, but I can't see her anywhere. I know Mom and Davery are somewhere above me, and she's probably still fighting, so I'm the only one who can help Mac now. If Mr. Charles grabs him and they fly away on the buzzard king, I may never catch up. I've got to do something.

I get down on my knees and stick my legs under the harness rope. I tap Rock Crystal Boy on the shoulder and motion for him to slow down. He instructs the herald, and we begin to decelerate.

This is it. I've got a single arrow left. One shot. I've hit all my targets so far today, and I only have to be perfect one more time. At least that's what I tell myself. But aiming at Mr. Charles feels different. Despite the fact that all my senses are telling me he's a monster under that fancy suit, he still looks human. How can I shoot another person?

Mr. Charles pulls something from inside his jacket. It's a knife—the same one he used to threaten me back at the house. I growl, feeling my anger rise. He intends to take Mac.

No way. I won't let him.

My hands are shaking as I draw my bow, nock the arrow, and take aim. Right at Mr. Charles's chest. But I'm in such a hurry and so nervous, I don't do my breathing exercise—I just let it fly.

Big mistake.

I watch the lightning arrow shoot forward, a perfect arc of

white fire. It zooms through the sky straight toward its target. Mr. Charles stops cutting the web around Mac and turns. His eyes widen. Then he lifts a hand, palm open, fingers spread as if trying to stop the arrow.

And he *catches* it.

I gasp. *No!*

His laughter rings through the canyon. He hefts the arrow a few times, checking its weight, and then looks up at me. We're still flying right toward him, and I'm close enough to see his red eyes. He seems to move in slow motion as he raises his arm, winds it back, and hurls the arrow—my arrow—straight at me.

I don't have time to do anything but watch it come.

It's a direct hit right over my heart. I scream as fire radiates through my body. I clutch at the shaft, thinking to pull it out, but I'm already losing strength in my arms. I struggle to breathe, my pulse beating too loud in my ears. Someone calls my name. I turn my head and Rock Crystal Boy is reaching out for me. But we don't connect.

I fall to the canyon below.

FORTY-FIVE

◆

Dead, Dead, Dead

I wake up, the world blurry around me, the feel of the dry desert ground at my back. I hear footsteps coming toward me, the *click-click* of a businessman's fancy shoes. I should feel more pain. Or maybe I should feel no pain at all, because I'm dead. Either way, I should definitely have less sand stuck up my nose. I sneeze some of it out, a wholly undignified move, and long for a tissue and a nice cold drink of water. Strange that the mind and body can still want stuff when you're dead.

I reach for the place over my heart where I was hit and discover the arrow is gone. All that remains is a warm spot that feels like I'm wrapping my hands around a mug of hot chocolate. I sense that if I kept my fingers there too long, they would get burned. I wonder what happened to the arrow, but I don't have time to wonder for long.

"Well, Nizhoni," comes a voice I'd hoped never to hear again. The voice of a shape-shifting red-eyed monster in a black suit. "It seems you can't be killed by your own arrow, which is a shame. I guess I'll have to do it the old-fashioned way."

Good news: I'm not dead, or even dying. Bad news: Mr. Charles is standing above me, ready to finish the job.

"Kill me all you want!" I shout, hoping he doesn't take me at my word. "At least you'll never get Mac!"

Mr. Charles laughs, a cold ugly sound. "On the contrary, I already have him. Spider Woman even wrapped him up for easy carrying. I'll have him in my fracking fields, drawing water from the earth, in no time."

I push myself to a sitting position and crab-walk backward, putting some distance between the monster and me. I try to peer past him, to see if he does, in fact, have Mac trussed up and ready to go like a stuffed turkey. But my vision is still messed up and everything beyond Mr. Charles is a big blur.

"I've collected many children with unique abilities over the years, but I've been looking for someone with Mac's particular talent for a long time," he murmurs, sounding pleased. "I told you your family was special."

I assumed Mr. Charles was a one-time kidnapper. The thought of him dragging kids with ancestral powers to Oklahoma and making them toil for him makes me shiver.

"Even if you take him, I'll find him. And my dad! You'll never be able to hide them from me."

Mr. Charles sighs. "Ah, sibling love. How touching. But here's the truth, Nizhoni Begay." His face grows dark and his words come out as sharp and cutting as the knife in his hand. "You are only a child yourself, and now you are a child all alone."

I look up, trying to find my mom, but the sky is filled only with black forms—buzzards, circling the top of Shiprock.

The land force of monsterslayers apparently never showed up, either.

"Your words are brave enough, but the fact of the matter is, you cannot defeat me. I have a very big knife." He holds up his stone knife, and I watch as it transforms into a huge sickle. A sharp curved silver blade on a wooden pole twice as tall as me. With his skeletal figure and his black clothes, clutching that giant scythe, he looks like the grim reaper.

"And you have nothing," he hisses. "You *are* nothing."

"You're wrong!" I say, because every minute he's been talking, my head has gotten a little clearer, and the place over my heart has gotten warmer. My whole body is filling with heat. And everywhere it flows, my muscles seem stronger, and my blood feels brighter. I flex my hands, and tiny sparks dance across my fingertips.

Now I know what happened to my arrow.

Łizhin's words ring in my mind. *Just be who you are. You were born for this.*

"You're wrong," I repeat. "I've never been alone. I have my best friend and my family . . ."

"Oh?" He looks around, raising his hand theatrically to shade his eyes. "I don't see them anywhere. Where are they?"

". . . and I have the heralds and the guardians . . ."

"Who will all be dead shortly."

". . . and I have the love and wisdom of my ancestors . . ."

"Now I'm getting bored."

". . . and I have one other thing you didn't count on."

He stops pretending to yawn and narrows his eyes at me. "And what, pray tell, is that?"

I raise my hands, palms up. "I have the lightning."

I release the fire that's been building in my blood.

And I blow Mr. Charles to smithereens.

FORTY-SIX

◆

Reunion

There is a deep silence, like the whole world is holding its breath. And then a sound like a bubble popping. And then more pops as all the bináá' yee agháni in the sky above me burst in a blaze of white lightning and turn into ash that rains down on me. It's pretty much the grossest thing ever. Even the king buzzard explodes, becoming a black heap on the red desert floor.

Flapping wings draw my attention as Tsídii comes to a soft landing beside me. Yellow Corn Girl helps Davery slide off the back of his herald and he runs over. "Did you do that?"

"Yup. Pretty sure that was me."

"That was amazing!"

"Thanks." I try to stand, but my legs don't seem to want to work. "Little help here," I say, holding out my arms.

Davery grabs my hands and pulls me to my feet. I almost fall over. Using that lightning power must have taken a lot of my energy.

"Just lean against me," he says. We hobble over to where Mr. Charles used to be. All that's left of him is the stone handle of his small knife and a pool of black oil.

"He was a monster, not a human," Davery says, guessing what I'm thinking. "You had to kill him."

"I know," I say. "But it still feels weird. I wish my shimásáni were here to say a little prayer or something."

He nods, totally understanding.

A loud victory cry draws our attention, and we turn to see Łigai land and my mom hop gracefully off his back. She must have switched back to the White Mountain herald while I was fighting Mr. Charles. She has a huge bloody scratch on one cheek, and her hair is looking extra punk, sticking up like she put her finger in an electrical socket. Her leather jacket is toast, but she's still carrying her lightning sword.

"Nizhoni!" she shouts happily. "I saw what you did. I'm sorry I couldn't get to you in time to help, but I'm so proud of you." She reaches out to hug me, and this time I let her. It's a little awkward, since she's still holding the sword, but it works. And I get a warm fuzzy feeling that has nothing to do with lightning and everything to do with having my mom back. My arms tighten around her.

"You did what I couldn't," she says in an amazed tone. "You defeated the monsters."

"You were awesome, too!" I say, stepping back from our hug. "I've never seen anyone fight with a sword in real life. It was badass!"

She laughs and lifts the sword slightly. "Wish I'd had something like this way back when, but I didn't finish the trials, so there were no sacred weapons for me." She glances admiringly at the guardians and heralds that surround us. "And I definitely didn't have this kind of backup."

"I *do* have the best backup," I say, grinning at Davery.

"But where's Mac?" he asks, snapping me back to reality.

"Right here," says a familiar friendly voice. Spider Woman, still wearing her rock-climbing gear and carrying Mr. Yazzie, approaches us. Walking next to her, his black locks gray with webbing, is my brother.

I grin, relieved to see him in one piece, but hesitate when I see the expression on his face. He looks a little green around the edges, like he's going to puke.

"Mac, are you okay?"

He nods glumly and runs a hand through his hair, dislodging a few strands of spiderweb. "Did you know she was going to wrap me up like a tasty fly?"

Spider Woman grins, looking not sorry at all. "I told him it was the only way." She shrugs.

We all laugh and group-hug Mac until he finally relaxes and smiles a little, too. But not without one last shudder at the horror of it all.

"We're not done yet," I say. "We've still got to find Dad. With Mr. Charles and his henchmen dead, how are we going to do that?"

"We'll search everywhere," Davery assures me.

"No need," Spider Woman says. "I found him, too. They had him all tied up in a big black SUV just over the Chuska Mountains. Thought he might belong to you."

"Dad!" I shout. He comes around from behind Spider Woman, where he was hiding. He looks a little banged up, his Albuquerque Scorpions hockey T-shirt torn at the collar and a few small bruises on his face, but he seems okay otherwise.

Mac and I rush over to hug him, and he laughs as he wraps us up in his arms.

"My kiddos," he whispers against my hair. "I'm so sorry. I never meant to leave you."

"You didn't leave us, Dad. Monsters kidnapped you," Mac says.

"It feels like I should have done more. I should have protected you. Believed Nizhoni."

"I did tell you that he was a monster."

"And you beat them all," he says, holding me out and looking at me like maybe he's never seen me—the real me—before.

I blush, feeling proud but a little embarrassed. "Well, Mac helped a little."

"Excuse me, I helped a *lot!*" Mac protests. "I saved your butt up there."

I punch him in the shoulder. "Of course you did. And Davery did, too." I step back so Dad can see Davery, who is offering his water bottle. But his eyes land on someone else.

"Bethany," he says, his voice soft with wonder. "You're alive!"

Mom steps up, tears in her eyes, her chin raised defiantly. But she pats down her hair and looks at Dad like she missed him, too. "I—I can explain—" she starts before Dad cuts her off.

He pulls her into an embrace, and I hear him say, "Tomorrow. We have time to talk about it all tomorrow."

Mac makes a face at me. "Gross. Are they going to kiss?"

I look. "Yep."

We all politely turn our backs, Spider Woman included. "What now, kids?" she asks.

My stomach growls, and I realize I haven't eaten anything since our morning Spam burritos. "Don't suppose you have any more burritos . . . ?"

"No, but if you want to come back to my place, I know a monsterslaying girl who can make some mean frybread."

"I'm not doing beans again," Mac groans. "I got the worst gas. Farted for days."

"Hey, who's that?" Davery asks.

We all look, squinting into the sun that's now halfway to its zenith. Coming down a dirt road, headed right toward us, is a bright green pickup truck. It's an old one, nothing fancy, and a cloud of dust trails out from behind it as it approaches.

"I recognize that truck," I say.

"Shimá," Mom says from behind me, her voice soft. "It's my mom."

My grandmother pulls up to stop in front of us, her old pickup rattling. "Hey," she says. "I heard there was a commotion out this way. Scared my sheep. Thought I better come check it out. Anyone need a ride?"

She gets out, and she looks just like she did in my dream—but without the apron. We all start talking at once. There's a lot of tears and hugging, and soon enough my shimásání is shooing us toward the truck, talking about getting us back to her house.

"We'll have a feast," she says. "In honor of Bethany coming

home and Nizhoni and Marcus discovering their powers. I'll make mutton stew and frybread."

"Did you know, Grandma?" I ask, curious. "About our family legacy?"

She nods, her face solemn. "I was never called on to fight the monsters. That was my brother, Eugene. And when your mom went missing, I knew she had been called, too."

"Maybe the family can finally enjoy some peace for a while," says my mom, putting her arm around my waist and squeezing. "Thanks to Nizhoni."

"Wouldn't that be nice," says my shimásání. "But that's not usually how it goes for our people."

That reminds me of something Mr. Yazzie said. I look around for him and see that he is perched on top of Spider Woman's helmet.

"Grandma?"

"Yes, Nizhoni?"

"Would you tell me more of the old stories sometime?"

She pats my shoulder. "Why, of course. We can all share stories after we eat."

"Hey, Grandma!" Mac shouts from behind us. "We found Eugene, too. He was in the Lost and Found with Davery and Mom and me. He's with the other slayers on the other side of Shiprock."

So they did make it after all.

Grandma blinks, surprised. "Is that so?" Her voice is matter-of-fact, but she rubs a tear from her eye.

"I bet he and the others need a ride," Mom says gently. "Wanna go get them?"

"I'm going to have to make two trips," my shimásání says, "but maybe I could fit one of them, at least."

"And which one might that be?" Mom asks with a laugh.

"How are we going to explain all these relatives?" Dad says, sounding bewildered. I think Davery tried to bring him up to speed while we were talking to Grandma, but the poor man still looks overwhelmed.

"This is the rez," Spider Woman says dismissively. "Stranger things have happened than a few missing relatives showing up. We'll figure it out." She gives us a wink.

"Are you coming?" I ask her.

"Why not? I'll hang around for a while. Make sure you show shimásání your bread-making skills. You better give me credit, though. That's my recipe."

Mom and Dad climb into the front seat, and Spider Woman and us kids hop into the open bed. Grandma turns the truck around and heads back down the road, the way she came. We bump along, holding on to the sides, the wind blowing our hair back.

"I love stew and all," Mac says, "but you know what I could really go for right now? Some Hot Cheetos."

While Mac babbles on about food, Davery touches my arm to get my attention. "What are you thinking about?"

"The song," I say. "The map of wonder the cart lady gave us."

"What about it?"

"It talks about the 'heir of lightning.' In that last verse."

"That's you," he says solemnly.

"Maybe not quite yet. But I'm getting there."

"Are you sad?" he asks. "That you're finally a hero but nobody back at school is going to know about it?"

"No screaming fans? No one carrying me on their shoulders? No YouTube or Insta to prove it happened?"

"Exactly."

"No," I say, shaking my head. I look at my mom, dad, and grandma chatting away in the cab, trying to make up for lost time. Mac, droning on about Hot Cheetos to Spider Woman and Mr. Yazzie, who are listening politely. Then Davery, my best friend, right beside me, still clutching his lightning book of knowledge.

"The important people know." I bump his shoulder with mine, and he smiles. "And even better, they're all here. What more could a monsterslayer ask for?"

GLOSSARY OF NAVAJO TERMS

ahéhee' (ah-HYEH-eh) thank you

bináá' yee agháni (bih-NAAH yee agh-HAH-NEH) the monsters that kill with their eyes

cheii (CHAY) grandfather (slang)

Dibé Nitsaa (dih-BEH nih-saah) the northernmost Diné sacred mountain

Diné (dih-NEH) the People, the name the Navajo call themselves in their language

Dinétah (dih-NEH-tah) the traditional homelands of the Diné

Diyin Dine'é (dih-yin deh-neh-EH) the Diné Holy People

Dólii (DOH-lee) bluebird

Dook'o'oosłiid (dooh-KOH-oos-CLEED) the westernmost Diné sacred mountain

hataałii (hat-tah-CLEE) medicine person

hogan (HO-ghan) traditional Diné house

Jóhonaa'éí (JOE-ho-nah-AI) the Sun

k'é (k-EH) kinship, relatives, family

Łigai (CLEH-gay) the color white

Łizhin (CLEH-zhin) the color black

na'ashjéii (nah-ush-JEH-ee) spider

Na'ashjéii Asdzáá (Nah-ush-JEH-ee as-ZUH) Spider Woman

na'ashó'ii dich'izhii (nah-ush-OH-ee dih-CHIH-zhee) horned toad

Nayéé Neizghani (Nah-YEEH nez-ghan-nih) Monsterslayer

Niłch'i (Ni-CLEH-CHIH-ee) the wind, who provided life to First Man and First Woman and helped the Hero Twins

Nizhóní (Nih-JHOH-NIH) beauty
shicheii (shih-CHAY) my grandfather
shimá (shih-MAH) my mother
shimásání (shih-MAH-SAH-NEH) my grandmother
Sisnaajiní (Sis-nah-ghin-NEH) the easternmost Diné sacred
mountain
Tsé Bit'a'í (SAY bih-TAH-ee) Shiprock, the volcanic pillar
where the original Monsterslayer imprisoned the bináá'
yee aghání
tsídii (SIH-dee) bird
tsiiyéél (see-YEH) a traditional Diné hair bun
Tsoodził (so-ZEH) the southernmost Diné sacred mountain
yá'át'ééh (YAH-AH-TEH) hello

AUTHOR'S NOTE

My ethnic heritage is Ohkay Owingeh and African American, but for the past fifteen years, I have been honored to be a part of my husband's big extended Navajo family, and for the last twelve, I have been the mother to a smart, funny, and beautiful Navajo daughter. When the opportunity to write a book for Rick Riordan's imprint arose, my daughter encouraged me to do it. Thinking of her, and all the Native kids this book could reach, and all the non-Native kids who know only the stereotypes associated with Natives, or, worse, labor under the belief that we're all dead, I knew I wanted to write this book.

Even before I met and married my husband, I studied Navajo law and lived on the Navajo Nation. It was in law school that I was introduced to traditional Navajo stories and fell in love with not only the adventures, but also the strength and messages about how to live one's life that they portrayed. I have continued to enjoy them as interpreted in comic books and popular storytelling by Navajo and non-Navajo artists and writers, and it is from the story of the Hero Twins that I drew inspiration for this book.

I am just a writer of fantasy, not a culture keeper or scholar. This book should not be mistaken for a cultural text. For those who are intrigued by the Hero Twins and Navajo traditional stories, I encourage you to seek out Navajo culture keepers and visit the Navajo Nation to learn more.

Thanks to Diné scholar and educator Charlie Scott for their insight and advice. Any and all inaccuracies and offenses are purely mine.

Thanks to my husband, Michael Roanhorse, and our daughter, Maya, for being my first readers and for seeing me through the storm.

Thanks to my incredibly patient and genius editor, Stephanie Lurie, who found all the plot holes and dug the story out of them many times. You are a goddess in your own right.

Thanks to my agent, Sara Megibow.

Thanks to the incredibly talented Navajo artist Dale Ray DeForest for that amazing cover art. Bringing you on the team was a no-brainer. You're brilliant!

Thanks to everyone at Rick Riordan Presents for all the hard work you put into bringing this book to readers.

And lastly, thanks to Rick Riordan himself, for allowing me to share some of what I know of the beauty of the Navajo culture with Navajo readers and the rest of the world.

OTHER RICK RIORDAN PRESENTS
BOOKS YOU MIGHT ENJOY

Aru Shah and the End of Time by Roshani Chokshi

The Storm Runner by J. C. Cervantes

Dragon Pearl by Yoon Ha Lee

Sal and Gabi Break the Universe by Carlos Hernandez

Tristan Strong Punches a Hole in the Sky by Kwame Mbalia